“Are you ready to meet your son?”

“In front of all these people?”

“These are Henry’s people. They only want what’s best for him.”

She led him around the outside of the group to where Emily stood. The vet’s eyes widened when she saw Liam. Carefully she lifted the baby off her shoulder, handed him to Trisha and went to join the others.

This was his son. Liam could only stand and stare as Henry shifted sleepily on Trisha’s shoulder and opened his mouth in a yawn as cute as a kitten’s.

He didn’t know what he was supposed to feel. New parents were supposed to fall in love, right? But he mostly felt disoriented. Disconnected. His body was here, staring at this baby, but his mind couldn’t connect the dots. How had his son been living, growing and learning in the world, and Liam hadn’t even known he existed?

D0059729

Dear Reader,

When Trisha Gilbert unexpectedly wandered into *Reunited with the Cowboy*, book one of my Heroes of Shelter Creek series, I knew that she needed her own story, but I didn't know what it would be.

Fortunately, while writing *After the Rodeo*, the second book in the series, I figured her out. Trisha is a careful, cautious person. But there were two occasions when she tried to be a little wild, and on both of those nights, huge, life-changing events occurred.

Living with the consequences of those events hasn't always been easy. But nowadays, she's finally found some balance and happiness...until Liam Dale shows up in Shelter Creek.

Liam is a Texas cowboy who heads to California for a fresh start, some peace and a little learning. Instead he finds Trisha, whom he met almost two years ago during one wild night in Texas. He was a different man back then, so he's not too surprised to discover that she isn't happy to see him.

Trisha and Liam have a lot to figure out about life, love and the meaning of family. I hope you enjoy their bumpy road to happily-ever-after.

Happy reading!

Claire McEwen

HEARTWARMING

Her Surprise Cowboy

Claire McEwen

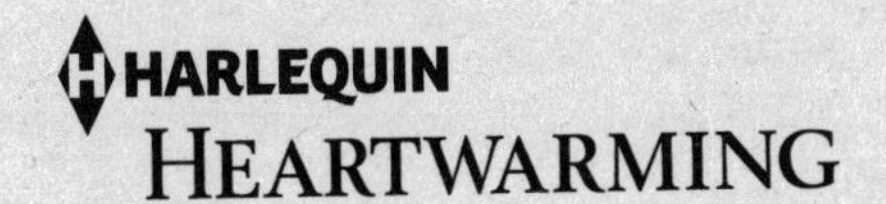

If you purchased this book without a cover you should be aware that this book is stolen property. It was reported as "unsold and destroyed" to the publisher, and neither the author nor the publisher has received any payment for this "stripped book."

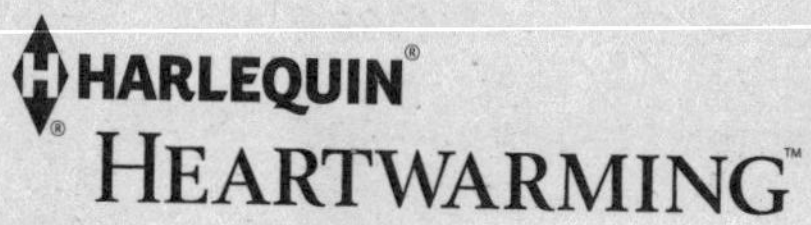

PLEASE RECYCLE
THIS PRODUCT IS RECYCLABLE

Recycling programs for this product may not exist in your area.

ISBN-13: 978-1-335-88967-6

Her Surprise Cowboy

Copyright © 2020 by Claire Haiken

All rights reserved. No part of this book may be used or reproduced in any manner whatsoever without written permission except in the case of brief quotations embodied in critical articles and reviews.

This is a work of fiction. Names, characters, places and incidents are either the product of the author's imagination or are used fictitiously. Any resemblance to actual persons, living or dead, businesses, companies, events or locales is entirely coincidental.

This edition published by arrangement with Harlequin Books S.A.

For questions and comments about the quality of this book, please contact us at CustomerService@Harlequin.com.

Harlequin Enterprises ULC
22 Adelaide St. West, 40th Floor
Toronto, Ontario M5H 4E3, Canada
www.Harlequin.com

Printed in U.S.A.

Claire McEwen writes stories about strong heroes and heroines who take big emotional journeys to find their happily-ever-afters. She lives by the ocean in Northern California with her family and a scruffy, mischievous terrier. When she's not writing, Claire enjoys gardening, reading and discovering flea-market treasures. She loves to hear from readers! You can find her on most social media and at clairemcewen.com.

Books by Claire McEwen

Harlequin Heartwarming

Heroes of Shelter Creek

Reunited with the Cowboy
After the Rodeo

Visit the Author Profile page
at Harlequin.com for more titles.

For Arik and Shane, my very own surprise family.

Acknowledgments

I'm grateful to my agent, Jill Marsal, for believing in this series, and to my editor, Johanna Raisanen, for her wonderful insight and patience. Many thanks to groups like WildCare and Project Coyote in Marin County, California; Native Animal Rescue in Santa Cruz, California; and the National Wildlife Federation for providing such helpful information about coyotes and other animals. I'm so thankful for all the readers who have embraced the Heroes of Shelter Creek series. Your enthusiasm, letters, social media posts and reviews warm my heart!

CHAPTER ONE

LIAM DALE OPENED his eyes and looked at the stubby straw between his fingers. Looked at his brother Boone's straw. *Long.* Looked at Tommy's. *Even longer.* "You've got to be kidding me."

"Looks like you'd better start packing your bags, little brother." Wyatt grinned at him with the smug face of someone who hadn't even had to draw a straw. As the oldest, Wyatt did the accounts for the Dale Cattle Company. His business skills were too valuable for him to be caught up in this absurd notion of their father's.

"You want to trade?" Boone leaned forward on the hay bale he was sitting on and offered his straw. When Liam reached, Boone pulled it away. "Just kidding."

"Jerk." Liam glared at his brother. He glanced around the barn. Leave here? With the early-spring sunshine lighting everything up, the air fresh and clean, it was the best time of year in Texas.

"Aw, don't be like that." Tommy, sprawled next to Boone, sent an elbow into his brother's ribs. "Poor Liam here has to go to California. Land of sunshine and surfer girls."

"You want to go?" Liam held out his small straw. "It's all yours."

"Thanks, but I'll stick around here, I think." Tommy glanced out the barn door like he had somewhere to go. "I've got a lot going on right now."

"Yeah, like chasing after Red Harris." Boone's grin had enough mischief to power a thousand pranks. "If he lets her out of his sight, she's likely to just forget he even exists."

"It's got nothing to do with her." Tommy tossed his straw on the ground. "I got over her a long time ago."

Liam caught the way Boone glanced at Wyatt. And the brief shake of Wyatt's head that meant *knock it off.* Red and Tommy had dated ever since high school, but a couple months ago, Red had decided she needed to spread her wings. Tommy had been moping ever since.

"It's okay," Liam said. "I'll go."

"You'll get to hang out with one of your bull-riding heroes," Wyatt reminded him. "You might have a lot in common."

"Except that Jace was never dumb enough to get stepped on." Liam glanced down at his leg, though from the outside, no one could tell that it was held together by pins and plates. The inside was a different story. He ran his knuckles alongside his knee, where it always felt tight.

"You're not dumb," Wyatt countered. "It was just luck. Yours ran out that day. Maybe this trip will help you move on from that."

Liam glanced at Wyatt suspiciously. "Did you rig this straw thing? Maybe we need a do-over."

"No way," Boone protested. "I'd never survive out in California. Too much tofu. Not enough steak."

"Jace raises cattle," Liam reminded Boone.

"Grass-fed. Organic. Humanely raised." Boone punctuated each term with air quotes. "Does Jace meditate with them, too?"

"Don't be dumb, Boone." Wyatt crossed his arms over his chest, which meant they were in for one of his pep talks. Or lectures.

"Jace is building a forward-thinking business. More and more people want to eat top-quality beef. That's why Dad wants one of us to work with Jace and bring his methods back here. We'll be able to sell a lot of meat to high-end restaurants if we change our ways."

"I get that Dad wants to raise niche beef. But I don't see why I need to move to California to make that happen." Liam stood, unable to contain his frustration. "Hasn't Dad ever heard of the internet? We can just look up whatever we need to know. Or give Jace a call and ask him."

Wyatt shook his head. "Nah. Dad wants one of us to really understand the ins and outs of this before we invest any money in it. There's a lot of innovation going on around Shelter Creek, the town where Jace lives. Methane capture, composting, stuff like that."

"I never thought I'd see the day when Dad got excited about going green." Liam couldn't shake the feeling that this trip to California wasn't really about Dad's business plans.

"The world's changing." Wyatt glanced around the barn with a grim expression, as if he could see the changes right there in front of him. "We've all got to rethink what we're doing. Better to be on the cutting edge than left in the dust."

Liam would bet his next paycheck that Wyatt had planted that smallest straw in his hand. In his older-brother, manage-everything way, Wyatt was trying to give Liam a fresh start.

But Liam was already working on his fresh start. Eighteen months out of rehab, learning to face pain instead of numbing it, *that* was his fresh start. Being free of the painkillers that had sedated his very soul was a fresh start. He was doing okay here at the family ranch. He was sober and productive and staying out of trouble. The last thing he wanted to do was step out of his comfort zone.

Working on the ranch, seeing to the cattle—it was simple and good and a routine he could manage. Sure, he was restless sometimes, but that just made him work harder.

Still, he owed his family. They'd pulled him back from the edge and got him clean. Probably saved his life in the process. So if Dad wanted him in California, Liam would go to California.

"I bet it's going to be nice out there. Good

weather, great scenery." Wyatt's compassionate smile couldn't hide the worry in his eyes. Ever since Mom passed away six years ago, Wyatt had tried to step into her shoes. Someone had to. Half the time, Dad was too obsessed with his ranch and business to realize he had sons. He mostly seemed to think of them as low-priced ranch hands.

"Kind of poetic, though." Boone's grin hadn't changed since he was twelve and Liam was eight and he'd put a frog down Liam's shirt. "Jace used to work for Dad during the off-season, and now you're going to work for him."

"Boone—" Wyatt pushed himself off the wall he'd been leaning on "—you're supposed to be seeing to that steer with the wire cut. It's about time to change the dressing."

Boone might have a smart mouth, but when it came to animals he was the most patient of all of them. He had no formal veterinary training, but he worked closely with the vet whenever he visited, and seemed to know intuitively what a sick animal needed. "You're right." Boone pulled out his phone and glanced at the screen. "I'd better get going."

Wyatt fixed his managerial gaze on

Tommy. "Did you get down there and fix that fence? We need to move it away from the edge of the wash. It's steep there. I think the steer slid under it somehow."

Tommy stood. "Will do." He put a hand to Liam's shoulder. "You gonna be okay? I'll go to California if you'd rather stay here."

Liam glanced at Wyatt, but his brother's face was carefully neutral. Still, he could practically hear his thoughts. That Liam had to step out of hiding at some point. He had to learn to face the world. Only then could he trust that he was really and truly able to live sober.

Jace's ranch was a safe space to do that. It also wouldn't hurt to see how Jace was adjusting to ranching life, now that his rodeo days were behind him. It might be nice to learn how to do something other than just hang on.

"Thanks, Tommy. I appreciate it. But I'm fine. A couple months in California is a couple months away from you clowns. It's going to be so peaceful, I might never come home."

"Can I have your room?" Boone clapped his hat on and disappeared out the door before Liam could get close enough to smack him. Tommy followed, and Liam could hear the two of them laughing as they made their way down to the lower barn.

"Are you going to be okay with this?" Wyatt fidgeted with one of the cuffs of his button-down shirt.

"I'm fine. It's a good chance to redeem myself. Contribute something to the family business, instead of robbing it." Liam's face heated, the way it always did when he remembered reaching into the safe in a 2:00 A.M. haze.

"Oh, come on." Wyatt's steady gaze met Liam's. "You wouldn't have done that if you hadn't been desperate. None of us knew what you were going through. We should have been paying more attention."

Liam shrugged, the shame sour in his throat. "I guess so. Still doesn't make it easy to live with."

"Another reason to take this trip. Get a change of scene and get a break from all the reminders of what you went through. I'll bet it will be good for you."

"I'll bet you arranged the entire thing."

Wyatt had the presence of mind to try to

look shocked. He was a terrible actor. “I’m just glad it worked out this way.”

“That, bro, is a nonanswer.”

Wyatt shrugged. “And you, bro, better get packing. It’s a long drive to California.”

CHAPTER TWO

TRISHA GILBERT TURNED onto the recently paved driveway of North Star Ranch and glanced up to admire the new metal sign that arched over the gateposts. Vivian and Jace had just had it installed and their new logo was really sweet.

A local metal artist had designed the arch, which met where a sun and a moon intermingled right at the top. Three stars surrounded the sun and moon. The big star on the left was for Carly, Jace's teenage niece. The two smaller stars on the right represented Amy and Alex, his younger niece and nephew. It was so lovely that Jace had honored his newly adopted kids this way.

A lot had happened since Jace returned to Shelter Creek and met Vivian, who worked with Trisha at the Shelter Creek Wildlife Center. Those two had fallen in love, gotten married and created a happy family with Carly, Alex and Amy.

The kids all loved to play with Trisha's baby, Henry. Trisha carefully accelerated up the steep driveway, wondering if she should have brought Henry with her today. But no, the kids might still be at school in town, and it would be hard to get any work done with Henry around. At eleven months, he was wiggly and reaching for everything. Better that she'd left him with Patty Clark, his babysitter.

In the pasture to her right, Trisha spotted a small band of tule elk grazing lazily on all the good spring grass. The elk were native to California and a protected species. She slowed her car to admire them before continuing on to park in front of Jace and Vivian's historic farmhouse. As she pulled her tote bag from the car, she admired the rebuilt porch and the new paint, yellow with white trim, that made the house look like a different building than the one Jace purchased over a year ago. Trisha knew that Vivian still had a long list of projects she wanted to do on the inside, but at least from the outside, the place looked beautiful.

Trisha's right knee twinged as she climbed

the porch steps, and she stopped to rub it in a motion that was really more of a habit. Her leg had never fully healed from the car accident in high school—the accident that she'd been in with Maya, who was her boss at the wildlife center now. Their friend Julie hadn't survived that night. Trisha straightened and forced herself up the rest of the stairs. At least she'd lived to feel her aches and pains.

The front door was open to let in the warm breeze. Northern California was indecisive in spring, bringing storms one day and sunny skies the next. Trisha tapped gently on the frame. "Vivian?"

"Come in." Vivian's voice emerged from the depths of the house. "I'm in the study."

Trisha wiped her feet carefully and crossed the wide plank floors of the hall and living room, admiring the high ceilings and tall windows of the Victorian era. She loved the house she and Henry shared in town—their bungalow was cozy and warm—but this old farmhouse had an elegance that truly was unique. "How are you feeling?" she called as she made her way down the hall. Vivian had caught a cold, and since her immune system wasn't that strong due to her lupus, she'd been working from home all week.

Vivian was at her desk wearing fleece pants and a sweatshirt, her long brown hair tucked up in a messy bun and black-framed glasses perched on her nose. She turned her chair to greet Trisha with a wide smile. "Better, now that you're here. Thank you so much for coming! Did you see our new sign?"

"It looks gorgeous. The whole house does. I love the paint."

"Me, too!" Vivian motioned for Trisha to sit in the armchair by her desk. "Jace sold his first group of calves, so we finally had some money. We figured we'd use it to get ourselves looking a little more respectable. Now I'm saving my pennies so someday we can fix up the kitchen. Though Jace is saving money for the composting area he wants to install, which will probably be a little more useful than new cabinets."

"You mean composting manure?" Trisha grinned. "He really is getting very eco-friendly. You've had a big impact on that cowboy."

Vivian's smile was lit with love for her new husband. "He's doing so much. He wants to get solar panels and a manure digester to make the whole ranch energy independent. Plus, he's adopted all of the wildlife center's recommendations for deterring mountain lions and other predators."

"I assume he didn't have much choice about that, seeing as he's married to the wildlife center's education specialist." Trisha tried to suppress the hint of envy that rose at the easy way Vivian talked about her husband and their goals. Henry was so perfect, so adorable, but sometimes Trisha couldn't help wishing that he'd come about a different way, in partnership with a man who loved her like Jace loved Vivian.

Trisha had allowed herself only two wild nights in her entire life. One had ended in that terrible car accident, but the other had given her Henry. In a way, it had been perfect timing. She was almost thirty years old and she had two great jobs doing what she loved. She owned her own house and she was more than ready to be a mother. And even if being a single mom was unexpected and challenging, lots of kids grew up without a father and did just fine.

Trisha focused on the reason for her visit.

"So, you wanted to go over the new video together?"

"Yes." Vivian scooted her chair closer to her desk. "I'm so excited about it. I'm gearing it toward educating adults, who will hopefully be inspired to donate to the center. It's great that Maya got that amazing footage of the mountain lion and her cubs from one of the wildlife cameras last week. I used it to start the whole thing off. Look."

She turned her monitor to face Trisha and clicked. A female mountain lion and her two cubs tumbled and played in the dim black-and-white footage. Then the video switched to color, and there was the golden eagle they'd nursed back to health a few months ago. Trisha flinched a little as her own face appeared on-screen. She was smiling and teary in the video as she stood on a nearby ridge and carefully released the majestic eagle from his cage.

Reliving that moment had tears welling hot in Trisha's eyes. The eagle had come in with lead poisoning, and he'd required round-the-clock care to get the heavy metal out of his system. It was a miracle that he'd recovered enough to return to the wild.

The video stopped abruptly and Vivian closed the file. "It's still really rough, but I wanted you to see it. We'll need narration about the wildlife rehabilitation you're doing, since it's the newest part of our mission at the wildlife center. If we can get new donors on board, maybe we can fund long-term habitats for animals that can't be released to the wild. Think of the education we could provide if people could visit us and actually *see* some of the animals that we work to protect."

"It would be amazing," Trisha agreed. "And maybe we could even pay to have a full-time veterinary staff."

Vivian nodded. "I know it's hard for you to juggle the wildlife center with your work at Emily's clinic."

"I actually really like the variety," Trisha said. "But I'm a technician, not a trained veterinarian, so I need Emily's help whenever someone brings an injured animal to the wildlife center. There have been times when she's not available. Last week she was in surgery when someone brought in that fox with the broken leg. Luckily I was able to get Doctor Farber to drive over from Santa Rosa, but he's not as experienced with wildlife as Emily is."

"We'll get there," Vivian said. "Think about how far we've come. Less than two years ago, it was just Eva's wild idea. Then all of our book club friends got involved, and they got Maya to agree to run it, and then they hired us." She smiled. "It's so exciting to be a part of something new, isn't it?"

"It's the best." Emotion rose in Trisha's throat. "I've always enjoyed working for Emily, but I felt kind of lost, you know? Like I was missing something important. Getting to know Maya, Eva, you and the other Book Biddies, and helping to start the wildlife center—it's all given me more of a purpose."

"I know exactly what you mean," Vivian said. "I moved to Shelter Creek thinking I was just taking a biologist's job. But it's more than that. It's become my mission." She glanced at the photo of Jace and the kids on her desk. "One of my missions."

Trisha reminded herself that she had a mission, too. Henry. So what if she didn't have some handsome guy whose photo inspired the look of adoration she saw in Vivian's eyes? Maybe she would someday, when

Henry was a little older and she had more energy to date. And maybe she wouldn't. That was okay, too. "Let's talk about what else to include in the video. It might be cute to add some footage of the baby bunnies. I'm still bottle-feeding them."

"I don't know how you do it," Vivian said. "You've got bottles to make for Henry, and bottles to make for bunnies."

Guilt tugged at Trisha's heart. She'd nursed Henry until last month and then he'd lost interest, maybe because he had to take a bottle at day care. If she'd been a stay-at-home mom he'd probably have nursed for longer. But that wasn't an option. And even if it were, would she have been willing to walk away from her work at the center? "Sometimes, when I bring Henry to work with me, he sits in his car seat and holds his bottle while I feed the bunnies their formula."

Vivian laughed. "We definitely have to get footage of that!"

They talked for several minutes, trading ideas about the video. Then Trisha glanced at the clock on Vivian's desk. "It's almost five. I've got to pick up Henry in a few minutes."

"Thank you so much for coming by. I

promise I'll be back in the office next week. I honestly think Jace and Maya are being overprotective, insisting I work from home right now."

Even though it had happened over a year ago, Trisha would never forget visiting Vivian in the hospital after she'd collapsed from the flu. That was when Trisha, Maya, Jace and all of their friends learned that Vivian had been quietly struggling with lupus. Everyone who cared about Vivian was a little overprotective nowadays. "We just want to make sure you stay really healthy," she assured Vivian. "It's better you're at home so you can be comfortable. And I don't mind driving out to this gorgeous ranch for a meeting or two."

Vivian stood, stretched and smiled. "It is a really nice place, isn't it? I feel so lucky to live here. Speaking of which, you should bring Henry by this weekend. We all need to get our baby fix and I'm sure this cold or whatever I have won't be contagious by then."

"I'm pretty sure Henry had it a couple weeks ago, anyway. I'd love to stop by. I swear, Henry already looks up to the big kids. He watches them nonstop when we're with you guys."

"He knows we're like family."

Trisha followed Vivian out of the study with a lump in her throat. She had family, technically. Her parents. But several years ago, they'd moved to a small village in Italy. They'd fixed up an old villa there and turned it into a hotel.

Trisha was glad they were following their dreams. Grateful that they'd flown home to meet Henry when he was born. But it had been clear, throughout their visit, that they loved their new life and couldn't wait to get back to Tuscany.

Outside on the porch, Trisha turned to hug Vivian goodbye.

"Hang on." Vivian put her hands up, smiling. "I don't want to make you sick."

"Oh, right." Trisha held her arms out. "Air hug, then."

Vivian blew her a kiss.

"I'll call you tomorrow. That's Friday, right?" Trisha clapped a hand to her tired brain. "I swear, this mom thing. Sometimes I don't know what day it is."

"Yes, tomorrow is Friday. Call me and we'll make a plan for the weekend. And kiss

Henry for me. Right on top of his curly little head."

Henry had the cutest brown curls Trisha had ever seen. Her own hair was blond, and just barely on the wavy side of straight. Maybe he'd gotten his curls from William, his father. William's hair had been brown, sun-streaked with blond. Had it curled? A little, she thought, at the nape of his neck.

Trisha wished her memories of him weren't so blurry. She'd been visiting an old high school friend, Becca, who lived in San Antonio now. They'd gone to a hotel bar, had a few drinks. Then Becca had this ridiculous notion to crash the wedding going on in the nearby ballroom. She'd talked Trisha into it, and after a few too many glasses of champagne, Trisha had met William there.

She shouldn't think about him. Or his hair. Or any part of that handsome, long, tall Texan thing he'd had going on. The whole thing was embarrassing—crashing that wedding, spending the night with a stranger. So totally unlike her. But in the moment, it had all seemed like a wild adventure—one night's escape from her small, predictable life. She'd felt exciting, interesting and oh so daring.

Until she'd woken up alone in William's hotel room in the shadowy dawn. Then she'd just felt hungover and ashamed.

Trisha realized that Vivian was waiting for her to say something. "Say hi to the kids for me. And Jace."

Vivian's gaze shifted to something beyond Trisha. "You can say hi to him yourself. Here he is."

Trisha turned and, sure enough, there was Jace, coming up the path from the barn with another man. The two were deep in conversation. Jace's companion was tall, even taller than Jace. He wore a brown cowboy hat, and he walked with his head inclined down, listening to something Jace was saying.

After a moment, Jace looked up, noticing them standing on the porch. "Well, you two are a sight for sore eyes," he said as they drew close. "Viv, I was just bringing our new ranch hand, Liam Dale, up here to meet you. Liam, this is my wife, Vivian. And this is our friend and Vivian's colleague at the wildlife center, Trisha."

Brown hair. Hazel eyes. Smile lines, engraved deep. His hair *was* curly. Trisha's heart stuttered in her chest. It couldn't be.

There was no way. Her stomach soured, driving the taste into her throat.

The cowboy hadn't noticed her. He was looking at Vivian, tipping the brim of his hat, saying, "Nice to meet you."

The two of them were shaking hands and Trisha glanced around in a panic, wishing there was some way to disappear. Could she run back into the house?

Then it happened. He turned his gaze on Trisha. His lips parted and his fingers froze, stuck halfway to his hat brim. He recognized her, too.

She tried to form her lips to make words, but they were oddly numb. Finally she managed "hello" but it came out as a small squeak.

He'd said his name was William. He'd said he lived in Texas. He had no idea that he was Henry's father. And he was right here, in Shelter Creek.

TRISHA'S BRIGHT BLUE eyes, wide with shock, mirrored Liam's own disbelief. How could she be here? Right here on Jace's ranch? Silence rang like static—Liam's uneven breath blocked out the breeze, the birds, all sounds except his heartbeat echoing through his veins.

He'd known she lived in California. She'd said so that night at the wedding, sometime between glasses of champagne and stints on the dance floor. He'd wanted to ask more, but it had been loud in the hotel ballroom. His college buddy Clint had gotten really into swing dancing, and he and his fiancée had hired one of those big bands with an entire horn section that blared out a riff every time Liam tried to ask her anything. They'd laughed about it then. Laughed about their silly attempts at swing dancing, too. It had been the most fun he'd had in forever. A reminder that some part of him was still alive.

She had movie star hair. Thick and blond and that night it fell in perfect waves just past her shoulders. With her sweet smile and big blue eyes, which seemed full of fun and mischief, he'd fallen for her instantly. And then there were her kisses, at the wedding and upstairs in his hotel room, that had haunted him every day since.

But still, he'd left while she was sleeping. She was too good for him, so wholesome and pure, while he was tainted, the pills corrupting him from the inside out. He'd walked out of that hotel room bone tired of the bleak Ferris wheel he'd been riding—dipping down so low when the pills ran out, wafting high with relief when he got his hands on some more.

It was as if Trisha's obvious goodness had brought to light all that was bad in him. All that was twisted and addicted and had him reaching, late at night, into the cash box in Wyatt's desk back at the ranch. Because numbing the pain in his leg wasn't enough anymore. He'd wanted oblivion so deep, it would numb his very soul.

He'd gone home that morning, straight from that hotel room to the ranch, and begged Wyatt for help. His brother had been happy to oblige, checking him into rehab the same day.

That night with Trisha had somehow saved his life. And now she was here. It was almost impossible to comprehend, but when he blinked and looked again, there she was, staring at him with a look that resembled horror.

Liam glanced around to see Jace and Vivian watching him with quizzical expressions on their faces. How long had he been standing here, lost in memories?

Trisha was so still, she looked like she'd

quit breathing. Liam pulled air into his lungs in silent sympathy. "Trisha." It wasn't much, but it was all he could manage.

His words seemed to startle her out of whatever trance she'd been stuck in. "Hello, *Liam*."

He didn't quite understand the extra emphasis she put on his name. But it was hard to understand much when she was standing right here in front of him. She'd seemed like an angel that night in Texas, come down to grant him another chance at life. Ever since, he'd wondered if she were even real.

"Nice to meet you." Trisha's voice was almost robotic. She was acting like they were strangers. But this was her. *His* Trisha. He was sure of it. His memories of that night were strangely clear, despite the pills and too many glasses of champagne.

And then he remembered. He'd given her his full name that night. *William*. Maybe because he'd been desperate to be someone else, the guy he'd been before the painkillers seeped like foul water into the cracks of his being. But from Trisha's view, he must seem like a jerk. He'd offered a fake name and disappeared at the first light of dawn.

If she wanted to be strangers, Liam owed it to her to follow her lead. He pushed away the questions piling up inside. "Thanks. I feel lucky to be here."

Trisha's eyes shifted quickly back to Jace and Vivian, dismissing him completely. "I'll see you soon, guys." She jogged down the porch steps, heading for a small red hatchback. And there was her limp, putting a tiny uneven hitch in her gait and chasing away any last doubts he'd had about her identity.

He watched as she got into her car and drove away, unable to tear his gaze away, even as she disappeared around the bend of Jace's driveway.

"You okay, there?"

Liam jerked his attention back to Jace, feeling heat flood his face. "Yeah. I'm fine." He forced a casual expression onto his stiff features and turned his attention to Vivian. "I truly appreciate you and Jace taking me on, ma'am. It's a nice piece of property, and I'm sure I'll learn a lot."

Nice was an understatement. Jace's ranch rolled out over green hills toward the Pacific Ocean, which Liam planned to visit on his first day off. Oak trees and cattle dotted the steep hillsides and small, seasonal creeks raced down gullies between the slopes. Jace's barns were new and his house was a fancy old building straight out of another era. Instead of a bunkhouse, Jace had given Liam a small, renovated cottage near the horse barn, with a view of hills and sky that he could look at all day long.

And now, by some stroke of luck or trouble, he'd found Trisha. Maybe drawing the short straw wasn't so bad after all.

Vivian was studying him carefully, a small smile tugging at the corner of her mouth. She was a pretty woman, with long brown hair. She had kind eyes behind her black-framed glasses. "I hope you'll enjoy working here. I know we're not paying you what you're worth."

"Please don't worry about that." His manners kicked in, though nine-tenths of his mind was busy trying to absorb the fact that his dad's whim and a short straw had led him to Trisha. "I'm not really here for the pay. I'm looking for experience raising organic, grass-fed beef."

"Well, we can certainly provide that. And dinner. Want to join us tonight? It would be nice to get to know you better, since you'll be a part of the ranch for a few months."

"That's kind of you. I'd like that." Through his haze of disbelief it occurred to him that he hadn't had a chance to stock up on groceries yet.

"Come on by at six thirty. Be warned, there are three kids who will want to know all about you."

He wouldn't mind chatting with the kids, but maybe he could find a way to steer the conversation to Trisha. He wanted to learn more about the person he'd held as a savior in his head for so long. It was a miracle she was here in Shelter Creek. An opportunity to get to know her that he'd assumed he'd never be offered.

At the very least, he'd have a chance to apologize for his bad behavior. Maybe he could even explain how she'd changed him, what she'd meant to him.

No. The word rose up from somewhere visceral. He didn't want her to know he'd been addicted. Didn't want anyone to know. Shelter Creek was supposed to be his fresh start—his chance to live without the shadow of those dark months looming over him.

Maybe he could find another way to explain why he'd left that night, because the last thing he wanted was to see any pity in Trisha's big blue angel eyes.

CHAPTER THREE

THE BUNNIES WERE drinking more now. Trisha smiled at the darker one, who'd had his fill and was nestling against one of his siblings. "Get some sleep, little one."

Found by her friend Annie, a local rancher, the rabbits had been tiny when they arrived at the Shelter Creek Wildlife Center. Trisha and Emily hadn't been sure if they'd survive at all. But all six of them were doing well, though little Peanut, the runt, was still the smallest.

Trisha filled the syringe with formula and picked him up, sitting the tiny bunny upright in her gloved hand. "Come on, Peanut. You can do it. Just a few more drops." It still amazed her how little nourishment a wild rabbit required.

Peanut's tiny pink tongue darted out to take a few more drops. With each cc he drank, his eyes closed a little more, instantly sleepy.

After she put Peanut carefully back in the

nesting box, Vivian added a little dish of alfalfa pellets, hay and carrot tops, just in case the bunnies wanted them. They were starting to get interested in real food, which was a good sign. As soon as they were big enough and fully weaned, she could release them back into the wild. Though it wasn't clear if Peanut would survive out there. One of his back feet was a bit deformed and he didn't move about nearly as much as the others.

Trisha and her boss, Maya, were wondering if Peanut should live here at the center. They'd build him a habitat, and visitors could see how rabbits lived in the wild. Trisha knew she shouldn't get attached to the animals she cared for. Returning Peanut to the wilderness where he belonged was the best possible outcome. But if the little rabbit couldn't run, he'd be an instant snack for a hawk or a coyote, which didn't seem fair.

Reaching for the disinfectant, Trisha wiped down the counters around the rabbit box and tried to stay focused on the long list of chores she had to do after work. But it was almost impossible to concentrate. How could William—no, *Liam*—be here, in Shelter Creek?

Had he given her a fake name that night in

Texas? Somehow the idea felt like a betrayal, even though Trisha had been crashing a wedding when they met—not exactly her finest moment of integrity.

How had he ended up in this tiny town in the coastal hills of Northern California?

It *was* true that Shelter Creek was becoming better known, thanks to the tourists who flocked to it on weekends to see the pretty ranches and vineyards, visit the wineries and hang out in the galleries and restaurants on Main Street.

And Jace's ranch had gotten some publicity thanks to his emphasis on sustainable ranching and his fame as a former bull rider. Jace had spent a lot of time in Texas during his career. Maybe that's how Liam knew him?

Ugh, there her mind went, zipping in every direction like a fly stuck in a jar. It didn't matter how Liam knew Jace. What mattered is that Liam had no idea he was Henry's father. And Trisha didn't know whether she wanted him to know.

She'd barely slept at all last night. Instead she'd stared at the ceiling, replaying the moment at Vivian's over and over again. All she'd been able to think about was that she didn't know Liam at all. When she'd seen him at the ranch, a fierce protective instinct had washed through her. No way did she want him to know about their baby until she was sure he was a good person. She'd been terrified that Vivian and Jace might inadvertently blurt out something about Henry. Or that Liam might blurt out something about their night together. So she'd pretended they were strangers.

Hopefully after she'd left, their conversation had moved on to some new topic that didn't involve her.

Anxiety crawled over her skin. This was intolerable. What was she supposed to do? Pacing the hallways of the wildlife center, Trisha made sure she was completely alone, then pulled out her phone and dialed Becca's San Antonio number.

Her friend's "hello" sounded muffled, like she'd just woken up. "Trisha? What's going on?"

Too late, Trisha remembered that Becca might have been on call last night. She was an emergency room doctor and kept insane hours.

"Did I wake you? I'm sorry, I can call back."

"No, I'm awake. My alarm just went off. I've got to get ready to go into work. What's up?"

"You're not going to believe this." Trisha stopped pacing and leaned against the wall, appreciating the cool cement so solid against her back. "Remember the guy I met the night we crashed the wedding?"

"Henry's mysterious disappearing daddy? Of course I do."

"He's here."

"Who's here?"

Trisha could hear Becca running the faucet, probably filling her coffeepot. The woman had a serious addiction to caffeine.

"That guy. Henry's father."

The sound of running water stopped abruptly. "He's at your house?"

"No, but he's living here in Shelter Creek. Working for some friends of mine."

There was a stunned silence on the other end of the phone. "I know it seems impossible, Becca, but he was standing right there in front of me yesterday. I swear!"

"Wait, Trisha—is he some kind of stalker? Or do you think he knows about Henry? Maybe that's why he came."

"There's no way he could know about Henry. He disappeared before we'd even told each other our last names." Trisha put a palm to her forehead and pressed, as if this way she could keep her head from exploding. "From the look on his face, I'm pretty sure he was as shocked as I was."

"I don't get it. How can he be in Shelter Creek?"

"He's working for Vivian and Jace on the ranch. I remember Viv saying that they were hiring an intern—the son of one of Jace's old employers. I guess maybe Liam's that intern."

"Liam? That's not the name he gave you, right?"

Trisha shook her head, forgetting Becca couldn't see her. "I thought his name was William."

"Right." Becca's sigh was audible. "This is unbelievable. What are you going to do?"

"That's why I'm calling you. I have no idea what to do! All I did so far was pretend that I didn't know him. That we were meeting for the first time."

"Did it work? Does he remember you?"

"I think so. But he went along with it."

When Becca spoke again, her voice was calm. She'd gone into her emergency room doctor mode, managing the crisis just like

Trisha had hoped. "You'll have to tell him about Henry."

Trisha slid down the wall to sit heavily on the floor. "I don't know."

"But he's the father." Becca coughed suddenly. "He *is* the father, right?"

"Yes! Trust me—he's the only one with the credentials for the job."

Her friend laughed. "At least you don't have any confusion on that front."

"Yeah. Things to be grateful for, I guess. But, Becca, what if he's a horrible person? What if he's mean? What if he hates children?"

"Most people aren't mean. He didn't seem mean the night you met, did he?"

Trisha pictured Liam's wide smile that night, his big laugh. His cute moves on the dance floor. "No, he wasn't mean. But he did walk out. He didn't even leave a note. So he doesn't seem like someone who'll be happy to hear that he has a baby."

"Maybe he won't be happy. That's his problem to deal with, not yours. But assuming he's a decent person, you *will* need to tell him." Becca's tone was firm. "He should know he has a child. Maybe he won't be interested in being a part of Henry's life. But he deserves a chance."

"The idea of letting a total stranger near Henry is so scary, Becs. I couldn't sleep at all last night, worrying. What if he has a temper? What if he's a terrible, damaging parent? What if I have to share custody of Henry?" Tears ran hot down Trisha's cheeks and she swiped at them with her sleeve. "I never thought I'd have to deal with this."

"Try to think of the positives. What if Liam turns out to be a good guy? What if he's a great dad? Wouldn't you want Henry to have a father then?"

Trisha's voice felt broken. "Yes."

"This is a really strange situation, for sure, but try not to panic, okay?"

Easier said than done. But listening to Becca's ideas had firmed up her own. "I'm not going to tell him about Henry quite yet. Maybe it's wrong, but I have to know if he's a normal, decent guy before I say anything."

"That makes sense. And if he's not a normal, decent guy?" Trisha's worries were reflected in Becca's voice. She adored Henry. She'd flown out to be with Trisha at his birth. She was one of his unofficial godmothers.

"I guess I'll consult a lawyer. Or just never tell him." Then it hit her. "Shelter Creek is a tiny town. He's going to find out I have a kid eventually. I'm sure he's smart enough to do the math."

"You'll have to move fast. Maybe ask a couple friends there in Shelter Creek to help you figure him out. What about Vivian? She's right there on the ranch with him. I'll search the internet. If there's any information on him and his family, I'll find it. Texas is like one big small town. There's got to be mention of him somewhere. What's his last name?"

"Dale. Liam Dale." It was some relief to have help. To have a friend who understood her fears. "Thank you."

"I got you into this with my silly wedding crashing idea, didn't I?" Becca's voice quieted. "I'm sorry."

"You have to stop apologizing. It was my choice. I was determined to prove that I could be wild and fun. And I can't regret Henry. He's the sweetest baby."

"He sure is. Trisha, I love that baby boy." There was rustling on Becca's end of the phone, and the sound of keys jangling. "I'm so sorry but I have to get to work. I'll be off tomorrow around noon. Call me and tell me how you're doing, okay? And try not to panic. Remember, this could have a happy ending."

"I guess so..." Trisha couldn't keep the doubt out of her voice. Liam was a stranger, and he might have rights to Henry. Her *baby.* It didn't feel happy—it felt terrifying. Panic fluttered anew. "Thanks for talking, Becca."

"Of course. We'll talk more soon. Love you."

"Love you back." The phone went silent and Trisha stayed where she was, sitting on the tile floor, sprawled against the wall.

In a perfect world, Liam had every right to know he had a son. Back when Trisha found out she was pregnant, she'd even tried to find him. At the time, she'd figured if she did manage to discover who he was, she'd have several months to get to know him. To make sure he was a good guy before she worked out any custody issues.

She'd never found him. With a name like William and just a guess at his age, figuring out his identity had proved impossible.

But now here he was, and every time she tried to imagine putting Henry in the arms of a virtual stranger, every protective instinct rose up, bared sharp mama teeth and screamed *no!* What if he tried to take Henry away?

Trisha scrambled up from the floor, her lungs desperate for more oxygen. She gasped, trying to get her heart to stop racing. *Breathe. Don't assume the worst.* Becca was right. All she could do now was keep Henry out of Liam's way and try to find out more about the Texas cowboy.

Glancing at her phone, she saw that there was no more time for this meltdown. Not if she was going to get to the store before she had to pick Henry up. She forced herself to focus on the routines of the wildlife center. She checked on the bunnies one more time, and peeked in at the fox, who was living in a pen outdoors now, his leg almost healed. They'd release him back to the wild soon.

Shutting down lights and locking doors, Trisha reminded herself that nothing had changed. At least not yet. She was Henry's mom, and Henry was safe with the babysitter. Her heart settled—her breathing returned to normal. She could handle this if she took it one step at a time.

TRISHA HADN'T EXPECTED her first step to happen so soon. She wasn't ready. Her emotions had been rubbed so raw during her conversation with Becca that the moment she spotted Liam in the Shelter Creek Market, she almost burst into tears.

That was why she was hiding behind the potato chip display, waiting for him to finish choosing milk in the dairy section. Trisha peered around the corner again. How could anyone take so long picking out a carton of milk? She pretended to examine the ingredients on a potato chip package while she waited, heart thrumming hard in her veins.

"No matter how long you stare at those, they're not going to get healthy."

Trisha started so violently, she hit the cardboard side of the display with her knee. Grabbing the swaying tower of chips to steady it, she glared at her friend Kathy Wallace from book club. "You scared me!"

Kathy's face creased into a mischievous smile. With her gray pageboy haircut, she looked like an elderly elf. She peeked around the corner of the chip display. "Who are we spying on?"

"No one!" Trisha's face heated. "Just craving chips, that's all."

"I don't blame you." Kathy grabbed a bag

and dropped it in her basket. "I love these things. Guilty pleasure."

Trisha forced herself to focus on Kathy's kind face and big smile. "How are you?"

"Doing well, sweetie. Are you coming to book club next week? It's at my house. And make sure you bring little Henry. I need my baby fix. Actually, I'm around this weekend, too, if you need a sitter."

Trisha glanced around, scared that Liam would suddenly peek over the stacks of junk food between them and the next aisle and ask, "Who's Henry?"

"Yes, I'll be at book club, for sure. And thanks for your kind offer. I don't think I need a sitter, but if you're around and have the time, maybe we could take Henry to the park together?"

"I'd love it." Kathy's smile crinkled around her eyes. She'd never had her own children. She was like a second grandmother to Trisha's boss and friend, Maya, and had pretty much adopted Trisha and Henry as family as well.

"I'll call you." Trisha peeked around the corner one more time, relieved that Liam had finally moved on and was out of sight. "I'm going to keep shopping so I can be on time to get Henry from Patty's house. But we'll definitely get together this weekend."

She gave Kathy a quick hug goodbye and started toward the dairy case, glancing down each aisle with trepidation. Fortunately, Liam was nowhere to be seen. Trisha grabbed a carton of milk and another of yogurt and turned away. In her hurry, the basket she held in front of her crashed into another shopper.

"Oof." The man staggered back a step, dropping his shopping basket. Cans rolled, milk spattered and the man put his hands on his stomach where she must have rammed him. A flat stomach in a black T-shirt with the shape of a Texas longhorn on the chest. Oh no. Trisha looked up. *Liam.*

"Should I take this personally?" Liam smiled faintly, though the expression in his eyes looked pained.

"Oh wow, I'm so sorry." Trisha stepped back and took in the mess all around them. Milk was pulsing out through a crack in the top of the carton like blood from a mortal wound. She knelt and set the carton upright to stop the flow. "I didn't see you when I turned around. I'm really sorry."

Mrs. Martin hurried toward them from the meat section. Her dog, Gladys, was a frequent visitor at the veterinary clinic. She put a gentle hand on Trisha's arm. "You poor thing. I'll just go tell Rhoda that we've got a spill back here." She turned to Liam with a kind smile. "Rhoda owns this market. You must be new in town. Welcome to Shelter Creek."

"Thanks." Liam glanced at the milk slowly surrounding his boots. "It's been eventful so far."

"Never a dull moment in this town," Mrs. Martin chirped, and bustled off to find Rhoda. Bless her heart.

Trisha set her shopping basket down and went to retrieve Liam's basket from where it lay on its side. She collected the cans that had flown out. "You have a dog?" She waggled the can of dog food she'd just found.

"Yup." He was looking at her with such a serious expression that Trisha braced herself. Did he know about Henry already? He was still standing in the milk. He gingerly stepped out of the puddle, onto dry linoleum.

"I'm truly sorry I bumped into you." She needed to leave, to get away from his hazel eyes, and the way he was studying her so carefully. It was disconcerting how familiar his face was. There was the curve of his lower lip, the faint stubble blurring the line of his jaw, the thick lashes and tousled curly brown hair. She remembered, suddenly, how soft it had felt under her fingers. Yet he was a complete stranger.

"Don't worry about it." He was looking at her so intently, it was possible he was doing the same thing she was—parsing through her features, finding what was familiar. What must he think of her? What might he remember? Heat flared over her face.

She handed him his basket and backed a few paces away. "I have to get going."

"Can I see you?" He glanced around, as if making sure no one was listening. "We should talk. Clear the air."

Her stomach lurched. Becca had said she should get to know him, and here was her chance. But talking with him would mean questions about her life, about what she did, how she spent her time. Which would mean telling lies of omission, big ones, about Henry. And she was a terrible liar.

She wasn't ready. She needed time. "I don't think we have to do that. The air's clear."

She waved her hand around as if to prove the point. "Perfectly clear."

"But… I left that night. I'd like to explain."

"Nothing to explain. Really. Totally understandable. No hard feelings." She was lying already. Of course she'd felt awful, waking up to find him gone. But there were more important issues at stake than her bruised ego. "Look, please don't worry about it. This is all just a strange coincidence, you showing up here in my hometown. But let's not make your stay in Shelter Creek awkward." Ha. If he found out about Henry, *awkward* would be the least of her worries.

"Won't it be less awkward if we talk for a bit?"

"What's there to say? There's no point in hashing over the past." Another lie, because their past had created an eleven-month-old cutie-pie, who was waiting for her at his babysitter's house. Trisha only had a few minutes to get there before she'd owe Patty a fee for late pickup. "There's somewhere I have to be. I'll just see you around. And sorry, again, about crashing into you."

Trisha hurried toward the front of the store and out into the cooling evening. It was supposed to rain again tonight and the clouds were rolling in, bringing dusk on early. She gulped in the damp air, relishing the scent of earth, of crisp, cool springtime.

Her hands were shaking, so she shoved them into her coat pockets, then drew in an equally shaky breath. Of all the people in Shelter Creek that she could crash into at the store, it had to be Liam? Was the universe trying to send her a message? If so, she had no idea what it was. At least she'd had a chance to set some boundaries. To let him know that there'd be no heartfelt talks or time alone together. At least, not until she figured out if it was safe to tell him about Henry.

Liam *seemed* like a fairly normal guy. He'd been polite just now, even while standing in spilled milk. But she needed to know more, needed to have some kind of plan, before she mentioned that they had a son together.

A son. That man in the store was Henry's father. Even though Trisha knew it intellectually, it was hard to fathom emotionally. She knew nothing about him except that he was from Texas, he knew Jace, he had a dog and he didn't lose his temper when someone rammed him with a shopping basket at the market.

She also knew that he was handsome, tall and thin with a lopsided smile and fascinating hazel eyes. But she'd known that already, from the moment she'd seen him at the wedding reception and Becca had given her a little shove and a dare. *Go talk to him.* Four simple words that had changed everything.

Trisha reached her car and climbed inside, locking her doors as if she could lock herself away from the reality of her situation. She'd left her shopping basket inside the store, sitting there beside Liam and the spilled milk. At least she hadn't added any diapers to her basket yet. Luckily she had a few left, and as for food… She'd just have to make do with whatever was in her cupboards tonight. No way was she going back into the market now. Not when the father of her baby was in there, boots soggy with milk, probably regretting that their paths had ever crossed.

CHAPTER FOUR

LIAM STOPPED HIS pickup near a few cows grazing in the pasture directly uphill from Jace's barn.

"Thanks for driving." Jace rolled down the window to get a better look at the cattle. "Can't believe my truck won't start."

"You just need a new battery," Liam assured him. "We can pick one up in town later on."

Ranger, Liam's Australian shepherd, sat between them, looking at the cows with mild interest. He might look the part of a herding dog, but the truth was, he was pretty useless on a ranch. Liam's dad had called him the laziest ranch dog in all of Texas and he probably wasn't wrong. Ranger was good company, though, and the perfect road trip dog, as Jace had learned on his drive out to California. Ranger was content to look out the window, feel the wind in his ears and take a short walk at the rest stops. He didn't need more than his food and bed to be happy.

"I'll get out here," Jace said. "Why don't you keep on driving to that far fence line?" Jace pointed across the pasture. "See what's going on with that clump of cattle. I'm going to check out a few of these cows and see if I need to bring them down to the barn tonight."

"You don't let them calve out here?" This was all so different than home. Jace's cattle got VIP treatment every day of their lives.

"We've got a lot of mountain lions in the area. I don't want them thinking my ranch is a beef buffet."

"Gotcha."

Jace stepped away from the truck. "I'll catch up with you in a few minutes."

Liam nodded and kept driving on the rutted track, noticing how Ranger immediately scooted over and took up the whole of the bench seat. "Couch potato." He scratched the dog's velvet ears, and Ranger sighed and put his head down, totally relaxed despite the bumpy road under their wheels.

Guiding his truck down the slope of a wash, Liam noted the trickle of water, remnants of last night's rain. Late March in

Northern California reminded him a little of a Texas springtime. Rain might wash across these hills in dramatic sheets, but it quickly gave way to blue skies again. Jace had mentioned that they sometimes got big storms at this time of year, but in the few days that Liam had been here, there'd only been some mild showers. And today, the thermometer in his truck read seventy degrees and the sky glowed such a rich blue it seemed like someone had gone up there and painted it that way.

He guided his truck up the other side of the gully and his thoughts drifted back to yesterday evening, running into Trisha in the grocery store. She'd been so cute in her dark jeans and tennis shoes, everything about her so neat and tidy. The problem was, she'd looked at him like he was a skunk who'd just wandered indoors.

Liam understood that he wasn't a total catch. On the surface, he was just a guy who loved ranches and rodeo. And if you went deeper, he had a leg busted to bits and the resulting penchant for painkillers. Though Trisha didn't know that. She didn't know anything about him because he'd fled like a coward in the dawn without leaving his name, or a phone number, or even a thank-you. Not one of his finer moments.

He could see why Trisha might not be happy to see him. But the way she'd acted in the grocery store yesterday evening, she'd seemed almost scared of him. Liam had been racking his memory ever since, trying to remember how he'd behaved that night in San Antonio. Had he come on too strong? Had he done something he shouldn't have? He hoped he'd acted the gentleman, but it was hard to remember the details. He'd been flying on Percocet that night, mixed with just enough alcohol to get a big buzz going.

Looking back now, he knew he was lucky he'd gotten through that lethal combo alive. That knowledge, that he'd been so careless with his God-given life, still scared him. It's what made him hit bottom with his addiction. That and the realization that the painkillers had been reworking his entire value system, so stealing was okay, a one-night stand was okay and life itself seemed less important than getting high.

He'd been inviting death, but something about Trisha that night had made him want to live. She'd saved him, turned his life around with her sweet smile, but she had no idea. Seeing her recoil at the sight of him here in Shelter Creek was a shock to his system. For some reason he'd thought, if he was ever lucky enough to see her again, that she'd smile at him. That she'd somehow know how much she'd helped him.

He'd been deluding himself, of course. That was his baggage, his mistake in building her up as this angel who had changed everything for him. She had no idea about any of that. In her mind, Liam was just the cowardly guy who'd disappeared at dawn.

She'd made it clear in the store that she didn't want to talk about the past. But the apology he owed for his behavior was burning on his tongue and needing to be said. Maybe he'd write her a note if that was his only choice. He'd have no peace until he explained how sorry he was. Running into her here in Shelter Creek was probably totally random chance, but it felt like the universe was handing him an opportunity to make amends.

Not for the first time he wished that things had been different that night. That he'd been sober and free of the painkillers. That he'd asked her on a nice date instead of bringing her up to his room. If he'd done things right back then, maybe everything would be different now.

No use wishing, though. He'd sown his misfortune and now he had to reap the harvest—her obvious wish to avoid him.

Liam parked his truck and bade Ranger to stay. The Australian shepherd yawned lazily, indicating he had no problem following the command. Liam noticed that the cattle near the fence were facing the bushes, moving restlessly. Something had them scared.

Exiting the truck, he grabbed his rifle from behind the seat and the box of ammo he kept with it. It only took him moments to load the gun. He held it at his side as he walked carefully up to the cattle. One cow was flat out on the ground. She was in labor and it looked like things weren't going smoothly. But that didn't explain why her buddies were so upset.

Liam scanned the scrub on the other side of the fence and spotted it. *Coyote.* A big one, sitting almost casually just a few yards away, watching the cow intently. It was probably waiting for that calf to be born, or for the right moment to go for the helpless cow's throat.

It was a part of ranching he hated, but it had to be done. Liam raised the rifle, got the coyote in his sights and fired.

The sound of the shot echoed off the hills and the cattle bolted, leaving the cow struggling to get up from the ground. Liam approached her and put a hand to her shoulder. "It's okay, girl." He kept his voice low and soothing, and she settled back down on her side again.

Rubbing the cow's back, Liam scanned the area where the coyote had been and saw it on the ground. For a moment he was sure he'd killed it, but as he watched, it lurched upright and hopped away on three legs, its front paw raised. Wounded. Suffering. It wasn't okay to leave it like that. Liam stood and raised the gun again.

"Liam, stop!" At Jace's shouted command, Liam lowered the rifle, set the safety and turned toward his boss.

"Coyote," he said as Jace ran up. "I nicked it. I need to finish the job."

"Don't," Jace gasped, winded from his sprint up the hill.

"What do you mean?" Liam pulled his gaze away from the spot in the bushes where the coyote had disappeared. "It was going for your cattle."

"This isn't Texas, Liam. We don't shoot coyotes around here."

Liam didn't even know what to say to that. Just stood there gaping at Jace like a landed fish. Finally, he pointed to the spot where the coyote had been and located a few words. "It was just waiting for the right moment to kill."

"Probably just curious. They like smaller prey."

"Like the calf she's about to drop." Liam knelt to check on the cow and Jace dropped to his knees next to him.

"This doesn't look like it's going so well." Jace pulled his cell phone out of his pocket. "I'm going to see if the vet can get up here. Maybe she can help your coyote, too."

Liam gaped. "Calling a vet for a coyote?" He almost laughed, then remembered that Jace was his boss and probably wouldn't like being laughed at. "They're just pests."

"Oh, they're pesky, all right." Jace put up a hand to stop Liam's response. "Hello, Emily? I've got a situation on my ranch. Can you get up here? It's a cow with a complicated birth, and possibly a wounded coyote, too."

Jace listened for a moment and then said, "I'll meet you at the barn and guide you out to the pasture." Hanging up, Jace gave his attention to Liam. "Can you stay here with the cow? Maybe take a look around for that coyote, too, and see if it's gone to ground nearby. If it has, don't kill it until Emily gets a look. Unless it's hurt real bad… Then you should finish it off."

Liam nodded, trying to take it in. Folks around here called the veterinarian to help coyotes? They just let them sit there and threaten their livestock? He truly was not in Texas anymore.

Jace stood and clapped a hand to Liam's shoulder. "I'm sure you did what you thought was right. But the gun is a last resort in these parts."

Liam nodded, not trusting himself to speak. During the two days he'd worked for Jace, ranching in California hadn't seemed all that different than at home. But now he realized he was in another world, with a very different set of rules. Every rancher he knew back home considered it a good day if he reduced the local coyote population.

"Mind if I use your truck to go meet the vet?"

"Not at all. Let me just get Ranger out." When Liam opened the door, the dog sat up and pushed his cold nose in Liam's face. It was slimy but comforting. "Come on, Ranger. You don't have to walk far. You can lie by this cow and scare off any other coyotes that might want to mess with it." Ranger would probably roll over for a belly rub if a coyote showed up, but Liam kept hoping some sort of herding instinct would emerge from the dog's DNA one of these days.

Ranger jumped out of the cab and lay down near the cow when asked. He looked around the pasture with a far more alert expression than usual. Maybe he could scent that wounded coyote. Or maybe there were even more coyotes lurking out there in those bushes beyond the fence.

Jace nodded his thanks when Liam handed him the keys to his truck. Liam watched his boss rattle back down the lane toward the barn, then knelt by the cow again, rubbing her belly. She was calmer now, but that wasn't necessarily a good thing. Her breathing was harsh in the quiet afternoon. "Don't give up, little lady," he told her, stroking her neck. "Help is on the way. Just hang in there and we'll get you sorted."

Giving her one last pat, Liam reminded Ranger to stay and went toward the barbed wire fence. He eased himself carefully between the wires. The grass was pressed down where the coyote had been and Liam saw a few small spots of blood. Maybe it was just a slight wound. Man, he was off his game to have missed it like that. Normally he could hit whatever target he aimed for, square on.

He wasn't a fan of coyotes. He'd seen them do too much damage and cause too much suffering. But he had to admire the way they survived, the way they worked together, the way they hung on, no matter if there was wildfire or drought or a bounty on their heads.

And he hated to make any creature suffer needlessly.

Liam made his way carefully around the bushes that dotted the hillside. No sign of the coyote. The brush was dense in places, almost impenetrable, a perfect hiding place for any animal.

Eventually he heard the sound of engines and emerged from the bushes to see his own truck arriving, followed by a white pickup. Jace and the vet were here. Liam climbed back through the fence and went to the cow. She was breathing unevenly, and she was quiet, like she'd given up on pushing her baby out.

A woman climbed out of the white truck. She was tall, with sandy-blond hair, and as Liam watched, she slung a big black bag over her shoulder and hurried toward him.

"You must be Liam. I'm Emily, the vet. What do we have here?"

"I think the calf is stuck."

"Right." Emily dropped to her knees next to the cow and put a hand to the animal's neck. "She's weak. We need to move quickly. Can you help Jace and Trisha unload some supplies from my pickup?"

Trisha? Liam's heart lurched in an uneasy beat. Didn't she work with Vivian at the wildlife center? Why was she *here*?

He jogged toward the vet's truck and sure enough, there was Trisha in the truck bed, loading a couple plastic storage bins into Jace's arms.

When she caught sight of Liam her eyes went wide with alarm. “Why do you have a gun?”

He’d forgotten he was still holding it. “Coyote.”

“*You’re* the one who shot a coyote?” Trisha’s hands went to her hips. “What is wrong with you?”

Jace walked by, his arms loaded with storage bins, and caught Liam’s eye. “Brace yourself. She’s not happy.”

Nothing about him made Trisha happy, Liam thought grimly. That night in San Antonio, she’d seemed almost ethereal in her sweetness. But so far here in California, she’d pretended not to know him, spilled milk all over him, refused to talk to him, and now she was looking at him like he was the lowest life form she’d ever encountered.

“I was doing my job.” He walked to his truck to put the rifle away, his pride bristling like the barbs on the thistles that grew around here. What was the deal with these people? Were coyotes sacred or something?

Trisha continued to glare at him until Emily called over her shoulder, “Trisha, grab the disinfectant, will you?”

"Sure." Trisha bent down and struggled to lift a huge plastic jug full of soapy-looking liquid.

Liam might be annoyed, but his daddy had raised him a gentleman. He went to help her.

"I've got it." She managed to pull it out of the truck, but staggered beneath its weight.

Liam put his hands beneath for support, his fingers inadvertently brushing hers. "Let me help you."

She stepped back hastily. "I'm fine."

He let go, watching her stagger along, barely making it to the veterinarian's side without dropping the container. Jace was there and he took the jug from her and received a sweet smile of gratitude. Apparently she didn't mind help, as long as it didn't come from him. A flicker of jealousy had Liam turning away, calling Ranger to get him out of the vet's way. He knelt to scratch the dog's soft ears and Ranger flopped at his feet as if he were too tired to resist gravity any longer.

Jealousy. Why? That night with Trisha might as well have been a dream, it was so removed from everyday life. And she wanted nothing to do with him now. They had no hold on each other, no obligation or real connection. So why did he feel like they should?

As Liam watched, the vet reached into her bag, pulled out a piece of plastic sheeting and looked at him. “Will you put this on the ground by the cow’s tail?”

Rising quickly, Liam grabbed the tarp and spread it on the ground while Trisha rummaged in the duffel, pulled out a stethoscope and handed it to Emily.

Emily glanced between Liam and Trisha. “You’ve met my assistant, Trisha?”

Liam watched Trisha’s face grow a shade paler beneath the baseball cap she wore over her ponytail. She *really* didn’t want anyone to know about their connection. Maybe she was married? She didn’t wear a ring, though. “I met her out here the other day.”

His lie earned him the faintest flicker of relief in the tight lines of Trisha’s face. “I thought you worked for the wildlife center with Vivian?”

Trisha nodded. “I do. I work for Emily, too.”

“You’re busy.” Maybe he’d hoped to make her smile with his admiration, but her mouth stayed in a tense line.

"Trisha's superwoman," Emily said. "I don't know how she does it all. Two jobs and—"

"It's nothing," Trisha interrupted her boss, and Liam saw that her cheeks had gone rosy. "Let's focus on this poor cow."

"Absolutely." Emily glanced at Jace who was standing just behind her. "I'm thinking that the calf's legs are tucked back. Okay with you if I take care of that?"

Trisha produced a clipboard and pen from the bag and handed it to Jace, on cue. These two ran a tight ship.

Liam watched as Jace scrawled his name on the form, allowing Emily to get to work. While Jace signed, Emily pulled on a pair of long gloves and coated them in gel. Then she lay down next to the cow.

Liam averted his eyes while she pushed the calf back and got it situated. He'd seen calves being born many times, had even needed to jump in and handle the delivery on occasion, but somehow it all seemed a lot more awkward with Trisha right there. She was really under his skin if he couldn't even witness a cow giving birth.

He wasn't needed here, so he walked over

to the fence and looked out over the scrubby fields. The sun was dipping down toward the horizon and that poor coyote was suffering out there. Liam heard a sound, a whimpering noise, and turned back toward the cow in alarm. Was she in trouble? Maybe the diagnosis was wrong. But Emily had a smile tangled up with the grimace on her face.

"I've got it," she was saying. "His legs are set. We should be ready to go."

Liam heard the sound again, kind of a squeak, coming not from the cow but from somewhere uphill. There, where the hill got so steep that it was more like a cliff, rising up far too sharply for a horse or cow to navigate.

Could it be his coyote?

"Good girl!"

Liam turned at Jace's shout to see him and Trisha crowded around Emily, watching as she shepherded the calf down onto the plastic sheet, a slippery mess but kicking, moving, alive.

Liam jogged over to help. Trisha pulled the lid off a tub of clean rags, and Jace grabbed one and started rubbing the baby down. Emily cleaned the calf's nostrils and checked its breathing, then sat back on her heels, an expression of relief softening her features. "It never gets old, does it?" she said to Jace.

Jace grinned, showing the megawatt smile that had graced a few billboards in his rodeo heyday. "It never does. Liam, get over here and let's see how the mama is doing."

Liam joined him by the cow's head. She was exhausted, but her eyes were clear and she was looking over at her calf with interest.

"I think she'll be getting up soon." Liam stood and Jace did, too, and in a moment, sure enough, the cow rolled onto her belly, got her legs under her and stood.

"Good mama," Emily said.

Liam glanced at Trisha. Her face was lit by a sweet, rapt smile as she watched the mother nuzzle her new baby, blowing her grassy breath over its face and body. The cow's big tongue came out and she licked her calf, starting the essential bonding process.

Liam felt his shoulders slump with relief. "I guess one thing's going right today," he muttered to Jace.

"You did what you've been taught to do," Jace said quietly. "You came here to learn different ways, right? Well, one way we're different is that we try to manage predators without killing them. I should have warned you about that."

Liam pointed toward the hillside. "I heard some sounds coming from up there just now. If you don't mind, I'll walk up and investigate. It might be that coyote."

Trisha had overheard, apparently. Disdain carved a line between her eyes. "You mean the one you shot?"

Jace intervened. "Trisha, Liam was doing what he thought best."

Jace's reasonable tone didn't seem to have much effect on Trisha. "If we find it, I'll be the one trying to help it survive."

Liam figured it was time to fight his own battles. "Look, Trisha, I'm sorry to upset you. But it was threatening the cow. That's why I shot it."

"Why didn't you just scare it away?"

Her self-righteousness was starting to grate. "I did what I've always done. They're a threat to livestock, they breed like crazy and at home we shoot them on sight."

"That's wrong!" There was so much anger in Trisha's eyes, Liam half expected to see blue sparks shooting out of them.

Emily joined them and put a hand on Trisha's arm as if to restrain her. "Let's focus on a solution here. Liam, where did you look for it already?" Emily shaded her eyes against the setting sun as she scanned the brush where Liam had searched earlier.

"All through that area over there. I looked under bushes, all around, but I couldn't spot it."

"They're hard to spot when they don't want to be found." Emily sighed. "The thing is, even if we find it, an adult coyote doesn't rehab well. They can panic in captivity."

"We can try, right?" Trisha gave her boss a pleading look. "We're doing great with the fox. Maybe we can trap this coyote and get him healed up. Liam says he heard something up the hill there."

Emily nodded and headed for her bag. She pulled out a flat plastic case. "I'll bring the tranquilizer gun just in case. Let's see what we can do." She quickly assembled the gun. "Jace, can you stay here and keep an eye on baby and mama?"

Jace nodded. "Will do."

Trisha grabbed what looked like a folded tarp and a small medical bag from Emily's truck. Emily looked at Liam, her eyes kind enough that he could tell she didn't blame him too much for what he'd done. "Show us where you heard the noises."

He led her and Trisha toward the barbed wire fence, feeling like a tightrope walker crossing a chasm. He'd already messed up today. Now he dreaded seeing what condition that coyote might be in. He'd never meant it to suffer.

At the fence he stepped through the wire and then turned to hold it up so it would be easier for Trisha to step through.

"I'm fine," she said curtly. "You don't need to do that."

He dropped the wire, but not before he caught the slight smile on Emily's face. "Go easy on him," Emily murmured to Trisha. "He's from Texas."

Liam fell into step next to Emily, who at least wasn't looking daggers at him the way Trisha was. "I don't really get why you all want these coyotes around. They're a danger to livestock and pets. Even people sometimes."

"There are ways to manage them so they don't bother the livestock," Emily said. "And predators are an important part of the ecosystem." Emily froze, then put her hand out, motioning them to stop. "Maybe we can save that lesson for later. I think I heard something."

They all stood quietly. Liam heard the breeze rustling the bushes, the call of a blackbird farther down the hill. And then it was there. A squeak so small it was almost a whistle. Another sound, a tiny yowl.

"We've got a den," Emily breathed. "That coyote may have been the mother."

The look Trisha sent Liam's way could fell men far tougher than he was. If she hadn't completely hated him before, she certainly did now.

"I bet the pups are right at the base of the cliff, behind those bushes." Emily started forward. "Let's walk as quietly as possible."

Liam hung back, letting Trisha follow Emily. They knew what they were doing, while he had no clue. He couldn't help noticing the way Trisha favored one leg as she climbed the hill. What had happened to her?

Not his business. She clearly wanted nothing to do with him. Except it was a strange kinship, both of them injured that way. His own leg ached a little as he climbed the steep slope.

Liam focused on keeping his footsteps silent as they climbed the hill. A mother. He'd wounded a mother coyote, leaving her pups to suffer. He thought of other coyotes he'd shot, back in Texas. He'd never considered the ripples he'd made in their world. The idea of pups being left to starve didn't sit so well.

Emily stopped at the base of the cliff, then carefully pulled aside the bushes. "There it is," she whispered as Trisha and Liam approached. "A good place for them to hide."

Sure enough, behind the bushes, dug into the cliff face, was a tunnel. And emerging from inside were the high-pitched yowls and yelps.

"Notice the prints?" Emily pointed to the earth around the tunnel, covered in doglike tracks. "These pups are pretty big for this time of the year. Must have been an early litter."

"I wonder how many are in there." Trisha knelt to examine the prints more closely. "It's hard to tell."

"Let's move away," Emily directed, so Liam walked several yards back down the hill, Trisha and Emily following. He stopped by the fence and waited for them to catch up. When they did, Trisha had tears in her eyes.

"Emily," she said, "I just remembered. A male coyote was hit by a car near here last week. The one Liam shot might be their only parent."

He'd orphaned them. The guilt seeping in was disconcerting. These were *coyotes* and yet, he felt awful. Meanwhile, Trisha was layering blame on him like mortar, cementing him firmly into the bad-guy category.

Liam waited for Emily's answer. The vet looked back at the bushes shielding the den. "We need to get a camera set up here. If they're part of a pack, that might not have been the mother you shot, Liam. Or if it was, she might return. Or another pack member might adopt the pups."

Liam took heart at her words. Maybe he hadn't wreaked total havoc on the babies' lives.

"Trisha, can you call Maya and let her know what's going on? Ask if we can get a camera out here." Emily turned to Liam. "Maya runs the Shelter Creek Wildlife Center. Her husband, Caleb, is good friends with Jace, so you'll probably meet them soon."

Great. So now he was going to upset his boss's best friends. Plus, Jace's wife, Vivian, also worked for the wildlife center. Liam had already seen how protective Jace was of Vivian. He was surprised Jace hadn't fired him on the spot when he shot the coyote.

His brother Wyatt and his dad should have explained a little more about Jace's ranching methods before they sent Liam out here. He'd been expecting to learn about grass-fed beef and organics. He hadn't known he was in for a hard lesson on wildlife management. Or that he'd become the villain in a coyote family's life story.

They walked back to where Jace stood watching as the calf drank milk from its placid mom. Ranger lay close by, his head raised at a proud angle, as if he'd had a hand in making all of this work out.

"Nursing already. Looks like you've got a good, strong baby boy here, Jace." Emily patted the cow's shoulder with a satisfied smile. "We found a den up there."

Jace glanced up the hill, though there was

no way to see the den from where they stood. "How many pups?"

"More than one, that's for sure." Trisha turned to Emily. "We can only give it about twenty-four hours before we have to intervene, right?"

Emily nodded. "About that. Two days at the most. If the parent doesn't come back, we'll have to consider trapping the pups and bringing them to the wildlife center. Do you have adequate housing for coyotes there?"

Trisha's frown crumpled the pretty arches of her brows. "We've talked about it but we don't have it yet. It's not easy to build. We have to dig out a bunch of soil, then build a cage with a wire floor or the coyotes will just dig out."

"I'll build it." Jace nudged Liam in the arm with his elbow. "This weekend. He'll help."

"I will?" Liam glanced at Jace and saw the stern look in his eyes. "Yes, I will." Really? He was going to spend his first days off in California building accommodations for coyotes? He'd been hoping to drive around the area and get to know it a little. Check out the coast, which was only about a twenty-minute drive west of here. But clearly all that would have to wait. Jace was the boss.

"You don't have to." Trisha's words came out in a rush and her cheeks were pink. "Jace, that's so kind, but we have a carpenter we've relied on before. We can just use him."

Jace shook his head. "That money can be better spent on something else. This problem originated on my land, so we're going to fix it. Right, Liam?"

Liam nodded, resigning himself to not just building a coyote shelter, but doing it under Trisha's disapproving eyes. "Absolutely."

"We might not need it, though, if the parents come back." Trisha's face was downright flushed now, and she looked like she might cry. Was he so intolerable to her that she didn't even want his help?

"Well, if we get lucky and you don't need it now," Jace said, "I suspect you'll need it down the road. Coyotes are known for getting themselves into trouble."

"I think it's a great idea," Emily added. "The wildlife center should be ready, in case we need to move these pups."

Trisha blew out a soft breath, like she was giving up. "Okay, then. Tomorrow's Saturday—how about we meet up in the morning, at the Wildlife Center? Emily, could you come and advise us on the design?"

"As long as there are no emergencies at the clinic. Speaking of which—" she glanced at Trisha "—we'd better get back."

"I'll talk to Vivian," Jace said, "and figure out what supplies we'll need."

"We'll be in touch," Trisha assured him. She and Emily gathered up their gear and loaded it in their truck.

Liam knew better than to offer to carry things for them now. These ladies were tough and they seemed to want to prove it, every moment. He turned to Jace instead. "Do you have a plan for getting these two down to the barn?"

"They're bonding well, so I figure we can put you and this baby in the back of the truck. If we drive slowly enough, Mom can keep up just fine. Do you have any hay or pellets, in case she needs some encouragement?"

"I've got pretty much everything in this truck." Liam pulled the lid off the plastic feed tub he kept in the truck bed.

"Including a rifle." Jace's dark brows creased together in concern. "I'll ask that you keep it unloaded and the case locked. I've got three curious kids in my care. I don't want any accidents."

"Of course. Absolutely." Liam felt like he needed to apologize, but he wasn't sure what he was apologizing for. If he saw a coyote around his livestock at home, would he still shoot it? Probably. He settled on "I'm sorry to cause you trouble today."

"We'll get through it." Jace took the container of pellets from Liam and fed a few to the mama cow. "Look, I know how it is where you're from. I worked on your family's ranch, remember? But around here, local people love wildlife. And folks really like the tourists who come out here on weekends to see it, too."

"So it's part of the economy?"

"Just like the wineries and the scenery. I know it's hard to understand. Trust me, I had a real hard time with it when I first bought this ranch. But the best thing you can do, if you run into wildlife around here, is stop and think about a way for both of you to go on your way safely."

"Got it." A part of him was still incredulous. How could any cattle rancher in his right mind encourage coyotes to hang out on his property? But, hey, it wasn't his problem. He was just here to visit and learn enough to satisfy his dad, then he'd be heading home.

Except there was Trisha, who was not just the sweet thing he'd imagined that night in Texas—she was also strong and tough and not afraid to speak her mind. Liam had to resist the urge to ask Jace about her. Or to tell him everything—about Trisha, about their night together and about how she seemed to hate him now.

But his mama had raised him a gentleman. He might want to talk about it, but it wasn't just about him. Trisha was entitled to her privacy. So he picked a different topic. "What happened when you first bought your ranch?"

Jace shook his head slightly, as if he still couldn't quite believe what he was about to say. "When I bought this land, it had been abandoned a long time. Wildlife had taken over. Those tule elk you see grazing around? Turns out the best pastures on this property were their only option for water in the summer and fall. Then Vivian discovered an endangered salamander in that same valley, and I didn't know what I was going to do. Anyway, it's a long story, but eventually the town bought that valley from me and it's a wildlife preserve now. Folks around here might seem a little overenthusiastic about wildlife, but they walk their talk, you know? So most ranchers try to find a way to coexist."

"Like bringing your cows down to the barn before they calve."

"Exactly. Except this girl here got started a little earlier than I expected. Just shows that even the best-laid plans go awry."

Liam pictured that coyote, suffering right now because of his bad shot. "They sure do."

Jace must have caught the gloom in his voice, because he put a hand to Liam's arm. "Hey. It might be too late to do anything for the coyote you shot, but at least we'll build that pen and do right by those babies."

It was some comfort, but Liam was still struggling to wrap his mind around the situation. "What will you do when those coyote pups grow up, get set free again and start hassling your cattle?"

"I've been meaning to get some livestock guardian dogs. Maybe it's time I made that happen."

Liam gaped at him. "Let me get this straight.

You'll raise these coyote pups up, send them back to the wild, then spend the rest of your days trying to scare them off?"

"That's pretty much it." Jace grinned. "Welcome to California."

"I don't know that I'll ever get used to it."

"You never know. It just might grow on you."

"I doubt it." Liam grabbed the old horse blanket he kept in his truck. He laid it out, wool side up, in the truck bed. "I've got that square peg, round hole feeling."

Jace grinned. "I've had that ever since I moved here and became a parent. Don't worry—you'll get used to it." He clapped Liam on the shoulder. "Come on. Let's get this calf riding in style. You got any rope we can use?"

"Sure." Liam climbed into the truck bed and searched his storage box until he found a length of rope. Jace lifted the calf and laid it on the blanket. Gently, they tied the little guy's feet together so it wouldn't hurt itself trying to get up. Then they folded the blanket over it for warmth. Liam sat down next to the calf, keeping a firm hand on its shoulder.

The cow hovered close by, mooing anxiously as she kept an eye on her baby. Jace scattered some pellets on the tailgate for her and she settled down, reaching for a few bites.

"Looks like we're set." Jace opened the door of the cab and Ranger heaved himself up from the grass and hopped in. The truck made slow progress across the pasture toward the barn, mama cow walking right behind. Liam held the calf tight, its body wiggly and comforting against his. There was something nice about bumping down the dirt track in the dusk, with only one task: keep this little calf safe. Liam knew how to do this. He knew the rules.

Ever since he'd left rehab, he'd been on shaky legs. Feeling like everything he thought he knew about himself was wrong. Until his injury, he'd never imagined he'd get addicted to anything. But somehow he became a guy who lied and stole, just so he could have one more pill.

Coming to California, working for Jace, was supposed to be a way for him to find his feet. But right now his feet felt less trustworthy than ever. His most basic instincts didn't work here. Trying to explain himself to the woman he'd treated badly. *Wrong.* Defending a ranch from predators. *Wrong.*

A wave of homesickness washed over him. Not for Texas, really, but for the familiarity. For the small amount of confidence working on his family's ranch brought him.

No use crying over it, though. He'd just have to find his footing. He'd help get the coyote pups set, and he'd find that coyote he'd hurt. And he'd smooth things over with Trisha. Because when he made mistakes he made things right again, no matter how long it took.

CHAPTER FIVE

THEY WERE PLANNING the new coyote enclosure, but Trisha was having trouble focusing on the meeting. Maybe because it was still early on Saturday morning and she hadn't slept well last night. Or maybe it was because Liam looked so much taller indoors. He even dwarfed Emily, who he was sitting next to, and she was tall and athletic. He'd removed his hat, and his hair curled around his ears and down to the nape of his neck.

Stop. Why was she paying any attention to Liam's looks? Maybe she was just shallow. Here was a man who'd walked out on her that night in Texas. Who drove around with a gun in his truck. It didn't matter what he looked like. He was obviously not the kind of person she should be involved with.

That gun was pretty much all she'd thought about last night, which was why she was even more sleep deprived than usual, huddled in a chair, sipping her coffee. Yesterday's events had shown her that she and Liam might as well be from different planets. What kind of person shot a coyote and acted like it was no big deal? That coyote hadn't even been hurting the cattle. Of course it had probably been thinking about it—but that wasn't the coyote's fault. Everything in the wild had to find its next meal. A cow lying right there on the ground must have been awfully tempting.

Liam should understand. He had a dog, after all. Dogs were predators by nature. Though his dog didn't seem very predatory. The chubby Australian shepherd was sprawled on the tile floor, snoring softly.

"Trisha, what do you think of this layout?" Maya pointed to a rough sketch on the whiteboard.

Trisha had been so caught up in her churning thoughts that she hadn't been paying any attention. Quickly she scanned the drawing. "Um...it looks good."

There was an awkward silence while everyone looked at her expectantly. As the person who cared for the wildlife, normally she'd have a lot of ideas about what types of facilities they needed. But this week hadn't been normal. Not at all.

She stared at the diagram, praying that an original thought would enter her head. Her bad leg ached above the knee. Maybe she'd twisted it on Jace's ranch yesterday. She rubbed it absently. *Think, Trisha, think!* Finally an idea coalesced. "It might be worthwhile to add a storage shed adjacent to it, for cleaning supplies and any other equipment we might need. Otherwise we'll have to make more frequent trips from the main building to the pen, and the coyotes will have more exposure to people."

"That's a good idea." Maya sketched a box onto the den area of the diagram to represent the shed.

"You *could* build it at the back of the main building so they wouldn't see you at all, if that's an issue," Liam suggested. "You could feed them through an opening in the wall, so you'd be totally out of their sight."

"This wildlife center is brand-new. We can't just go around cutting holes in it." Trisha's words came out more sharply than she meant them to and *Maya shot her a questioning look. Heat washed over Trisha's face. Why did she snap almost every time she spoke to Liam?* Maybe keeping such a big secret made her irritable. Or maybe she was angry because he was Henry's father but he didn't seem to be the kind of guy she wanted him to be.

"No, we can't cut holes," Vivian said thoughtfully. "But Liam has a point. We could build the pen *near* the back of the building, and the shed could be right by the back door."

"It makes sense." Maya started scribbling on the board. "There are oak trees behind the building, and no one goes back there. We could plant some bushes around the pen to isolate the coyotes even more."

"Can you really build something like that?" Emily turned to Liam. "We know you want to help, but if it's too much…"

Liam studied the design. "I wish Jace were here to see this, too, but it looks pretty good to me."

"He'll be here soon, with the kids," Vivian assured him. "The main thing is, in your experience with construction, is this something we can build quickly?"

"I think so. The most time-consuming part will be digging out the soil and pouring and setting the posts. If Jace and I can get some extra help, I think we can get it done."

"I can help," Maya offered. "My husband, Caleb, probably can, too."

"Carly needs some service hours for school. Maybe she and a few of her friends can pitch in," Vivian said. "I'll call Jace, since they're together right now, and see what we can do."

"That would be perfect." Maya turned to Liam. "See? You have helpers."

"Okay, then." Liam went to the whiteboard. "What dimensions are we talking about?" Soon he was in an animated discussion with Maya and Emily about the ideal size for a coyote enclosure.

Trisha took the opportunity to step into the clinic to check on the bunnies. She'd switched their heat lamp off when she arrived—now she looked at the thermometer just to make sure they weren't getting cold. They were spending time out of their nesting box now, hopping around to investigate the chunks of wood, plants and branches Trisha had placed in the cage. She'd also added plastic tubes to simulate tunnels. She was trying to re-create a natural environment, leaving food scattered around for them to find just as they might in a natural setting. She'd even given them a big tub of dirt to dig in.

Trisha sent a quick text to Lillian, Maya's grandmother, who was watching Henry for her. Normally on a Saturday she'd just bring Henry to work with her, but since Liam was here working on the coyote habitat, that option was off the table.

Lillian texted back a photo of Henry crawling in her dining room, with the caption *adventures under the table*. Trisha bit back the urge to type *make sure he doesn't hit his head*. Her friends teased her about being overprotective of Henry, so she was trying to let go a little. At least outwardly. But it was hard not to worry. Especially when Trisha knew, firsthand, how life could go very wrong, very quickly.

"Hey, do you have a minute?"

Trisha spun around at the familiar voice. "Hey… Liam." She shoved her phone into her back pocket as if he'd be able to see the photo of Henry from across the room. "What's going on?"

"I was hoping I could talk with you for a moment."

"Um...okay."

"What's in the cage?"

"Rabbits. Babies. We're hoping to release them in the wild once they're a little older."

He came closer and bent to peer through the wire mesh. "They're cute little guys. Have you been looking after them for long?"

"Since they were tiny. I bottle-fed them for a few weeks."

He glanced at her in amazement. "You're a good mama apparently. They look like they're in great shape."

She was a good mama. Oh my lord, if he only knew. Flustered, she pointed to the rabbits. "See the largest one, nibbling that oat grass? I call him Robert. Amelia has a funny white splotch on her nose. That's her, lying alongside that branch. Maybe she's practicing her camouflage skills." She was babbling but she couldn't seem to stop. She reached into the cage and scooped up Peanut, who had come over to say hello. "This is Peanut. We won't release him into the wild because he has a bad leg."

Cradling Peanut close to her chest, she stroked the bunny's soft fur. He was the only one she ever handled now. She wasn't happy that his foot hadn't healed well, but she was glad she wouldn't have to say goodbye.

"He's pretty lucky. He'll probably have a much better life here with you than he would out in the wild."

"Maybe. I hope so." She stood there awkwardly, stroking Peanut's back, waiting for Liam to say what he'd come to say.

"Can I pet him?"

"Sure."

He reached out, just two fingers extended, to brush the tiny rabbit. He was so close she could feel him, his heat, his energy, even though he was keeping it in check so he wouldn't scare Peanut. "It's been a long time since I touched a little animal like this. Usually I'm around cattle and horses. And Ranger."

"Where is he?"

"Snoozing in the other room. He is the laziest ranch dog I've ever known. My dad got him, planning to train him to work cattle, but Ranger could never muster up the interest. My dad doesn't have a lot of patience for things that don't fall in line with his plans, so I took Ranger on. Which basically means

I provide him with dog food and places to sleep. He's a freeloader."

Despite her nerves, she couldn't help but smile at his fond description. Clearly he loved Ranger despite the dog's flaws.

Liam took a step back and cleared his throat. "Look, I just wanted to say that I'm sorry if me being here in your town makes things awkward for you. Seems like you'd prefer to forget about what happened between us, and I'll try to do that, too, if that's what you truly want. But before we forget, I want to apologize if I did anything that night that I should not have. Or if you feel like it was all a mistake."

And there was her dilemma. She couldn't say she was upset that he'd walked out without a note or a word. That would imply that she cared, when that night had obviously had meant next to nothing to him. And she couldn't say that she regretted it. Not when it brought her Henry. "I don't want you to think I'm that person you met. Someone who crashes weddings. Who…well…" She couldn't even finish the sentence. Might actually implode with embarrassment if she did. "That night was so out of character for me.

It's almost like it happened to someone else." Except she had the proof, waiting at Lillian's house for his mama to pick him up and take him to the park.

"I don't think you're like that. And for what it's worth, I'm not usually like that either. I was a different person back then."

"So was I." It had been an attempt to feel young, because the accident and Julie's death had made her feel so old. And it had backfired spectacularly, because it had made her a mom. She loved it, but it didn't exactly lend itself to feeling young and carefree.

Trisha set Peanut back in the bunny cage, because she needed something to do. This was the perfect opportunity to bring up Henry, but she kept picturing Liam as he'd been on the ranch yesterday, trying to justify why he'd shot that coyote. No, she couldn't tell him. Not yet. Maybe never.

"I need to get going—I have errands today. Is there anything else you wanted to say?" It was polite, but still a dismissal. Trisha saw Liam's affable expression falter just a little and felt guilty for making him feel so unwelcome.

He wasn't satisfied with their conversation—she could tell by the trouble clouding his gaze. "You're angry at me, and I don't think it's just about that coyote." His gaze sought hers, and it was impossible to look away.

"It's just the coyote."

He didn't believe her. She could tell by the way he studied her so closely, as if he was looking for clues. But there was too much he couldn't know. "I really do need to leave now."

Disappointment flickered across his expression for a bleak instant. "Okay, then."

He started back toward the conference room and Trisha followed. When she went to Vivian to say goodbye, her friend put a hand to her arm. "Are you doing okay? You seem stressed."

"What?" Trisha pulled her gaze back from watching Liam say something to Maya and forced a smile onto her face. "I'm fine. Just a little tired, I guess."

"Can you still come to book club tonight?"

"Yes…sure!" She'd been so busy obsessing about Liam, she'd forgotten about it. She'd also forgotten her promise to Kathy—that they'd take Henry to the park today. "I should get going, actually, if I'm not needed here now? I have to go pick up…" She let her words trail off, not wanting to say Henry's name in front of Liam.

"Oh right." Vivian glanced at her watch. "Of course. Thanks for stopping by for this meeting. It's sad about the coyotes, but I'm glad we're getting this habitat built."

"Did Maya get the camera set up?"

"She and I set one up yesterday evening. The pups have poked their heads out a few times. That's it."

Trisha scrubbed a hand across her eyes. Between worrying about Liam, and Henry's inexplicable need to wake her up at three in the morning, she was wiped out. This news didn't help. "How long before the pups get malnourished?"

Vivian sighed. "Not long. We'd better get the pen built this weekend. We'll have to get them out of the den first thing Monday morning if nothing changes."

"So do you think the coyote Liam shot is dead? Is that why it's not coming back?" Trisha asked. Vivian and Maya were both trained wildlife biologists and sometimes Trisha envied them their wealth of knowledge.

She loved animals, but she'd never been to college.

"It could be dead." Vivian's expression was grim. "Or it could just be injured and scared. Disoriented."

Trisha glared at Liam, though he wasn't looking at her. "Aren't you angry? He should have asked Jace before he shot at it."

Maybe Liam wasn't looking her way but he still heard what she'd said. Trisha could tell by the way his shoulders squared under the fabric of his T-shirt. But he didn't turn to look at her. Keeping his dignity despite her jabs. He'd been right just now. She *was* angry. Angry that he'd walked away that night, leaving her no way of reaching him, leaving her pregnant.

But how could she carry such anger, when that night had created Henry?

Vivian put a gentle hand on her arm and led her a few paces away. "It's a bad situation with this coyote, and we all feel upset about it. But we have to remember that it's different where Liam is from. It was different where I used to work in New Hampshire, and where Maya worked in the Rockies. Ranchers shoot coyotes in those places all the time. Even here in Shelter Creek, ranchers have the right to shoot a coyote if it's threatening their livestock. We hope they'll call the wildlife center first, but they don't always."

Maya glanced their way from where she was still scribbling notes on the whiteboard. She must have read something in Trisha's body language—her yearning to be anywhere but here. "Are you taking off, Trisha?"

"Yes, I have to go."

Maya nodded. "I'll see you tonight at book club, right? And make sure to bring Henry with you."

"Who's Henry?" Liam asked.

Trisha's heartbeat jumped into her ears, followed by a strange rushing sound. Was she going to faint? Is this what fainting felt like? "He's my cat," she croaked, trying to ignore the way Maya's eyes opened wide in surprise.

"Your cat goes to book club?" Liam was smiling warily, like he wanted to laugh but wasn't sure it was safe. "That must be some cat."

"Right, yes. He is...very special." Trisha's face was flaming hot and she could feel Vivian's incredulous gaze boring into her side.

Emily's and Maya's identical shocked expressions would be funny if all of this wasn't totally awful.

"Well, I'll see you all later." She shot a pleading glance in Emily and Maya's direction, trying to make them understand that they had to go along with Henry the cat. Then she turned and fled, Vivian right behind her. They went out the door to the parking lot, and Trisha thought about running to her car, jumping in and zooming away before she had to explain anything to her friend. But that was ridiculous and she needed Vivian's help. She stopped and turned to face her.

"Trisha, what is going on? Why would you say that?"

"Viv, I need you to go along with the cat story for now, okay?" A *cat*. What had she been thinking? Now it was all going to come out.

She'd never shared who Henry's father was with anyone, not even with Vivian, Maya and Emily, her closest friends in Shelter Creek. She'd been ashamed of her one-night stand—a little horrified that she'd been so intimate with a stranger. She'd been desperate for something that night in San Antonio. Adventure, a break from the quiet of her life, an escape from the guilt over Julie's death and the way her past mistakes chipped away at any happiness she found.

Tears steamed behind Trisha's eyes and she blinked them back. She'd been happy being Henry's only parent, making all of the decisions on her own, loving her boy enough for two people. Every time she encountered Liam it felt like Henry's life, his well-being, was slipping a little more out of her control.

If she told her friends, it was one step closer to telling him—gun-toting, coyote-shooting, one-night-stand-abandoning Liam—that he was the daddy of her baby.

But she *had* to tell her friends. She was panicking and she needed their help to figure out what to do. Not now, though. Right now she needed to hug Henry so tight, to cover his soft curls with kisses, to hear his delighted laugh when she pushed him on the baby swings at the park.

"I have to go. I'll tell you tonight, at book club. I promise. Just don't tell Liam anything else, okay?"

"You want me to keep pretending that Henry is a cat." Vivian studied her carefully, a worry line creased between her dark eyes. "I don't know *what* is up with you. I'm worried, frankly. But I'll make sure the others know to stick with that story. For now."

"Thank you, Vivian." Trisha swiped at the tears that were starting to spill over onto her cheeks. "I know it doesn't make much sense, but it will. At book club."

She ran for her car and started the engine. Soon she was pulling up to the curb in front of Lillian's house. She raced for the front door, desperate to cuddle her son close.

LIAM TRIED TO focus on what Maya was saying about the placement of the coyote pen. He was standing behind the wildlife center with her and Emily, measuring out the distance from the building to the shed they planned to build.

In the few minutes since Trisha had left, they'd all been a little distracted. Liam didn't know what was causing Maya and Emily to exchange such questioning looks, but he knew how he felt. That he'd done damage by walking out on Trisha that night. Damage that his apology might never be able to repair. Shooting that coyote had made things even worse. Trisha loathed him now, if she didn't before…

He'd been wrong, thinking their night together had forged a connection between them. He needed to let that idea go and let her have her peace.

It should feel like a relief. He didn't need the headache that was Trisha. There was plenty to worry about without her. Boone had called last night and mentioned that Dad had been acting real tired lately. When their mom had gotten badly fatigued, it had turned out to be cancer, fatal cancer, so Boone, Wyatt and Tommy were all worried. But, of course, Dad wasn't listening to anyone and wouldn't go to the doctor.

After they'd hung up, Liam had gone back to the pasture near the coyote den with a big flashlight, hoping he could find the wounded coyote. There'd been no sign of it, so he'd gone back again at dawn today, roaming farther and farther along the steep hills.

It was ridiculous to lose so much sleep over the fate of a coyote. But he'd learned in his recovery program the importance of making amends. Even if he didn't feel he'd been completely wrong to fire at that coyote, clearly everyone else around here did. So he had to try to make it up to them. But it hadn't worked. He couldn't find the poor animal anywhere.

Just after dawn, Maya had shown up and lowered some kind of fancy camera into the den. The adult wasn't there either.

"How's it going back here?" Jace came around the side of the building, holding hands with Vivian. They were followed by his nieces and nephew. His oldest niece, Carly, was pushing a wheelbarrow full of tools.

"Are we glad to see you!" Maya hugged Jace and Carly, and high-fived with the two smaller ones, Alex and Amy. Carly set down her wheelbarrow to give her a hug. Then Maya peered past them. "Did Caleb come with you?"

As if in answer, a funny-looking shepherd mutt came bounding around the side of the building and launched himself at Maya.

"Einstein, down!" But she was laughing as the ecstatic dog put his paws on her chest. It was only then that Liam realized the dog was missing a back leg.

Ranger got up from his place in the shade to visit the canine newcomer, but Einstein was only interested in greeting his mistress.

"That's enough," came a deep voice and Einstein immediately sat. Ranger sat, too, looking mildly alarmed.

Liam turned his head to see who'd spoken. A big, bulky man with tattooed arms was walking toward them.

"You made it," Maya exclaimed. "Liam, this is my husband, Caleb. He's going to help out today."

Caleb's big hand enveloped Liam's in a firm grip. "Good to meet you. Heard there's been a little trouble with a coyote."

"My fault." When Caleb released his hand, Liam squeezed his fingers into a fist to make sure they were still working. "We do things differently in Texas."

"That's the way it's done most places. Come on by our ranch later in the week. We can teach you a lot of wildlife management methods that don't involve guns." He glanced at Maya with a wry smile. "Like it or not, it's become one of my missions in life."

"Now, don't pretend you don't like showing folks around." Maya hooked her hand under her husband's arm and looked up at him with laughter in her dark eyes. "You're practically getting long-winded on those tours of yours.

I'm pretty sure I saw that rancher from Fort Bragg stifling a yawn during your talk about sheep the other day."

Caleb's laugh boomed out in stark contrast to his stern features. "Yeah, I might have gotten a little carried away when I was talking about the dogs."

"Our livestock guardian dogs," Maya explained. "Caleb adores them, maybe a little too much. I have to remind him that they're not pets."

"They were one of the best investments I've made." He winked at Liam. "You'll meet them, of course, when you check out the ranch."

"I look forward to it." Liam still felt like a fish out of water, but Jace and his friends were kind. They barely knew him, but they were going out of their way to make him comfortable.

"Where are you at with this pen?" Jace came forward to examine the stakes they'd driven into the ground to mark where the posts should go.

"We've got chain-link fence and metal posts being delivered in a couple hours,"

Liam told them. “I figure I’d better start digging so we’re ready when they arrive.”

“I rented a mini loader,” Jace said. “We’ll get this done a lot faster that way.”

“Can we drive it?” Little Amy looked so eager to get started that they all laughed.

“I’m not sure you’re old enough.” Carly smoothed a gentle hand over her little sister’s hair.

“You and Alex are going to help me cut the edges so the whole thing is just the right shape,” Vivian told them. She pulled a shovel out of the wheelbarrow and shoved it in the soil right next to the stake Emily had left there. “We’ll start here.”

“I’ll do that,” Jace and Maya said in unison.

Vivian straightened, wielding the shovel like she might smack them with it. “I am fine. All better. No fussing.”

Jace and Maya glanced at each other ruefully, and Maya held up her hands in a gesture of surrender. “Sorry, Viv.”

Jace crossed over to his wife and kissed her on the head, whispering something in her ear that made her smile. Then he handed the other shovels to Amy and Alex. “You’d better get started or Vivian will have this all dug up before you get your chance. She's tough that way."

Giggling, the two kids pushed their shovels into the ground next to Vivian.

Something was going on there, to do with Vivian's health, but Liam had no idea what it was. Nor was it his business. He took advantage of the moment to move closer to Emily and ask the question that had been bothering him. "Is Trisha okay? She seemed like she ran out of here."

Emily's cheeks suddenly flushed pink. "Trisha? I'm sure she's fine. She just had a lot to do today."

It was silly to keep asking about her, like a kid with a crush in junior high or something, but he couldn't help it. "Have you known her a long time?"

"Yes. At least… Well, Trisha's pretty private." Emily looked past Liam for a moment, and Liam followed her gaze to catch Vivian mouthing something to her. "I mean, not private in a bad way." Emily looked flustered, which was odd. Liam hadn't seen her get rattled before. "Why? Is there something you want to know?"

What *was* he hoping to know? "Just curiosity, I guess. She seems so upset at me. I guess it just made me wonder about her."

"She loves animals. She's a natural caretaker, an amazing parent—" Emily broke off for a moment, a strange expression flitting across her features "—to her cat. To all the animals she meets, really. So she takes it very personally when an animal gets hurt. It's one reason why she's so good at her job. She'll forgive you for that coyote, eventually. Just give her some time."

"Thanks," Liam told her. "I appreciate your understanding." What Emily probably didn't realize was that there was so much more for Trisha to forgive. Why hadn't he just left a note that night in Texas? Or even better, stuck around and said goodbye? He'd been a coward. Afraid to let her know what a loser she'd hooked up with. The old familiar shame crawled up his spine. He glanced at Caleb. "Can I give you a hand with unloading that digger?"

"Absolutely." Caleb grinned. "But I get to drive it first."

It felt good to joke. To lighten the mood. "You sure about that? I drove across California just last week. There are some lousy drivers in this state."

Caleb took the bait. "You're talking to an ex-marine, my friend. I can drive any rig, anywhere."

The straightforward banter was a relief. "I won't argue with that. You drive first." Still laughing, Liam followed Caleb around the side of the building, ready to dig, to build, to lose himself in this project and try to forget about Trisha, at least for a little while.

CHAPTER SIX

MAYA CUDDLED HENRY CLOSE, planting a gentle kiss on his brown curls. "Trisha, what was going on today? Do you want to talk about it?"

Trisha glanced around at the members of The Book Biddies Book Club who were lounging and chatting in Kathy's comfortable living room. They'd talked about the book, a historical mystery, and now everyone was immersed in their own conversations. Emily and Priscilla Axel, Trisha's former third grade teacher, were sunk into Kathy's big slipcovered armchairs. Annie Brooks, dressed in her usual jeans and a flannel shirt, was seated cross-legged on the floor talking with Vivian. Maya's grandmother Lillian and Eva, a local gallery owner and founder of the Shelter Creek Wildlife Center, were sharing a love seat, deep in an animated discussion. Monique, the owner of the local beauty salon, was helping Kathy clear the dessert plates.

"Everyone looks like they're busy," Trisha wavered. "Maybe I should just wait until another time."

Maya skewered her with a look. "I had to make sure my husband did not mention Henry when we dug out the coyote pen today. Poor Emily got so flustered when Liam asked about you that she started babbling about your love of cats. If you don't want to talk about it with the whole group, I understand. But I wish you'd let me, Vivian and Emily know what's up."

"Liam asked about me?" Trisha blushed when she realized how teenage she sounded.

Maya's brows rose a little more. "Why, yes. Apparently he was worried because you seem to dislike him so much."

Trisha was silent, taking that in. She'd seen Liam as this one-dimensional person so far. Handsome, callous, and now, a threat to her and Henry. It hadn't occurred to her that he'd spend time worrying about her feelings.

"You do seem to have a problem with him," Maya went on. "Is it the coyotes?"

"That's definitely part of it." Trisha looked at Henry, who was getting sleepy in Maya's arms. The lids of his eyes looked puffy. Maybe she should just take him home and put him to bed and avoid this whole problem for a few more hours.

"And the rest? I'm not trying to pressure you, Trisha. But you told him Henry was a cat, and that fib isn't going to hold up for long. Do you like him? Are you afraid he won't like you back if he knows you're a mom?"

It was tempting to take that idea and run with it. But it would be another dead end.

"Okay. Here we go." Trisha stood up, a little dizzy with nerves, but determined. "Excuse me, everyone. May I have your attention?"

The chatter in the room petered out. Kathy and Monique appeared in the wide doorway from the kitchen and leaned on either side of the doorframe. The two looked like complete opposites—Kathy with her gray hair cropped sensibly short, in her loafers, slacks and cardigan; Monique dressed like she should be going to a nightclub in platform shoes, black leggings, a fitted top, full makeup and all kinds of jewelry. Yet their love of books and gossip and friendship brought them together.

Everyone waited, watching Trisha expectantly. She should have rehearsed this, should have thought about what she would say. "Um…hi."

"Hi, Trisha," Eva called from her spot on the love seat. Everyone laughed, except Maya, who gave her a look that clearly said, *Go on!*

"I'm dealing with a bit of a dilemma that I'm hoping you all can help me with." There, they were nodding. At least that was a good start.

"I've never told you who Henry's father was. But I'm going to tell you now."

Every eyebrow in the room went up. The Biddies had been so polite about not asking, but they must have been curious all this time. Trisha took another deep breath, trying to steady her careening heart. "He was a man I met in San Antonio, when I went to visit my friend Becca. She and I went to a hotel bar and ended up crashing a wedding in the ballroom next door." She flushed. "Becca is a little wild like that."

"Apparently you are, too," Kathy said, and Trisha glanced at her, afraid to see censure on her face. But all she saw was warm support.

"Anyway, at that wedding I met a guy and

I…" Oh gosh, her face was so hot it might just melt off. "… I went to his hotel room. When I woke up in the morning, he was gone. I never got his last name. It turns out I didn't really know his first name either, until recently. That night, he said his name was William. Now I know he goes by Liam."

"Oh my gosh." Vivian gasped out the words. "*Our* Liam?"

Trisha nodded. *Ugh*, she felt so exposed. She suddenly wished there was a way to take the words back. As if they were butterflies she could trap in a net and set free outside in the empty, anonymous night.

Vivian glanced around at the group. "We have a guy named Liam working for us," she explained.

A thick silence coated everything. Trisha could hear the grandfather clock ticking off seconds in Kathy's hallway.

"What a bizarre coincidence." Emily leaned forward, elbows on knees, and clasped her hands together. "What are you going to do?"

"I don't know. I mean, I never thought this would happen. He just disappeared that morning. I've always felt like Henry was all mine. *Only* mine."

"And now you might have to share him," Maya said softly. "Oh wow."

The tears that never seemed far away these days started rising in Trisha's throat. "I feel like I need to tell Liam. But I barely know him. My friend Becca called me last night. She did some online research. His family is well respected among the Texas ranching community. She found some information about his bull-riding career, but that's it. I looked online a bit, too. He doesn't have social media accounts, apparently. So all I really know about his character is that he didn't stick around that night. And then he shot a coyote on Vivian and Jace's ranch."

"Charming," Monique drawled, her expression of distaste making it clear she found it anything but that. "In my opinion, you're under no obligation to tell him anything. He walked out on you. He didn't make any effort to stay in touch."

"He's a father," Lillian said quietly. "And he has no idea. It seems like he has a right to know."

"Maybe even a legal right," Eva added.

Trisha looked around at her friends, trying to read their expressions. "Do you all think I'm awful? I mean… I had a one-night stand!"

"We know you're not awful!" Priscilla exclaimed. But she'd been Trisha's teacher. Of course she'd say that.

"We all know at least a little about biology, Trish." Monique's lipsticked mouth tweaked into a wry smile. "We figured there had to be a guy involved somehow."

"I had a one-night stand once," Kathy said.

The entire group turned to stare.

"Kathy Wallace, all these years we've been good friends and neighbors, and you never told me." Lillian started laughing. "You wild girl."

Kathy's pink-cardiganed shoulders lifted in a shrug. "It was decades ago. On a business trip. And it wasn't glamorous like they make it seem on the TV shows. A very off-putting experience, really. Never wanted to do anything like that again."

"I've had one, too," Monique confessed easily. "Though it sounds like mine went far better than Kathy's."

"Okay, before we all start confessing

things we shouldn't, let's figure out how to help Trisha." Annie, always restless, stood up and started pacing the rug in front of the fireplace. "Vivian, what do you know about this Liam guy. Is he a good egg?"

Vivian stood, too, and shoved her hands into the pockets of her sweatshirt. "I don't know him well yet. Jace used to work at Liam's family's ranch when he had time off from the rodeo circuit. He told me that Liam got into bull riding and was doing really well for his first couple years. Then he got stepped on. His leg was crushed."

"Ouch." Emily winced.

The poor guy. Trisha could empathize with him on that issue. She looked over at her sleepy baby cuddled up to Maya. "You hear that, Henry? Both your parents have messed-up legs. Once you learn to run, we'll never be able to catch you."

"Trisha!" Maya looked shocked, then dissolved into quiet giggles. "Is it weird that I appreciate accident humor these days?"

"I know!" Trisha grinned at her friend. "And then I feel horrible. So guilty." But it felt good to laugh after the tension of the last few days and nights.

"Julie loved to laugh. She would probably appreciate a joke now and then, too, if she were with us," Maya said, sobering. "And we've both certainly done our share of crying about it."

"Not to change the subject, but I have to see Liam almost every day, so we need to figure this out." Vivian sat up straighter and put out her hand, counting off thoughts on her fingers. "We know he's from a good family, in Texas. We know he was badly injured in a rodeo. We know he did not stick around the night he met Trisha."

"I honestly do not like the sound of that." Priscilla folded her arms, her eyes stern behind her blue-framed glasses. "It doesn't seem honorable."

"We also know he shoots coyotes," Trisha added, the thought making her even more glum.

"But he spent today building a coyote pen," Maya added. "I think he's open to learning, Trisha. He's trying to adapt to our ways here. Maybe you need to give him a break about the coyote."

"He's handsome." When the whole group turned to look at her, Emily put her hands out in an exaggerated shrug. "What? I just spent the whole day with him. You think I wouldn't notice?"

"He's nice to the kids," Vivian said. "He works very hard and he's good with the animals around the farm. And he's kind to that ridiculous lump of a dog, Ranger." She smiled gently. "About all the ranging *that* dog does is from the couch to his food bowl."

"Plus, you *have* to tell him," Emily said. "We can't keep pretending Henry is a cat."

"What? How is Henry a cat?" Lillian asked the question, but all of the older Book Biddies were gaping at Emily in astonishment.

"Henry's name was mentioned this morning, at the shelter, when Liam was there," Trisha explained. "He asked who Henry was and that was the first thing that came into my mind."

"It was actually pretty funny," Vivian added. "Except that we were all so confused."

"I panicked." Trisha glanced around at the group. "I'm still panicking. Henry is *my* baby. It's my job to protect him. I can't just let some random guy into his life because he happens to be the father."

"Overall, he sounds like a good guy."

Maya's grandmother Lillian turned in her seat to face Trisha directly, her eyes as kind and sweet as always. "I know this is scary for you, Trisha. And it sounds like Liam isn't perfect. He's certainly made a couple choices you don't like. But you have to do what's best for Henry."

"But what if he *isn't* what's best for Henry?" Panic brought tears along with the words. "What if Liam is mean or impatient or resents him? What if he tries to take him away from me?" Trisha buried her head in her hands for a moment, trying to get a hold of her fear.

Kathy appeared at her side, put a gentle hand on her shoulder and handed her a box of tissues.

"Thank you," Trisha choked out.

"Let us check him out," Vivian offered. "I can learn a lot since he's working for us. I can talk to Jace. Do you mind if he knows the real situation?"

"Will he keep my secret? Or will he be bound to some man code and decide to tell him?"

"Hmm." Vivian worried her lower lip. "Let me think about that. Maybe I won't tell him."

"How about we all keep Henry a secret for one more week," Priscilla said. "We can use that time to find out more about Liam. Then maybe Trisha will feel better."

"I'll stop by the ranch," Annie offered. "Jace borrowed a pair of hoof trimmers from me a while back. Maybe I can find a way to run into Liam under the pretense of collecting them."

"I have a cousin who practices family law," Eva said. "Would you like me to ask her what custody issues might come up?"

Trisha smiled gratefully and wiped her eyes again. "That would be helpful. Thank you."

"We'll probably be working with him this week to trap those coyote pups," Maya reminded them all. "We just have to avoid mentioning Henry. Not even feline Henry. But we can try to get him talking about other stuff and see what he's really like."

Something in Trisha's chest that had been tangled in knots ever since she'd first realized that Liam was in Shelter Creek unraveled a bit. Just enough easing of tension that she could breathe a little more deeply. It was a good thing she'd told her friends. She needed their common sense. She didn't have family. She was an only child and her parents lived in Italy now. But this group of women felt more like her family every day.

"I say we meet in a week and share what we've learned," Kathy said. "You all are welcome to come here again."

"Next weekend is the Spring Art Fair," Eva reminded them. "I'll be displaying a bunch of art from my gallery there. Can we meet at my booth? I'll provide wine. How about at five o'clock?"

"That sounds fun. After we've gossiped about Liam, we can walk around," Emily said. "Maybe I can find some nice animal art for the clinic waiting room."

Priscilla clapped her hands together. "I love the Spring Art Fair. Several of my former students will be exhibiting. I've been looking forward to seeing their work."

"This is really nice of you all," Trisha said. "I can't tell you how much I appreciate your help."

"We will always be here for you." A mischievous smile lit Annie's face. "And it will be fun to play detective."

"I just wish I had a reason to run into him." Lillian sighed.

"Me, too." Kathy looked at Lillian, her expression brightening. "We could deliver cookies."

"Ooh, good idea." Lillian looked at Vivian. "Can we bring you and the kids some cookies? And perhaps drop some by the barn while we're at it?"

Vivian giggled. "This is getting ridiculous. But yes, you are always welcome. Especially when you bring cookies."

"I've been knitting that shawl for you, Vivian," Priscilla said. "And I'm almost finished."

"Well, I guess you'll have to deliver it," Vivian replied, her dark eyes sparkling. "Perhaps Wednesday? I believe the cowboy in question is going to dine with us that evening. If you arrived at six o'clock, you could stay for the meal."

"Perfect." Priscilla sat back in her chair, a satisfied smile deepening the lines of her face. "As a former teacher, I'll ask all about his education."

Her friends were amazing, finding fun in what had felt so heavy and impossible until now. And surely Trisha could keep Henry away from Liam for one more week. She'd just have to be careful doing errands around town. Especially at the grocery store.

For a moment she pictured herself handing Henry off to Liam in some awful custody agreement, and stress shot through her veins. *Don't think about that. One thing at a time. Find out if Liam is a decent person. Find out what my legal situation is. Then I can make some decisions about what to do next.*

As if sensing her worries, Henry woke up from his snooze on Maya and immediately started crying. Trisha went to collect him, cuddling him close, kissing his sweet head, inhaling his lovely baby smell. Just holding her son calmed her down.

"He's tired. I'm going to take him home." Trisha looked around the room, taking in the comforting sight of her fellow Book Biddies. "Thank you all so much for helping me."

"We're so happy, too." Kathy picked up Henry's diaper bag, brought it to Trisha and planted a kiss on her cheek. "That's what we're here for. To support each other."

Trisha blinked tears and kissed her friend back. "I'm so lucky to have you." She waved to everyone else, not trusting that she could say more without crying. Gratitude…relief… worry… It was a potent emotional cocktail.

The drive home through the quiet streets of Shelter Creek made Henry sleepy again. But it also gave Trisha's thoughts room to grow into bigger and scarier worries.

At a dark and deserted intersection, Trisha stopped at the stop sign and rolled down her window. She peeked up at the stars, needing to see some light, however distant. Hopefully, The Book Biddies would discover that Liam was a good person. Hopefully they'd learn that the custody laws were on Trisha's side. Right now she had to try to stay calm and believe that maybe, somehow, everything would be okay.

CHAPTER SEVEN

LIAM GAVE WILD BILL a pat on the neck and tied the bay quarter horse to a wooden post. "You're a good guy, Bill. Thanks for the ride."

Vivian jumped lightly down from the palomino she was riding. "I think W.B. likes you. Maybe he should be your horse while you're staying here."

"I'd like that. W.B., huh? That's what you call him?"

"We have three kids. We're always in a hurry. A lot of stuff gets abbreviated around here."

Liam laughed. He liked Vivian a lot. She was real and unpretentious. They'd become easier with each other on the ride across the ranch this morning. Vivian had suggested this outing yesterday, when they'd both been down at the wildlife center working on that coyote pen. At first Liam had wondered if they'd have anything to say to each other, out riding together in the early morning. But he shouldn't have worried. Vivian was a chatterbox and somehow she'd got him talking, too. She sure asked a lot of questions. Maybe that was a California thing. People in this state certainly had a reputation for wanting to connect to the world on some deeper level.

"Too bad the kids have school today." Vivian led her horse to the next post over. "They were sad to miss out on coyote trapping. They've been glued to that wildlife camera feed."

"I bet they are." Jace and Vivian's kids seemed really smart and curious. "Living out here, they probably get plenty of chances to see wild animals."

"We've all learned a lot." Vivian tied her horse and turned to Liam with a smile that was full of gentle compassion. "When Jace first moved here, he saw the wildlife as one big annoyance. Not unlike you."

"You all sure do like your wildlife. But I guess I'm starting to understand a little. I keep worrying about that coyote I shot." He shook his head at his own growing softhearted ways. "That's different, for sure."

She laughed softly. "That seems to happen here in Shelter Creek."

A noise had them both looking toward the track they'd just traveled. A black pickup was clanking up the rutted lane.

"That's Maya and Trisha," Vivian said. "I guess Emily couldn't make it. She's probably got a surgery scheduled at her clinic."

Liam had expected to see Trisha at the wildlife center at some point yesterday, but she had never shown up. Instead, Maya, Vivian and Emily had lent a hand and given him plenty of advice. Come to think of it, all of them had asked a lot of questions then, too, about how he learned carpentry, and the way his family managed predators at home.

It had been kind of flattering having three smart, pretty women hanging on his every word, but that, combined with Vivian's questions this morning, had him wondering. Maybe Trisha had mentioned what happened in Texas. Maybe that's why they wanted to know so much about him. Could it be possible that she was actually interested in him, and had her friends checking him out?

He'd barely let himself imagine the possibility. Trisha had been so industrious about building walls between them ever since they'd first seen each other here in Shelter Creek. Somewhere, behind all that, could she want something more?

No, that was his own wishful thinking. Trisha was beautiful and unique, and any guy would be a fool not to want to spend more time with her. But she could barely tolerate him. Maybe her friends were just curious. They were all scientists, after all.

Maya parked the truck, and she and Trisha hopped out. Everyone looked just a little ghostly in the dim light of dawn. Liam touched the brim of his hat. "Morning, ladies."

"Morning." Each of them hugged Vivian hello. It was clear these gals were a lot more than colleagues—more like best friends who worked together. Liam couldn't seem to keep his eyes off Trisha. She wore a fitted pink parka and her long blond hair was under a blue beanie. The cold air tinted her cheekbones and the tip of her nose. When she smiled at her friends, her whole face lit up with warmth that Liam suddenly wished she'd show him. But he could waste a whole lot of days wishing for something like that.

"So—" Maya gestured to all of them to

make a circle around her "—we've got a problem. The cameras haven't shown any sign of an adult coyote. Ideally we'd wait longer, because sometimes parents stay away for a while, but when Vivian sent a camera into the den last night, the pups seemed listless. They're probably dehydrated and hungry."

Liam pulled off his hat and ran a hand through his hair. This was his doing. He glanced at Trisha and she looked away quickly, like she'd been watching him.

"It's a tough call," Maya continued. "We can bring them to the wildlife center now that we've built the enclosure. We can feed them, raise them and try to keep them wild so we can release them back out here. But with no adult coyote around to teach them to hunt, their chances of survival are much lower than they would be if raised out in a pack."

"But there is no real pack, right?" Vivian waved her hand to encompass all the wildland on the other side of the pasture fence. "If there were, one of them would take over parenting, right?"

"Most likely." Maya looked at the group. "What do you think?"

"I was doing some reading last night," Trisha said. "If we choose to take them in, and if the parent never returns to this area, we have to be prepared for raising them long-term. That means feeding them live animals when they're older, so they can learn to hunt. Things like rats and gophers, rabbits and even quail. Are we willing to do that?"

"We can't feed them Peanut!" Vivian looked distressed.

"It doesn't have to be Peanut, but it has to be *some* animals. Raising coyotes for release into the wild isn't for the faint of heart."

"Let me get this straight." Liam looked from one woman to the next in astonishment. "You're going to kill other animals just to save coyotes? Isn't that basically exchanging one animal for another?"

"Yep," Maya said. "We're making a value judgment that having wild predators like coyotes around is more important than the lives of a few gophers or rats, or even bunnies."

Liam whistled low. "I'm not sure I'll ever quite understand you all. It just seems like you're exchanging one type of vermin for another."

"Hopefully we can find their parent and release them before we have to teach them to hunt," Trisha said. "Right now they'll eat a stew made of meat and some vegetables and fruits, so that's a lot easier to provide."

"What do you all think?" Maya looked around at the group. "It's going to be a challenge to raise them, but I don't think they'll make it through another day out here on their own."

"I think we should go for it." Trisha looked troubled. "Though I'm not looking forward to feeding them rats and things."

"I say let's do it." Vivian looked at Liam. "What do you think?"

"I get a say in this? Last I checked, I'm the one who caused this problem."

"Which is why you get a say in fixing it." Vivian looked at Trisha. "Right?"

Trisha's brows lowered as she shot a speaking glance at her friend that Liam didn't understand. "I think so."

Liam took the easy way out. "I think when two biologists and a wildlife caregiver tell me that we need to capture these pups, then we'd better go get 'em. What can I do?"

"Carry the trap." Maya went around to the tailgate of the truck and pointed to a rectangular wire cage. "We're going to bait it and hope the pups are hungry enough to go right inside."

The cage wasn't heavy, but it was long and awkward, and Liam staggered with it as he followed Maya, Trisha and Vivian toward the pasture fence. Maya climbed through the barbed wire, then reached over to take the cage from Liam so he could follow her. He noticed that Trisha was holding a bucket. "What's in there?"

"A couple dead gophers," Trisha answered. "Coyote snacks."

"Didn't you just say they'd eat some type of stew?" Liam took the cage back from Maya.

"I'm not totally sure how old they are," Maya said. "But from what I could see on the camera I sent down, they're at the age where their parents would still regurgitate food for them. The pups should recognize the gophers' smell, since it's a big part of the coyotes' diet out in these coastal hills. Hopefully it will lure them into the cage. And if they *are* ready to eat whole gophers, they can start snacking on the drive to the wildlife center."

"And," Vivian added with a sly wink, "I caught these little devils myself. They happened to be eating all the carrots in our garden, so it's a win-win."

"Who knew you were so bloodthirsty!" Trisha gaped at Vivian. "Usually you're so sweet with everyone and everything."

Vivian shot her an evil grin. "The California pocket gopher will make the kindest, most sane gardener hard-hearted eventually, my friend. Just wait until you start up a garden with—"

"Carrots." Maya cut Vivian off abruptly. "When you grow carrots and other root vegetables, or anything, really. Then you'll hate gophers as much as we do."

"Right. That's what I was going to say." Vivian gave Liam a strangely troubled glance, then pointed uphill toward the den. "Let's get going, shall we?"

Trisha glanced into her bucket with a sigh. "If we have to kill gophers for these pups, I'm just glad they're gophers with a history of theft."

"Just like coyotes have a long history of livestock theft." Liam shot her a wink when she glared at him. "Just saying."

"We could debate the merits of coyotes

versus gophers for hours," Maya said. "But let's not, since we're getting near the den."

Liam followed the women up the slope until they reached the bushes that masked the den's entrance. Vivian moved the camera out of the way, and Maya held the branches back so Liam could position the trap.

"Hang on," Trisha whispered, and slid the cage door up. She tipped the gophers in, and then glanced up at Liam with a grim smile. "Breakfast time."

"Mmm…" he whispered back. "Don't tempt me."

She laughed. Just a little huff of a laugh, but he'd charmed it out of her and he felt like he deserved a medal or something. He knelt with the cage and maneuvered it so the open door covered the den's entrance.

"Okay," Maya said quietly. "Now for the tricky part." She pulled a thin rope from her jacket pocket and attached it to the top of the cage door. "If I do this right, we can drop the door once they're inside." She played out the rope for a few yards along the ground. "I'm going to hide in these bushes over here. Vivian, will you stay and help me?"

"Sure." Vivian's smile was bright with excitement. “It’s been a while since I’ve done any fieldwork. I actually miss lying around in the bushes.”

Trish put a hand on Liam’s arm. Just a brief touch, but he felt it right through the sleeve of his sweatshirt. “Let’s move back down the hill.”

He reached out, offering to take the bucket for her, but she moved it out of his reach. “I’ve got it.”

Of course she did. Even if she needed help, she’d never admit it. Walking behind her, Liam could see how she put most of her weight on her left leg. He wished he could offer his arm. Though he probably wouldn’t be much use. His own leg felt weak, too. Most of the time he was fine, but on rugged slopes like this, he felt an odd sort of weakness. He probably needed to do a little more physical therapy. Or maybe this was just as good as it got. Hard to say.

Down by the trucks, he noticed a few of Jace’s cows grazing along the far fence line. It was a good excuse to give Trisha the space from him that she so clearly wanted. “I’m going to go check on these gals. Jace will want a report on how they're doing." He started toward them, but Trisha called out.

"Can I speak to you?"

He stopped, heart banging oddly in his chest, and turned to face her. "Sure. What's up?"

She took a few steps to close the distance between them. Her hands were clasped in front of her, fingers twisted together, betraying her agitation. "I feel like I've been rude since you arrived here in Shelter Creek. I want to apologize." Her wide blue eyes looked even bluer against the beanie she wore. He had a sinking feeling he could forgive pretty much anything, when she was looking at him like this.

"I've given you a couple good reasons to dislike me."

She nodded slowly and glanced around as if to make sure no one could hear them. "Can I ask you something?"

"Go ahead."

"Why did you just leave that morning?" Her cheeks, already pink in the cold air, went a little pinker.

What could he tell her? Standing in this cow pasture with just a few moments alone probably wasn't the best place for the full ugly truth. "I had some stuff I needed to take care of. Some personal stuff."

"And you didn't want to leave a phone number?"

"Ah. That." He looked out over the green hills, with the early-morning fog clinging close to the ground.

"Yes, *that*," she echoed.

"I wasn't in a good place in my life back then," he answered carefully. "I wasn't able to start a relationship. I shouldn't have gotten as involved as we did."

"So…you regret it?"

This was like walking through a field of cow pies in the dead of night. No matter where he stepped, things were going to get messy. "No, it's not like that. Not at—"

"Trisha! Liam!"

Liam looked up to see Vivian on the hill, waving her arms around.

"They must have caught the pups!" Trisha started toward her friend and Liam followed, relieved that he hadn't had to answer her question. Did he regret what happened between them? No. He was pretty sure it had saved his life by making him realize how much he wanted to be worthy of someone like her. Did he regret behaving like a jerk? Absolutely. And he sure regretted the way she resented him. The way he must have hurt her.

Trisha led the way through the barbed wire fence and up the hill.

"We got three of them," Vivian said as they approached. "They walked right into the cage. Two are still inside."

"Can we see?" Trisha's face was lit with an eager smile.

"Of course. Come on."

Maya was kneeling down, looking at the pups. "Their ears are pointing up," she said quietly. "And they're interested in the gophers, so they're probably a few weeks old."

Liam and Trisha knelt down side by side to see them more clearly. They were varying shades of gray and brown.

"Whoa, that one has blue eyes," Liam whispered. The one he pointed to let out a squeaky yelp and cowered in a corner with its littermate.

"No way." Vivian glanced at Maya. "Do you think it could be one of them?"

Maya leaned over to peer at the pup. "It's

possible. Or its eyes may change to brown later."

"What do you mean, *them*?" Liam studied the blue-eyed pup more closely.

"It's a genetic mutation that's been showing up on the California coast. No one knows why, but some coyotes here are now being born with blue eyes."

"That is so cool," Trisha breathed, leaning next to Liam to get a better look. "I hope they stay blue—that is really gorgeous."

"We've got to get the other two out of the den." Maya's practicality brought them all back to the task at hand. "I'm going to grab a flashlight and a few other things from the truck."

"I'll help you," Liam offered. The pups were incredible. Like little dogs, yet also some other animal entirely. More feral, more wild in both their looks and energy. He hadn't expected to be so intrigued by them.

Maya started down the hill, motioning for Liam to follow. He fell into step beside her and said what he'd been wanting to say. "I'm sorry my actions have caused you and your wildlife center so much trouble."

"I appreciate that. But I've worked with

wildlife and ranchers all over this country. I've seen the bodies stacked up on ranches before. It breaks my heart that coyotes are hunted like that, but it's not new to me."

Liam was silent, processing the image she'd planted in his mind. They'd never had a full-scale hunt on their ranch before, just shot at any coyotes who were actively threatening the livestock. But he knew that other ranchers took a more proactive approach and tried to eliminate all the coyotes on their land.

Maya glanced his way with interest. "What did you study in college?"

"Animal husbandry, what else? I was born and raised on a ranch. It's what I've always wanted to do. Well, that and rodeo."

"Vivian mentioned you were in some kind of accident."

"Yup. Got stomped on by a bull with a mean streak and something to prove."

"I'm sorry to hear it."

Liam shrugged. "When you sign up to ride them, you know it's a very real possibility."

"Are you planning to get back into rodeo?"

It pained him to say it, but he'd thought long and hard and come to his decision. "I don't think so. Not sure my leg could heal from another run-in with a bull."

They'd reached the truck and he waited while Maya chose what she wanted. She handed him a shovel, a pickax, a rope and a pole with a noose of rope on it. She grabbed a few more things for herself. "Okay, we're set."

They started back up the hill, and the questions continued. What were his hopes for his family's ranch? Did he enjoy travel? You'd think they were on a first date or something. He wasn't used to talking about himself like this. He was a little relieved when they got back to the den.

"What should we do next?" Vivian motioned to the cage holding the pups, which she and Trisha had moved a few feet away from the den entrance.

"Let's take a look." Maya lay on the ground and beamed the flashlight into the tunnel. "I can see them. It's not a deep den at all. I think if we can just make the entrance a little wider, I can use the catch pole and grab them."

Trisha took the shovel from Liam. "Okay, let's do it."

He gripped the pickax. “Let me loosen the soil up first.”

Maya scooted out of the way and Liam went to the den entrance and carefully chipped away around the edges. The cliff was rocky—it was amazing that the coyotes had found a spot with soil soft enough to dig through.

Liam wedged the pickax behind a rock and levered it forward. It gave suddenly, breaking free from the soil and sending him staggering back into Trisha. She stumbled, too, and he reached for her shoulders, steadying her so she didn’t fall.

He wished he could hold on longer—it felt so right. “Sorry about that.” Liam released her and stepped back. “Didn’t mean to knock you over.”

“It’s fine,” she muttered, moving to stand by Vivian and Maya. “I’ll just stay over here until you need some shoveling done.”

Liam kept working, loosening rock. He tried not to eavesdrop but he could hear a little of what the women were saying as they spoke quietly.

“Where’s our little friend this morning?” he heard Vivian ask.

"Priscilla came by to watch him. She's always up so early. She said it's because of all those years of getting up early to teach."

"She loves kids," Vivian said. "She watches Alex and Amy for us a lot. We tease her that she could have a second career."

Maya glanced at Liam. She must have noticed that he'd been listening. "Pet sitting," she said. "Priscilla pet sits. And babysits."

"Right," he grunted, heaving a big rock a few feet away from the entrance. Trisha sure did love animals if she hired a pet sitter for her cat when she went to work. That was going a little overboard. Maybe the cat was sick or something. Or maybe she was one of those cat ladies people were always joking about. "I think we're ready for that shovel now."

He reached out his hand, but Trisha was determined to shovel on her own, so he stood back and watched her scrape and slide dirt out of the way.

Maya came forward with the pole and flashlight. "Let me see if I can get them." She lay down on the ground and trained the light into the den, then set it down and slid the pole in. She kept one hand on the rope she'd pull to tighten the noose around a pup. "Yikes," she said after a long moment. "This is impossible. I can't get any leverage and they're scooting away so quickly." She pulled the pole back and stood up. "One of us is going to have to reach in there. And, Liam, you're tallest. Can you do it?"

"Reach in there and grab them?" He gaped at her. "Won't they bite me?"

"Oh right, you don't have a rabies vaccination. Trisha, you're the next tallest. Are you willing to try?"

"Of course." Trisha pulled off her hat and set it in the grass. "Anyone got a ponytail holder?"

"Take mine." Maya pulled her brown hair loose and handed a rubber band to Trisha.

Trisha quickly bound her hair back and slid on the long leather gauntlets that Maya handed her. "Can someone shine the flashlight?"

It was on the ground next to Liam. He tried to hand it to Maya but she shook her head. "You go on. Once you see these pups in the den, I bet you'll never want to shoot a coyote again."

"You're determined to convert me, huh?"

He smiled at her and flopped down on the ground next to Trisha. A mistake because he immediately remembered the last time they'd lain down together. *No.* This was not the time. It would never be the time to think that way. He had to keep in mind that Trisha didn't like him much. That night was clearly something she'd prefer to forget. He just wished he could.

Liam switched on the flashlight and lit up the den. It was just a hole dug into the cliff, and not that deep. And then he saw them, cowering in the back corner. Two balls of fluff with eyes lit green by the flashlight, their ears too big for their heads, like someone had stuck big furry tortilla chips on top of them. It was their fear that got him, though. They shook, knowing they were trapped, and he had to swallow down a lump that rose in his throat. What was wrong with him? He was getting soft after just a week in California.

"They're beautiful," Trisha murmured reverently, peeking in, too. "Okay, can you put the light all the way into the den? Otherwise I'll just block it when I go in."

Liam shoved his arm into the den entrance,

wondering if he'd get a coyote bite for his troubles. Not that he didn't deserve one.

Trisha slid forward into the den and Liam realized that the hole they'd dug wasn't quite big enough. She was lying on her stomach, her side pressed against his arm, and he could feel her warmth. He bent at the waist, scooting his body away from her.

"Hold the light still," she hissed, so he did, and she wriggled farther into the den. He heard a high-pitched squeal and then Trisha was sliding back out. She emerged with a squirming pup caught by the scruff of the neck. As soon as she was out of the tunnel, her other hand moved to support its little bottom.

"Make sure the other one doesn't get out," she told Liam and clambered to her feet. She hurried to meet Maya at the cage, where they put the pup inside with its littermates.

"One more to go." Trisha's face was bright with joy. She was in her element here. All her animosity toward him, the stiff, self-protective way she'd been acting, had vanished in this moment.

Liam could rescue coyotes all day, just to see her like this.

She flopped down on her stomach again. "Ready?"

He put the flashlight back in the den and she scooted in on her stomach, and quickly there was another yelp from inside, as if the final coyote had given up on hiding and accepted its fate. Trisha came back out with the last pup, a lighter tan color than its brothers and sisters. "What a cutie," she said breathlessly as she scrambled to her feet. "Here's the last one." She put it in the cage and Maya locked the door. Vivian sat down on the ground next to Liam. "Can you hold the light for just another moment? I want to get some photos of the den."

"You thinking of redecorating?"

She giggled. "It's science. We want to learn as much about our local coyotes as possible. Plus we'll put photos and video on our website to educate the public about our work." She sat up again, finished with her photos. "The more people understand about coyotes..."

He got her drift. "The less likely they'll be to take a shot at them."

"You learn fast. I'm glad Jace hired you."

"Really?"

"Yes. Really. Except for the shooting, it's been nice having you on the ranch." Then she stood, brushed off her jeans and went to join the others.

Liam sat for a moment, looking at the den. Just over a week ago he was in Texas, pulling out of the ranch, waving goodbye, starting his trek for California. Now he was here, rescuing coyotes with a bunch of scientists. He'd gone down a strange rabbit hole, for sure. He glanced at the den. Coyote hole might be more accurate.

But maybe it wasn't such a bad place to be. For the first time since he got here, it felt like maybe things were looking up. It was nice that Vivian was warming up to him, especially because she was married to his boss. Maya was friendly and even Trisha was smiling today.

Liam heaved himself up off the ground and gathered the tools. Vivian helped, while Maya and Trisha carefully lifted the cage of coyote pups and started down the hill. As he followed, Liam glanced out over the hillside, half expecting the adult coyote to be there, mourning the loss of its pups. But there was nothing but grass and brush and some patches of blue sky where the fog was lifting, moving back toward the coast, letting in the light of day.

CHAPTER EIGHT

"I CAN REPORT that Liam's got a good way with horses." Annie topped off her wineglass and took her seat in the circle of lawn chairs set up behind Eva's gallery booth at the Spring Art Fair. "I went by to pick up that hoof trimmer and Liam was up on Jace's horse, Wild Bill, bringing in some cattle. That horse has been on three ranches and not been willing to do much work for anyone. Jace only took him because he was so broke at the time, he'd have accepted anything with hooves. But he hasn't gotten much use out of him either, until now."

"That says something about a man, if he can get a skittish horse to settle down." Maya looked at Trisha reassuringly. "I knew Caleb couldn't be totally lost to me when I saw him working with his rescue horse, Amos."

"I agree. Horses are more people-smart than people are." Annie looked at Trisha.

"We're not trying to pressure you. Just reporting what we've noticed."

Trisha nodded and bounced Henry gently on her knee. Her sweet baby giggled in delight, giving her a big openmouthed smile with two bottom front teeth just poking through his pink gums. "He was really helpful with the coyote pups."

"How are they doing?" Monique folded her perfectly manicured hands in a plea. "Can I come see them?"

"We've got a video camera on them, so you can see them on the wildlife center's website. But you can't come visit them personally," Trisha told her. "We need to limit their exposure to humans as much as possible. We try to never let them see our faces or hear our voices."

"Then how do you feed them?" Kathy glanced up from the blanket she was crocheting for Henry. It had rainbow colors in a patchwork pattern.

"We slide their food through a hatch that Liam built into the solid wood wall in their pen," Maya explained. "It lands in a shallow trough. That way they don't see us and associate us with food."

"Folks have been very helpful with trapping gophers for us and dropping them by," Eva added. "I love this partnership we've created with the community." She jumped up as someone stopped by her booth. "Gotta go. Time to promote the gallery." She shook out her brightly patterned dress and smoothed her sleek, short haircut as she went to meet her potential customer. Eva always looked like a walking work of modern art.

Trisha turned to Vivian, who was sitting beside her, and put a hand on her friend's arm. "What's your take on Liam? You've probably spent the most time with him."

"I really like him." Vivian looked around the group with a warm smile. "He's been to dinner at our house a couple times and he's sweet with the kids. He's patient with the little ones and very polite to Carly, who I suspect might have a bit of a crush on him. Annie's right—he's got Wild Bill eating out of his hand and no one else has been able to earn that horse's trust. And he has a nice sense of humor." She glanced over at Trisha with a grin. "Listen to me. Maybe I'm getting a little crush on him, too. He sure is handsome with those unique eyes and all that wavy brown hair."

"You've already got one gorgeous cowboy." Emily shook a finger from her seat across the circle. "Don't get greedy, now."

Everyone laughed, and Vivian raised her water bottle in a toast. She never drank alcohol. "Can't blame a girl for trying."

"He told me a lot about his family's ranch back in Texas," Maya said. "It sounds like they want to make a lot of positive changes there."

"And Jace tells me he's always looking for an excuse to go out to the pasture by the den, so he can keep looking for the coyote he shot," Vivian said. "I'm glad he is. If it isn't wounded too badly, it might come looking for the pups."

Trisha looked at Maya, who was a national expert on predators. "What are the chances of that happening?"

"Not high. But I like that Liam's not giving up. It could happen, and that would be excellent news for the pups. If we could successfully reunite them, they'd have an adult to teach them how to hunt properly."

Trisha turned Henry so he was facing the

group. Instantly all The Book Biddies' expressions changed to goofy, as they all waved, smiled and cooed. She laughed along with her baby. "This little boy is going to grow up thinking that all women adore him, and will wave and talk to him in sweet singsong voices. Is it possible for a baby to have too many aunties and grannies?"

"Never," Lillian said adamantly. "In fact, I think he needs a cuddle from his grandma Lillian right now."

"As long as Granny Priscilla is next." Priscilla smiled. "And to add my two cents, when I had dinner with Vivian and her family the other night, Liam was very kind. He told me stories about his former teachers. It sounds like he really enjoyed school."

Trisha brought Henry over to Lillian, who quickly snuggled him in her arms and booped his nose, making the little boy giggle in delight. "Your cowboy certainly was appreciative of the cookies Kathy and I delivered yesterday," Lillian said. "He seemed very touched that we'd brought him his own special tin of them."

"Oh, he's very sweet," Kathy added. "And all that *yes ma'am* and *no ma'am* in his Texas accent…" Her voice trailed off and she pretended to fan herself. All the other Biddies laughed.

As Trisha returned to her seat, Vivian looked up at her. "It would be great for Henry to have a daddy," she said quietly.

She was right, of course. "So why do I feel so scared?" Trisha rubbed at a tear that had trickled down her cheek. "I don't know what's wrong with me."

"A mother's instinct is a powerful thing." Vivian took Trisha's hand in hers. "You've been Henry's sole protector for his entire life. You've been his person."

"And you've been able to parent him exactly how you want to," Emily added. "Without having to compromise or take anyone else into account. It must be really scary to think about having to listen to someone else's opinion on how to raise your baby."

Now the tears were really coming. "That's just it. And then there's all those panicky thoughts I told you about at the book club meeting. What if he's short-tempered with Henry? What if he doesn't think about safety when he's with him? What if he wants to take Henry to Texas or something?"

A soft hand rested on Trisha's shoulder. It was Eva. "I researched all this. He can't take him out of state unless a judge approves it, and why would they? You will have to work out some kind of custody arrangement, eventually. But that could be a good thing for you and Henry. Single parenting is intense. Trust me, I know."

"No one is going to let anything bad happen to Henry," Lillian said. "We will be the first to stand behind you if Liam sets a toe out of line. But you have to look at the long game. A child should know both their parents." She glanced at Maya, the granddaughter she'd raised. "If possible."

"I agree." Maya smiled at Trisha. "Try to think about what Henry would want, as he gets older." Maya didn't know her own parents at all—they were very troubled and had been homeless for decades now—so Trisha knew her friend was speaking straight from the heart.

All of them were right. It would be completely selfish to keep Henry a secret any longer. This was a moral choice. The universe had thrown Henry's dad right up on her doorstep. It was completely unexpected, but Trisha still had to do the right thing.

"You could tell Liam right now, if you're up for it." Vivian pointed to the pretzel booth. "It looks like Jace talked him into coming along."

Trisha scanned the line of people waiting for pretzels and there were Jace and Liam, and Ranger, who stood calmly at Liam's feet. Both cowboys were gently guiding Alex and Amy forward for their pretzels. Trisha's heart did an unexpected flop when Liam knelt down and listened attentively to whatever little Alex was saying. Alex hadn't spoken much when he first came to live with Jace, and he was still shy. If he felt comfortable talking to Liam, that meant something.

She looked at Lillian. "Do you mind keeping Henry for a bit?"

"I'm still waiting for my baby fix," said Priscilla.

"Me, too." Emily glanced at her watch with mock outrage. "I'm pretty sure Lillian has gone over her allotted time."

Everyone laughed, and Trisha stood, feeling like, if she took one step outside this circle of friends, she'd be stepping off a cliff. She had no idea how she'd land.

"You've got this." Maya stood up. "Do you want me to come with you?"

The tears that had sunk below the surface rose again. Of course Maya would offer. She and Trisha had survived that horrible accident together when they were teens. They'd each had to find a way to live on after their friend Julie died, and it had forged a bond between them that ran deep. "Thank you so much. But I think I should do this alone."

"I understand." Maya opened her arms, and Trisha stepped in for a hug. "We are all right here," Maya said quietly. "If he gets weird or you feel worried, The Book Biddies have your back."

"Hear, hear." Annie rose from her seat and hugged Trisha, too, which was unusual. Annie wasn't much of a hugger. "You be strong, okay? You set the rules for how you introduce him to Henry. He walked away that night, so you get to call the shots."

Annie was one of the strongest people Trisha knew. She ran a successful ranch on her own and she organized all the local ranchers to support each other. For the past couple years, she'd been in love with another rancher in Shelter Creek, Juan Alvaro, but despite their close relationship, she never gave up her independence. Maybe Trisha could channel some of Annie's toughness when she talked with Liam. She didn't want to cry, or fall apart, or show her fear. "I'll keep that in mind. Thanks, Annie."

She went to Lillian and picked up Henry. Hugging her baby close, she inhaled his special scent, rejoicing in the feel of his small body against her chest. His little fist tangled in her hair. These were her last moments of being his only parent. She swallowed hard. "I'll keep you safe, baby," she murmured. "No matter what. I promise." She untangled her hair from his fingers and passed him back to Lillian. "I'd better go do this, before I lose my nerve."

"I'm so proud of you, Trisha," Lillian said. "You always put your baby's well-being first. You are a great mother."

Now the tears would not stay back. Trisha admired Lillian and her words felt like the highest praise. "Thank you."

She stood, gave Henry a last wave and went to have a talk with his daddy.

"HERE'S SOME CHEESE sauce for your pretzel, Amy." Liam handed the little girl her requested sauce. "I brought some extra napkins." He handed the pile to Jace.

"Thanks for the help." Jace passed a couple napkins to Alex and sat back in his chair with a sigh. "My wife is over there having wine with her book club. I'm here with you, navigating kids and messy pretzels. What am I doing wrong?"

Liam glanced in the direction his boss was pointing, surprised to see Trisha wending her way through the crowd. She was dressed in slim dark jeans and a cute pair of white tennis shoes. She wore her pale pink parka against the chill.

He remembered how she'd looked the last time he saw her, up at the ranch, after pulling coyote pups out of the den. She'd had dirt all down her front and side, and some on her cheek. He'd pointed it out, resisting the temptation to brush it off for her.

"Good evening," Jace called as Trisha got closer. "Are you coming to tell me that you're keeping my wife for the rest of the evening?"

Trisha laughed, a light musical sound. "The

Book Biddies official meeting has adjourned. You can go crash the after-party anytime."

"And where is young—"

She cut Jace off. "Liam, may I speak with you?"

Her rudeness to Jace seemed unlike her. Come to think of it, she was as stressed as he'd ever seen her, her whole body vibrating with it, like a wire that had been pulled too tight. "Sure, I guess. Is it okay if I leave you on your own for a bit, Jace?"

Jace grinned, his easygoing nature moving on from the awkward moment. "With these two hellions? You'd better believe it. As soon as they finish their pretzels, we're going to go see how much mischief we can get into."

"I'm not sure how much mischief is available at the art fair," Trisha said.

"Oh, we'll find it, trust us." Jace ruffled Amy's and Alex's hair. "Right, guys?"

"You know it!" Amy had cheese sauce on her nose, so Jace leaned over with a napkin and wiped it off.

"Okay, then. Ranger, come." His dog emerged from beneath the table looking guilty. "Were you scavenging under there again?" Liam ruffled the dog's ears and clipped a leash to his collar.

"Hi, Ranger." Trisha held out her knuckles. It was sweet to see her interact with his dog. All of her prickly defenses went down when she was around animals.

"Where do you want to go?" Liam asked as they walked away from Jace and the kids.

She motioned to the street that ran along one side of the town square. "There's a park over there. Would that be okay?"

He nodded and they walked there in silence. Liam kept glancing her way, waiting for her to say something, but she didn't. Instead she chewed her lower lip, her skin so pale, he wondered if she was ill. It was odd that she'd seek him out tonight, when all she'd done since he got to Shelter Creek was try to avoid spending much time around him.

Liam glanced around the town, still getting used to its quaint feel. They were walking on Main Street, with the square behind them. The buildings were Victorian era, as far as he could tell, all painted in pretty, festive colors, with flowers spilling out of gardens and window boxes. Some old cottages had been converted into shops and restaurants. There were also gift shops, a couple of wine tasting rooms and some galleries. Shelter Creek definitely catered to the tourists, who seemed to love it here.

"It's a nice town," he attempted by way of conversation.

"It is."

"Have you lived here a long time?"

"All my life." She walked on in silence again, then seemed to realize that she was being so quiet. "It's changed a lot. It was a lot less fancy when I was younger. But a few years ago they started offering flights from Los Angeles into the Santa Rosa airport. That's not too far from here and it helped make Shelter Creek a tourist destination. Plus, we get weekend visitors from San Francisco, too."

"It must be great for the economy."

"It really helps." She left the sidewalk and led him through a small park in a redwood grove. There was a picnic area and a playground farther on, but Trisha went down the slope toward the creek that rushed around rocks and rippled into eddies beneath the overhanging tree roots. "This is Shelter Creek. Not the town, the actual creek." She sat on the ground beneath an enormous tree and indicated that he should do the same.

"It's pretty." Before Liam sat, he ran his hand over the thick redwood bark and peered up, trying to see all the way to the top. He couldn't. The branches went on and on, though he caught glimpses of the dim evening sky somewhere up there. It would be getting dark soon. "These trees are amazing. You realize that, right?"

"Is this your first time seeing a redwood?" She looked up at him with obvious disbelief.

"My first time seeing one up close. The bark is really weird." He pushed on it. "It's kind of like a sponge or something."

"It's fireproof. The inside of the tree might burn in a forest fire, but the outside layer will still stand, letting the tree live. It makes these amazing tree caves. There's a forest just west of town that has some. We used to play house in the trees when I was little."

"We?"

"I'd play with my parents. I'm an only child."

Liam remembered the loud chaos of his own childhood. "I can't imagine. Were you lonely?"

"Sometimes."

He sat beside her at the base of the tree, and Ranger settled at his side with a happy sigh. Liam ran his hands over Ranger's velvet ears and watched the creek go by. It smelled good here, the ground still damp from recent rains. Little green plants that looked like giant clovers pushed up through the red-brown soil beneath the redwood trees. When he couldn't take the suspense any longer, he leaned over and bumped his shoulder gently into Trisha's. "Are you going to tell me why you brought me down to this creek?"

The breath she let out was shaky. He glanced down at her. She had a dried-up redwood frond in her hand and she was twisting it into knots. She glanced at him and her lip trembled and he hoped she wouldn't cry. Was this about that night? Had he been so very terrible to her?

"I have a son," she said quietly.

That definitely wasn't what he was expecting. "You're a mom?" He didn't quite know why she was telling him, so he didn't know how to answer. "That's great. Kids are awesome."

"You think so?" Her eyes were sparkling in the dusky light.

Were those tears welling up? He barely knew her, didn't know how to handle all this emotion with her. "What's wrong, Trisha? You're upset."

She swallowed hard and threw the redwood leaf into the creek. "He's yours."

Liam's heart gave a lurch, like it had missed a beat or two. His muscles went oddly still. His ears had a strange ring in them, or maybe that was the sound of the creek. It was all sort of blending together into a strange internal roar. He watched Trisha warily, but she didn't look at him. "Mine?"

She finally looked at him and, yes, there were tears. She was crying silently, with no sobs, just pure emotion pouring over her skin. "I got pregnant that night in San Antonio. I had a baby boy. His name is Henry and he's just turned eleven months old."

He stood, her words propelling him forward into action, though there was no real action to take. He walked a few paces away, Ranger at his heels. A kid. A baby. She'd had his child.

He'd never considered the possibility, never

considered the consequences of that night. In those days, the only consequence he cared about was the high that he got from taking another pill.

He turned back and Ranger whined in confusion. Trisha was still sitting, her knees up, her arms wrapped around them as if she needed to hold herself together physically.

He was a father. He had a little boy. "Eleven months old?" It was a stupid question, something to anchor him while the world spun around him. He wasn't questioning his role in this. He was there that night. He could count.

She nodded, but said nothing.

He sat again and closed his eyes, pressing his hands to them as if the pressure could slow his racing thoughts. Ranger flopped down next to him again, a warm comforting presence along his thigh. "I left without telling you how to get hold of me."

Her voice was calm, almost wooden. "I looked on the internet. On social media sites. But there are so many people when you search the name William."

The wrong name. He'd given her the wrong name, and no last name. Then walked away from her, and his child. He took his hands away so he could see her profile. "I am so sorry."

She was still looking straight ahead, studying the water, as if hypnotized by the current, but he heard the hurt behind her words. "I figured you wouldn't be interested anyway."

"I wasn't in good shape at that time. I had problems I had to work out. But, Trisha, I am interested. I'm… I'm blown away." He paused, trying to pin his thoughts into words, but it was impossible. "I don't really know what I am. But I *am* interested."

A baby. He was a father. He'd never even considered being a dad—it was something far off in the future, once he met someone, fell in love, got married. But it had happened, was already happening. He'd missed her pregnancy, and most of the baby's first year. "Why didn't you tell me sooner?"

"You've been here for two weeks. I had to make sure you were a somewhat-decent human being."

Liam stared at the water, questions flooding his mind. He wasn't sure which to ask and which to keep to himself. "You're doing well? Having a baby and all? He… Henry… is healthy?"

She smiled then, as if the mention of Henry turned a light on inside her, creased her cheeks and crinkled her eyes. She was so beautiful, the mother of his child, the angel who, back in San Antonio had somehow made him realize it was time to get help.

"Henry is a beautiful, chubby, happy baby. And I'm fine, too." She pulled her phone out of her back pocket and opened the photo app. And there he was. Liam's son. Brown hair like his, but more curly, like Liam's mom's had been. The baby's smile had a hint of Boone's mischief. But the sweetness in his blue eyes was all from Trisha.

He couldn't stop staring at the photo. Their child. "I can't believe we have a son together."

"Me neither, really."

A lump was growing in his throat. "Where is he?"

"Back at the art fair."

He looked at her, startled that the baby was so close by. "With who?"

"Maya. Her grandmother. Emily. Our book club friends. They're like Henry's extended family."

Family. Until now the word had meant his brothers. His parents. The ranch. Texas. Now he had a son just a few blocks away. Here in California. "Can I see him?"

"You can meet him, yes. But there's a lot to figure out, Liam. You have to realize, he's my baby. *Mine.* I carried him. I've raised him until now. I don't know what role I want you to play in his life."

He was still trying to take it all in. "I get it. I do. We both need to think about it."

She rose stiffly from the ground. "I'll take you to him, if you want."

He stood, too, and Ranger, ever patient, followed suit. "Yes, I do. I want to." His heart was racing and he had to force himself to take a deep breath. It was a lot to take in, almost too much to fathom.

They started back toward the town square and what she'd just said sunk in. Vivian, Maya, Emily—they all helped her with Henry. "Your friends. Do they all know about me? Does Jace know?"

"Jace doesn't know, and neither does Caleb. I'd never told anyone who the father was, and my friends were kind enough not to pressure me." She glanced his way briefly. "But last weekend, when you'd been here for a few days already, I did tell my book club.

So Maya, Emily, Vivian and everyone else in The Book Biddies have known for a week."

"Ah." It all made sense now. "That's why they were asking me all those questions."

"I wanted to make sure you were a good guy. I mean, you showed up in town and shot a coyote."

Her words hit hard in the most insecure spot in his soul. He hadn't been a good guy for a couple years after his injury. He'd done so much he was ashamed of. He should tell her right now. Just spit it all out and let her know the kind of man she'd gotten herself caught up with. But then she might change her mind about letting him see Henry. And he had to meet his son, even if it was only this once. So he took the lighter route. "I take it you don't have a cat? Or at least not one named Henry?"

She gave him an apologetic glance. "No cat. I'm sorry for the lie. I wasn't ready to tell you, and once his name was mentioned, I had to think of something."

"I'm actually kind of relieved that you don't bring your cat to book club meetings. It's not really my business, but it did seem kind of odd."

"Why would you care?"

"Because I like you." There. He'd said it. Though now, whatever he'd felt for her before was buried in layers of complication. They had a child. A baby.

She looked surprised at his words, but said nothing. They'd reached the edge of the art fair. She gestured for him to follow. "Come on." She hurried forward as if determined to get this meeting over with.

Liam and Ranger followed Trisha through the crowded fair, Liam's pulse thrumming with anticipation and something else. Disbelief? It was almost dark now. White lights had been strung between trees and along paths and the booths for the art fair were all lit up. On a normal night it would be pretty, but the way his life had just changed in the course of a sentence lent a surreal quality to everything around him.

He saw a circle of chairs behind the Shelter Creek Gallery booth. Jace was there, sitting with Vivian while the kids played behind them. Maya and Caleb were next to each other holding hands, and Liam recognized Annie Brooks, who'd come by Jace's ranch the other day. And there was Emily, the vet, standing off to one side, cuddling a sleepy-looking baby wrapped in a blanket.

Liam put a hand on Trisha's arm. "Is that Henry?"

"Yes." She looked up at him. "Are you ready to meet your son?"

"In front of all these people?"

"These are Henry's people. They only want what's best for him."

She led him around the outside of the group to where Emily stood. The vet's eyes widened when she saw Liam. Carefully she lifted the baby off her shoulder, handed him to Trisha and went to join the others.

It was his son. Liam could only stand and stare as Henry shifted sleepily on Trisha's shoulder and opened his mouth in a yawn as cute as a kitten's.

He didn't know what to feel. New parents were supposed to fall in love, right? But he mostly felt disoriented. Disconnected. His body was here, staring at this baby, but his mind couldn't connect the dots. How had his son been living, growing and learning in the world when Liam hadn't even known he existed? If he hadn't drawn the short straw in the barn that day, he might never have known.

Panic jolted his senses. It was all so random, that he was here at all. He'd come so close to going through life never knowing about this baby. He took a step back.

"Liam, are you okay?" Trisha was watching him carefully and he remembered that this was a huge moment for her, too. That she'd been forced to include him in the life she'd carved out for Henry all on her own.

"It's a lot to take in."

"Do you want to hold him?"

"I haven't had much practice." He tied Ranger's leash to a nearby light post. Then he reached awkwardly for Henry. He didn't know where to put his hands. They looked so big next to the baby. He pulled them back. "I don't want to hurt him."

"Here." Trisha turned Henry carefully so he was on his back, cradled in her arms. "Hold your arms like mine."

Liam tried to imitate her position, bending his elbows, and she laid the baby in the crook of his arm. "Support him underneath with the other arm." She kept her arms under Henry until she was sure Liam had him, then she stepped back and Liam was holding his son.

The soft weight in his arms was unfamiliar

but somehow an enormous comfort. Henry blinked at him with mildly curious eyes, like he was trying to decide whether this new person was worth waking up for. “Hey, Henry,” Liam whispered. “I’m your dad.” The sudden lump in his throat had him holding back any more words he might want to say. Not that there were words adequate for this moment anyway. Henry’s nose was tiny, his cheeks round. Liam had next to no experience with babies, but his son looked like a beautiful one to him.

A big hand came softly down on his shoulder. “You okay?” Jace’s gaze was full of concern. “Vivian just let me know what’s going on over here.”

Liam nodded, not trusting himself to speak.

“Okay. Let us know if you need anything.”

“Thanks, Jace,” Liam managed. “I appreciate it.” He turned to Trisha. “What do we do now?”

“I’ve got to take him home to bed. Want to walk us to my car?”

“Yes. I’d like that.”

She went over to one of the chairs in the circle and came back with a tote bag. “Good night, everyone," she called out. "Thanks for all of your support tonight." Everyone waved and called out good-night, but thankfully, no one said anything about what had just happened. That all in an instant, right before their eyes, he'd become a daddy.

Trisha took Henry from Liam and the air was cool where the warmth of his son had been. "Will you carry the diaper bag?"

"The what? Oh yes." He grabbed the tote she'd set down and went to retrieve Ranger from the lamppost. Then he followed Trisha to her car, which was parked at the edge of the square.

She loaded Henry into the car seat and put the bag on the floor. Then she turned to Liam. "I guess we should talk a little more about this another time."

"Yeah. I'd like that. Soon, I hope."

"Tomorrow is Sunday. Want to come by my house in the afternoon? Vivian has the address."

"Sure. Yeah." The surreal feeling had returned and he had the sense that his life, which had seemed so simple just a few hours ago, had been broken up like the pieces of one of those giant jigsaw puzzles his brother

Wyatt sometimes did. There must be some pattern, some way to put it all back together, but Liam couldn't fathom it right now.

"Great. I'll see you then."

"Yeah. Good night, Trisha. Thank you." Maybe that was a weird thing to say. But she could have found a way not to tell him. She could have said that Henry belonged to someone else.

"Good night, Liam." She got into her little hatchback and started the engine.

Liam stood and watched until Trisha and his son had disappeared into the night. He walked back to the circle and sat down woodenly in the chair next to Jace.

"I don't know what to say."

"I became a father of three with one phone call," Jace told him. "You don't have to explain anything to me."

"Just tell me I'll start to feel something other than total confusion, soon."

Jace's laugh rang out, causing several people to look their way. "Oh, trust me, my friend. You will have more feelings than you've ever had before. Maybe just enjoy the daze while it's here."

Liam slid down in his chair and tipped his

head back so he could see the sky. The black silhouettes of redwoods rose impossibly high. Stars were coming out behind them. They were comforting. A reminder that no matter how overwhelming this news seemed, it was just a tiny blip in the cosmos. He had a son. And by some miracle, he'd met him tonight. He had a son. *He had a son.*

CHAPTER NINE

"LOOK AT HENRY, crawling so fast now." Monique pinned up a section of Trisha's hair. "Remember when he couldn't figure out how to use his back legs?"

"He'd scoot backward until he got stuck partway under the sofa, remember? I must have a million photos of him with his legs under there, looking totally confused." Trisha grinned, watching Henry do laps around her kitchen table. His little diapered buns waggled back and forth with every crawling step. She'd put him in pants that had a bear face on the seat, so the bear waggled, too. It had to be the cutest thing ever. Or maybe that was yesterday, when he was cuddling the stuffed horse Annie had given him. Or the day before when Trisha and Henry had stopped by Maya's ranch. Caleb had set Henry up on his placid horse Newt's back, then ducked down behind so Trisha could take a photo.

It almost looked like Henry was riding by himself, if you discounted Caleb's big hands holding him securely in place.

It was reassuring to remember all the good times. All the joyful moments since Henry had come into the world. Especially after last night, when everything changed forever.

"How was it, telling Liam?" Monique must have read her mind while she snipped away with her scissors.

Trisha watched her split ends fall to the floor. "Terrifying. Like I was throwing away the life I've built for Henry. I feel like I traded it in for the complete unknown."

"I can understand that." Monique put gentle fingers under Trisha's jaw to angle her head just so. "Sometimes the right thing is the hardest thing to do. At least Liam seemed to take it okay. I think it's a good sign that he wanted to meet his son right away."

"He seemed like he was in a daze. Who wouldn't be? One minute he was his usual carefree, Texas cowboy self, and the next, he was a father."

"He's tough—he can handle it." Monique gave a soft huff of laughter. "Isn't that a bit what getting pregnant is like? One minute you're just you, like you've always been, then you look at that stick and realize you're going to be a mom."

"Yes, but we do get several months to prepare ourselves."

"True." Monique came around to the front and started rearranging Trisha's hair. Her makeup was perfect as always, and Trisha admired the neat lines painted around her eyes, the shadow blended just right. She'd never been great at makeup, and since having Henry she didn't even bother. Monique had finally insisted on coming by today to trim her hair, since Trisha hadn't found time for the salon since Henry was born.

"I just hope he doesn't get weird. I want him to be a good dad, but I don't want him to try to change anything significant, you know?"

"And what about the fact that he lives in Texas?"

Trisha shuddered. "I can't think about that. All I know is that Shelter Creek is Henry's home."

Monique's expression became fierce. "No way is Henry-bug going anywhere. As his favorite auntie, I decree it." Monique was closer to great-auntie age, but she'd never acknowledge the "great" part. "Still," she went on, "you did the right thing, telling him. Keeping that secret any longer would have been cruel. And I trust it's going to work out well. It's a miracle that Liam ended up here in Shelter Creek. That has to mean something."

"I hope so." Trisha closed her eyes, trying to keep the confusion at bay. There was so much to think about. And worry about.

"Let's have faith. And if anything goes wrong, we'll stand together and make it right." Monique pulled Trisha's hair up straight off the top of her head and snipped some strands. "I'm giving you a few more layers around your face. Trust me—you'll love it. And it's time to end this parted-in-the-middle-straight-hair look. You're a confident young mama. You should be rocking some cool hair."

"Okay." Trisha barely heard what Monique was saying. What if Liam was a terrible father?

"Can I say something that's probably way too personal and might make you mad at me?"

Trisha glanced up to meet Monique's kind gaze. "Isn't that your specialty?"

Monique laughed—a low rich sound. "I guess it is. Look, you have to find your own way through this. You and Liam both. I've watched you in the last couple years. You were very quiet around town until you got involved with us Book Biddies. It almost seemed like you were trying to disappear, you know? Like you were apologizing for being here at all."

Trisha winced. Was that how she'd come across? Sure, she'd been quiet, content with her work as a veterinary technician, spending her free time reading and taking walks. Or at least, that's what she'd told herself.

"You've been coming out of your shell since you got involved with us Biddies, and Maya and the wildlife center. And Henry has been great for you, too. I guess what I'm saying is that all of these things were changes that you couldn't foresee, and yet they were all really good for you. Maybe having Liam in your life is another good change."

"Maybe. I hope so." It was certainly possible. "So why do I feel so scared?"

"Because it's normal. When you found out you were pregnant, I imagine that must have been scary, too, right? But look at you now, with this beautiful baby. And you've been making it work as a single mother."

They both looked at Henry, who'd found his favorite cloth baby book. He'd opened it to the page with the mirror and was watching himself with a drooly smile on his face.

"I mean, look at that baby. He's thriving. You've built a loving community around him. Even if Liam isn't the perfect father, Henry will be fine. And you will be fine, too."

"Thanks, Monique. You know you could change your salon to a therapist's office and charge a lot more money."

Monique smiled as she tugged at the hair on either side of Trisha's face, running it through her fingers to make certain it was even. "Hair is way more fun than therapy. And if the cut is good, the results last longer, too." She ruffled Trisha's hair and removed the black poncho she'd put over her shoulders. "Go look in the mirror."

"Keep an eye on Henry?"

"Absolutely. I'll make sure he doesn't actually eat that book."

"He's teething. If you look in the freezer, there's one of those iced chewy things. Maybe he'd like it." Trisha went to the bathroom, saw her reflection and froze. Monique had added layers from her jaw to the ends of her hair, which still fell well past her shoulders. Her normally stick-straight hair, which she usually kept back with a headband or ponytail, looked thicker. Flowing. More interesting.

"What do you think?" Monique called. "Do you look like a sophisticated mama?"

"I look like a grown-up," Trisha marveled, turning her head to see the way she looked from the side.

"It's about time." Monique's dry humor meant no insult and Trisha didn't take it that way. Monique called her salon Monique's Miracles and she'd certainly worked one today.

"Do you feel more confident?" Monique asked. "Ready to spend some time with the father of your baby?"

"I guess so."

"I hope so, because he's sitting in his truck outside."

Trisha followed Monique to the front window and there was Liam, sitting on the tailgate of his truck, with Ranger at his side. He was rubbing the dog's ears, staring absently into space.

"Girl, you sure do know how to pick a baby daddy. That is one handsome cowboy."

Trisha smiled ruefully. "He is that. Good genes."

"Any chance you'll rekindle the fire that caused all this?"

"What? No! That was just too much alcohol. And he probably had his beer goggles on." But she remembered what he'd said last night. That he liked her. Her skin felt warm every time she pondered those words.

"He looks lost, sitting out there."

Trisha agreed. "Maybe I should go out and talk to him."

"I'll do it. I've got to get going anyway." Monique bustled back to the table to collect her scissors and other supplies. "Let me talk a little sense into him on the way out?"

"Sure. Maybe he needs a little Monique therapy."

"Oh, trust me, honey, everyone does." Monique stooped down to kiss Henry on the head and then blew another kiss to Trisha. "You look gorgeous. Shoulders back, keep your confidence up—you've got this." And then she was out the front door and gone.

Trisha watched by the window as Monique approached Liam at his truck. Liam scooted over as the hair-stylist-slash-therapist sat right down on the tailgate beside him. Trisha smiled. “Poor Liam won’t know what hit him,” she told Henry, and went to get the broom.

LIAM WAS PETTING Ranger’s head and pondering a tree when the unfamiliar woman sat herself right down on his tailgate.

“That’s a pretty nice tree,” the bleached-blonde lady said as she sat down. “A coast live oak. I love their twisting silver trunks. This one must be a few hundred years old.”

Startled by her presence, Liam scooted over to make more space for her. “I was just thinking that. How much it’s seen. All the weather and people’s lives…” Liam realized he was revealing his inner thoughts to a total stranger. “I’m sorry, I guess you caught me in a strange mood. What can I do for you?”

“I’m Monique. A friend of Trisha’s. I was just leaving her house and I saw you sitting out here.”

Liam tipped his hat and turned his body to see her a little better. It was weird sitting in such close proximity to someone he didn't know. "Nice to meet you, Monique." His mama, rest her soul, would be proud that her boy was keeping up the manners he'd been taught, even when his mind was reeling.

"I'm sure it's a shock to find out you have a child." Monique's voice was matter-of-fact, as if they were still chatting about the tree.

"Yes. No disrespect intended, ma'am, but that's kind of personal."

"I'm one of Henry's honorary aunties, so it's personal to me, too."

"Ah. Okay." This town had more meddling ladies per square foot than any place he'd ever been.

"I want Trisha and Henry to be happy. I want Henry to know his father. As long as his father is a good man." She gave Liam a long, assessing glance. "You *look* like a good man."

"Looks are deceptive." As soon as he said it, he regretted it. What was it with this woman, getting him to be so honest? Maybe because she was so blunt, it made him that way, too.

"So that's why you're not inside with your son right now."

"It might have something to do with it." He'd woken up this morning thinking about his addiction. All that he'd done wrong as a result. What type of father did that make him?

"Did you kill anyone? Injure them? Commit any other major crimes?"

"Not really, no."

"Are you a danger to women or children?"

"No!" This lady was one of a kind. Perfectly dressed and made up on a Sunday morning, like she was going to some fancy event, yet here she was, getting her white slacks dirty sitting on his tailgate, giving him the third degree.

"And clearly animals like you. That dog seems devoted and I even heard that a horse aptly named Wild Bill has taken a liking to you."

"How do you know about that?" Liam had a weird feeling that Monique was some kind of fairy godmother, descending on him to put everything to rights.

"News travels fast in this town."

"I guess so."

"Anyway, Liam. You seem like a nice guy. I think you should go inside and share whatever is weighing on your mind with Trisha. She's the mother of your child and a great one at that. She has the right to know your secrets. You two will figure it out from there."

She slid off the tailgate and waited expectantly.

"You're saying I should go in there right now." It was hard to understand his own reluctance. His son was in there. He should be eager to go in. But to walk in that door was to assume a level of responsibility he hadn't thought to take on for years. He wasn't sure he was ready.

"No time like the present." She smiled brightly.

Liam stood up and closed the tailgate behind him. "Stay," he told Ranger. The good dog flopped down on the old horse blanket. Knowing Ranger, Liam figured he'd be snoozing in moments, oblivious to the life changes swirling around his owner.

"Thanks for the kick in the pants," he told Monique.

"Anytime you need one, cowboy, you just stop by my salon. Monique's Miracles. You're always welcome."

"I appreciate that."

"She turned on her high heels and walked quickly toward her little red sports car. Her pants were covered with dust, but she didn't seem to care one bit. She had class and guts, and she was demanding that he have that, too.

Brushing off the seat of his jeans, Liam squared his shoulders and walked toward Trisha's neat Victorian cottage. It was painted pale blue with white trim. A porch ran along two sides, with old ornate carved columns and a bunch of decorative trim along the roofline. There were flowers in pots and one of those hanging wooden porch swings with lots of pillows. A great place for a nap, and boy could Liam use one. He'd been up most of the night, trying to take it all in.

But tired or not, he'd heard Monique loud and clear. It was time to step up to his new life. He was a dad, and everything was different now.

CHAPTER TEN

TRISHA THOUGHT SHE was prepared for the knock on her door, but it rattled her down to her bones.

She'd almost hoped Liam wouldn't come by today. That maybe holding Henry last night had scared him off. Then her own world, so safe and cozy with just her and her baby and all of her friends for support, would stay intact.

His enthusiasm last night was lovely and she should welcome it. But instead it reminded her of the spot where a rock had struck the windshield of her car last week. The cracks were slowly spreading, breaking her view apart. With Liam in the picture, she couldn't see her way forward anymore. She took a deep breath and let it out.

"Okay, Henry. Your dad is here." Her voice sounded foreign—not just the words, but the tone, everything. Henry was too busy with his teething ring to pay much attention. She picked him up, needing the comfort of his solid little body against hers.

She opened the door and there was Liam—hazel eyes, tentative crooked smile. His hat was in his hand, the old brown felt and braided leather band worn with years of use. He had a few freckles on his tanned skin. She hadn't noticed that before.

He wiped a palm on his faded jeans. "Morning." He looked young. She'd never really considered his age, but now she did. "How old are you?"

He looked startled, and rightly so. She'd just blurted out her question. "I'm twenty-six."

Twenty-six? She almost slammed the door in his face right there and then. Her shock must have shown on her face, because he leaned an arm on the doorframe and gave her a nervous smile. "Let me guess. You're a very young-looking forty?"

"No! I'm twenty-eight."

There was a touch of relief in his eyes. "You've got two years on me. That's nothing."

"But twenty-six seems too young to have a baby."

"I think you're holding evidence to the contrary." He smiled at Henry, a gentle smile without his usual swagger behind it. "Good morning, little guy."

Henry regarded him solemnly, still gnawing on his icy toy.

"He's teething." Trisha pulled a tissue out of her pocket and dabbed at Henry's chin. "I need to put a bib on him. He's like a fountain of drool."

"He takes after his daddy."

At Trisha's surprised look, his smile went sheepish. "Sorry, dumb joke. I don't really drool much, that I know of. Maybe while I'm sleeping." Liam put a hand over his eyes for a brief instant. "Okay, can we start again, here? I think I'm off my game."

She couldn't believe he had her smiling despite all her anxiety. "I suspect we're both off our game today."

"Are babbling idiots like myself allowed inside?"

Oh gosh, she was just leaving him there, standing on her doorstep. "Of course. Please come in."

He leaned on the outside wall and yanked off his cowboy boots. He had gray wool socks underneath and seemed oddly vulnerable without his hat and boots. Or maybe it was his age. *Twenty-six.* Why was it bugging her? Had she been hoping somewhere deep down inside that he was older, and more established? That he'd jump in and take charge and make everything okay for her and Henry? That was ridiculous. She didn't need a man to take care of her. But she sure didn't need a boy hanging around either.

She led the way inside. "Do you want to sit down?" She motioned toward the sofa in her small living room.

"Sure. Thanks." He set his hat on the arm of the sofa and sat down.

"Can I get you some water?" This was so awkward. They weren't even friends. They barely knew each other.

"That would be great."

She kept Henry with her as she went to the kitchen. She put his teething ring back in the freezer and filled a glass of water for Liam. She grabbed Henry's green sippy cup as well. Back in the living room, she set Liam's glass on a coaster on the coffee table and sat on the floor with Henry next to her. The little guy took a few sips from his cup, then threw it down, so it rolled.

"We put the cup down like this." Trisha demonstrated by setting it upright.

"Teaching him manners already." Liam's tone held that teasing Texas charm she'd found so irresistible the night they met.

"Trying. I suspect it will take some time."

Henry waved his arms in delight and knocked the cup down again.

"Okay, you scamp." Trisha set the cup on the coffee table. "Let's get you blocks to knock down." She opened the drawer of the coffee table and pulled out the box of old wooden ABC blocks that had belonged to her when she was young. She set them up in a stack and Henry squealed in delight as he demolished her creation.

Trisha tried to think of something to talk about besides Henry. She wasn't ready to talk much about her son, even though he was the whole reason for Liam's visit. "How is your work going with Jace?"

"Good." He nodded. "I thought I knew pretty much everything about ranching, but he's got a different take on it. He's showing me how to make sure everything on the ranch is organic. There are lots of rules about that. And did you know he's getting this thing called a digester? It turns manure into methane gas and he's going to use that gas to power the ranch." He grinned and gave her a wink. "Sorry, I probably shouldn't be talking about manure here in your nice house."

Trisha smiled, surprised that he was so funny. "I work with animals—I know all about manure."

"That's right—you're Emily's veterinary assistant *and* you work at the wildlife center."

She nodded. "It keeps me busy, but I love both jobs."

"How are the coyote pups doing?"

"Great." Trisha brightened just thinking about them. "They're all really healthy, as far as we can tell. They're eating a ton and even practicing some hunting behavior in their pen. We watch them on the video camera so they don't get used to us at all."

"I go up to that pasture every day and take a look around for the mom."

She didn't want to say it, but someone should. "Liam, it's very possible that she's dead. You know that, right?"

He sighed. "Yeah, I know. But I just keep

thinking that I only nicked her. If that's possible, and she's out there somewhere, I need to make it right. I believe in righting any wrongs I did, Trisha. That's why I'm going to show up for you and Henry."

She stilled, wishing she could un-hear his words. "We are not a *wrong*, Liam. If you regret getting me pregnant, then please just leave. We don't need you to *show up for us*. This little boy is the best thing that's ever happened to me. There's nothing wrong about him."

He put his hands out, palms up, to stop her. "I just meant that I accept my responsibility. Henry's my son and I mean to do right by him."

If she had fur like the mama bear she was, it would be standing straight up right now. Instead, she stood up. "Maybe you should go. I'm not willing to be your responsibility, or some obligation you have to do right by. You should be here simply because you want to be. We were fine before you got to Shelter Creek and we'll be fine after you're gone. We don't need anything from you."

He stood, too. "Hang on. You're as prickly as a patch of nettles. Maybe it's coming out all wrong, but I don't mean anything bad. Remember, I'm still trying to get my head around all of this. Give me a chance to do it right."

Every muscle in her body ached to push him right out the door. But that wouldn't be fair to him or to Henry. She sat back down. "Okay, you're right. I'm sorry. But I *won't* be your burden." She'd felt like such a burden, all those years when her parents had to care for her, until she could walk on her leg again. Years when she could feel their resentment in every tight-lipped smile and heavy sigh. As soon as she'd been well enough, they'd been on that plane to Italy, to follow the dreams her car accident had postponed.

Pulling in a deep breath, she tried to calm her instincts and be rational. "Okay. Stay. Why don't you come sit on the floor with Henry? If you play with him, you two can get used to each other a little."

"Thanks." Liam folded his big frame to sit cross-legged. He seemed to take up most of the space in the living room. He set up some of Henry's blocks close to him. Henry crawled over and waved a pudgy arm to knock them down. Then the baby took a block and put it in his mouth. “I’m not sure that’s for eating, big guy.”

“It’s okay for now. I’ll get his teething ring back out of the freezer in a few minutes.”

Liam glanced at her ruefully. “I didn’t even know they got teeth this young. I have a lot to learn.”

“You didn’t have any younger brothers or sisters?”

“I’ve got three brothers. Boone is younger than me, but just by a year. I don’t remember much about him as a baby. Guess I was too busy being a baby myself.”

“I didn’t have brothers or sisters. I read a lot of books while I was pregnant, trying to get up to speed.”

“You got any you can lend me?”

She looked at him in surprise. “You want to read baby books?”

“I’ve got a baby now. I figure I’d better.” His smile had a lopsided, shy twist that tugged at her conscience. She wasn’t the only one struggling here.

Henry was clearly enjoying knocking over the blocks, but the real attraction seemed to be Liam himself. Henry gazed up at him with an adoring expression, as if he could sense some connection on a deep genetic level. More likely, Liam was the first man who had really sat down on the floor to play with him. Caleb and Jace were always kind and supportive, but they couldn't substitute for a father.

Trisha went to the bookshelf and pulled out a couple baby books. "These ones are pretty good." She set them on the coffee table and sat back down on the floor.

"Thanks. I'll return them as soon as I'm finished."

"There will be a quiz." She was only half joking. If he wanted to be around Henry, he had a lot of catching up to do. No way would she let her baby get hurt because Liam had suddenly decided to play daddy for a while. Still, there was something really sweet about the big cowboy wanting to read about babies.

Liam reached under the coffee table for Henry's red rubber ball. He rolled it to Henry, making a funny face while he did it. Henry squealed with delight and crawled after the ball. It was adorable, except Liam, making faces at Henry, looked like a big overgrown kid. Which he practically was.

Maybe she was only a couple years older,

but she felt a lot older than her age. The accident, Julie's death, the guilt, the years of rehabilitation—it had all grown her up fast.

"Henry," Liam was saying. "Can you roll the ball back?"

"He doesn't know how to roll it back yet."

"That's okay. I'll teach him."

"He isn't a dog, Liam. You don't need to teach him to fetch."

She saw annoyance in the sharp look he gave her. "I know he's not a dog, Trisha."

She was messing this up. What was wrong with her? Every nerve ending seemed to be raw and irritated. "I'm sorry. I just think that my job…our job…is to let him explore. If he wants to bang on the ball, it's because he's learning from it."

"I get it. You had Henry on your own. You've raised him on your own. But by some crazy coincidence, I'm here. Maybe I don't know anything about babies right now, but I can learn. It's fine to tell me when I'm doing something wrong, but I'd appreciate it if you didn't bite my head off."

Trisha drew in a deep breath, trying to steady herself. "I'm just so anxious about all this. I don't know how to explain it except to say that Henry is my world. He's been my world since I got pregnant. And when you have a baby, the most enormous protective instinct takes over. It's kind of primal. So I guess you coming into our lives has me on edge. I don't really know you. I don't even know if you're safe for us."

"Hey." Liam put out a hand, his warm gentle fingers resting on hers. "I would never hurt you. Or Henry. Please trust me on that."

"I'm trying. It didn't help that the first thing you did when you got into town was pull out a gun."

"I'm a Texan. There are guns everywhere back home. I've now learned, the hard way, that they are a way bigger deal out here in California." He opened his hands in a helpless gesture. "I can't undo what I did."

"You're right. I'm sorry. This is a lot to get used to."

"You're telling me. I barely slept last night, trying to get my head around this. Trying to figure out if I'm even fit to be a dad to Henry." He was silent for a few moments, stacking blocks again. Henry let go of the ball and crawled over to knock them down.

"Captain Destructo," Trisha murmured,

tickling Henry's tummy. He giggled and hit at the blocks, so they tilted and rolled on the rug.

Liam's voice was so quiet, she barely heard it. "I was a drug addict, Trisha."

A clammy feeling crept over her skin and settled cold and heavy in her stomach. "What happened?"

"I was a bull rider. I competed in college and for over a year afterward and it was all going pretty good, until I got stepped on by a bull. My leg was smashed and I was in a whole lot of pain. I got addicted to the painkillers they gave me after surgery."

Trisha remembered the medications from her own accident. The alluring sensation of drifting above the pain. "That happens to a lot of people. The doctors are supposed to wean you off."

"I didn't want to be weaned off. I just wanted that numb feeling again and again. I don't know why. My mom died while I was in college, from cancer—maybe I never really dealt with that. For whatever reason, I kept finding new ways to get the drugs. Going to different doctors, even buying pills on the street. I lost everything—whatever money I had, my friends. I even broke the trust of my family. I stole from the ranch."

Henry crawled over to say hello. Trisha picked him up and set him in her lap. She handed him a stuffed lamb that he liked to shake, taking comfort in his warmth and sweet wiggly presence. "What's going on with you now?"

"I've been off them for almost two years. I went to rehab, came home and worked on my family's ranch until I came out here."

"So this is the first time you've lived away from your family since it happened?"

"Yup. I think they figured it was time I proved to everyone that I could head out into the world and not run into any trouble."

"And you ran into a baby." It was a lot to take in. Too much. She almost wanted to laugh. A few minutes ago she'd been worried because he was young. That seemed like the least of her worries now.

He smiled ruefully at Henry. "I sure did. I want you to know that I don't crave the pills anymore. Or any drug. I don't drink or smoke or anything. But addiction, well, they say it's a lifelong battle. I could go back to it someday if I'm not careful. You're letting me into Henry's life, so you have a right to know who I am. Who I was. And who I could become again."

Trisha kissed the top of Henry's head, feeling the weight of Liam's words as further responsibility. "This is so complicated, Liam. It's my job to keep Henry safe."

"That's why I was sitting out in the truck today. I was trying to decide if I should even come in. Maybe I'm not the dad Henry needs."

Knowing that Liam had doubts increased her own. "I appreciate you telling me. I'd like to say it's no big deal. But of course it is." Suddenly it was all too much. He was a twenty-six-year-old former drug addict who was quite possibly here in Henry's life solely out of guilt and a sense of duty. When she strung it all into one sentence like that, their little playdate today seemed like a terrible idea.

"Can we just try this again another time? This is all a lot to process."

She saw the disappointment in his eyes before he hid it with his usual self-deprecating demeanor. "I'm not much of a catch—I understand that. But I will do my best to be what you and Henry need. Okay?"

She stood up, setting Henry on her hip. "Thanks for that."

Liam stood, too, and picked up the books from the coffee table. "Still okay if I borrow these?"

"Of course." Maybe her reaction was over-the-top. Lots of people had problems with pills after major accidents. But her mind was reeling. It felt like she'd gone too close to the edge of a cliff and was scrambling back to safety as fast as she could.

He reached over and picked up one of Henry's little hands with his first finger. "Bye, Henry. Great hanging out with you today." Henry's fingers curled around his. "Look at that. He's got a good grip."

Father and son had a little finger shake until Henry released him.

Liam's warm hazel gaze held Trisha's for a moment. "I'd like to talk to you soon. I hope this won't change everything."

"I don't know what to think." Emotion added a raw note to her voice.

"Let me know when you do." And then he was out the door.

Trisha watched him from the living room window as he pulled his boots on, clapped his hat on his head and went to his truck. He let Ranger out of the back and put him in the cab, and then dog and owner drove off down the street.

Trisha kissed Henry on the head and tried to believe she'd just done the right thing, taking a step back. What could be wrong with needing a little time to think? They had time. They didn't need to rush this.

Just because Liam had ended up here in Shelter Creek didn't mean Trisha had to bend over backward to make everything okay for him. Or put Henry in a situation that she wasn't comfortable with.

Except Liam wouldn't be in Shelter Creek for that long. So maybe she should figure out what she wanted sooner rather than later.

She carried her son to the kitchen and filled a bottle. "Let's tuck you up for a nap, little one." In the bedroom, they cuddled in the rocker while Henry drank his formula. Then she changed his diaper, put him in pajamas and set him in his crib. Exhaustion crept over her and she lay on her bed next to the crib, watching Henry watch his mobile. His eyes closed, then opened, then closed again. He huffed out a little sigh and slept.

Trisha closed her eyes, too—so, so weary. Maybe, if she slept, she'd wake up with more clarity than she had now. Or maybe sleep would just give her a much-needed break from her turbulent, troubled thoughts.

CHAPTER ELEVEN

LIAM TRIED TO focus on what Jace was saying but it was tough. He kept scanning the hills beyond the pasture. It had become a habit now, looking for that coyote. Hoping it might show up, miraculously healed.

"We've got to rotate this pasture sooner than we might otherwise," Jace was saying. "We want the grass to regenerate quickly and if the cattle cut it too short, or trample it to mud, that isn't going to happen. When you're raising grass-fed cattle, hay is always your last resort, used for emergencies."

Liam willfully dragged his focus back from his coyote search. "So basically, you're trying to give the cow the most natural life possible, start to finish."

"Right, but you can't just try. Not if you want to be able to market your beef as certified grass-fed. You have to *make* it work, and that takes a lot of planning."

"Okay." Liam saw a faint motion in the brush beyond the pasture. Could it be the coyote?

"But as a result of all the work, you'll sell your beef for a whole lot more than you might have otherwise." Jace paused. "Are you still following me?"

"I'm sorry." Liam forced his eyes away from the brush. No more branches had moved. Maybe he'd just imagined an animal going through.

"You're thinking about the coyote again?"

Busted. Liam's face heated. "Yup. And it's weird. Back home, I never gave much thought to killing animals who hassled the cattle."

Jace nodded. "It's different out here, isn't it? In Shelter Creek, we're surrounded by so much wild land, it sometimes feels like we're the trespassers."

Liam smiled, relieved that Jace understood. "It's true. Also, it bugs me that firing my gun was such a knee-jerk reaction. I guess I didn't realize it was so ingrained."

Like reaching for another pill. In rehab he'd vowed to become someone who thought things through. Someone who asked for help, instead of following every impulse.

"You've just found out you have a kid. That must make everything seem different. I know I had to examine a lot of my own behavior when I took on my sister's kids."

"How did you do it?" Liam felt dumb asking, but he had to know. "I mean, one minute you were traveling from rodeo to rodeo, the next you had three kids to look after. I can't even wrap my head around having one."

"Well, I guess I was a little less surprised than you. I knew my nieces and nephew a little, and I knew that my sister had some big problems. But it was still hard. I had to learn parenting fast—way faster than the folks who do it the normal way. I messed up a million times."

"The thing is, if I mess up, Trisha will just keep Henry away from me."

Jace shook his head. "Trisha is one of the sweetest people I know. She's scared right now, and trying to figure out how to do right by both you and Henry, but you two will work it out. Just take it slow. Give her some space."

"I told her about my past. That I'd been addicted. I assume my dad mentioned something to you about that, before he sent me out here?"

Jace nodded. "He did."

"It doesn't bother you?"

"You're not still using, right?"

"No, sir. Absolutely not."

Jace nodded. "You seem all right to me. Look, Liam, we've all had problems we had to overcome. You know me—I was always drinking and fighting when I was younger. And my buddy Caleb won't mind me telling you that he's sober and goes to AA. In fact, he'd probably be happy to take you to his next meeting. Might not be a bad idea… and it would show Trisha that you're serious about maintaining your recovery."

"That would be great. I'd appreciate it." He'd do whatever it took to show Trisha he'd changed. That he took his role as a father seriously.

"I think it's better if we all judge each other on our present selves, rather than our past." Jace fixed Liam with a stern look. "But…if you hurt Trisha or do wrong by her and little Henry, then that *will* be a problem."

"I want to do the right thing." Liam remembered the shock on Trisha's face when he'd told her his age. "She thinks I'm too young."

Jace laughed. "She doesn't know the way you were raised. Your dad gave you the responsibilities of a full-grown man when you were still in grade school. I was there—I saw it."

"Well, if it comes up, feel free to mention it to her."

"I could, but it would be better coming from you. Talk to her. Let her get to know you. She'll see your age isn't an issue. Unless…it is. Being a dad is not something to take lightly. If you get involved in Henry's life, you have to commit to *stay* in Henry's life."

"I'm just not sure how that's going to work, since I live in Texas."

"People have been known to move." Jace glanced around the pasture and then put a hand on Liam's arm. "Hang on, what's that?"

He pointed toward the bushes Liam had been watching before. "I'm pretty sure I just saw a coyote over there."

"I knew it." Liam wanted to jump up in the air, pump a fist, but he forced himself to stay calm, squinting at the bushes. "I thought I saw something over there earlier. I wonder if it's *my* coyote."

"I don't see it now. Don't get your hopes up. There are plenty of them out there, waiting to move into new territory if it opens up. Did you know that if you kill off a bunch of coyotes, the ones left over will just start having bigger litters? You'll end up with more coyotes than you started with."

"I didn't know that." Liam had lost count of all the things he didn't know. It seemed to be the theme of his life right now. "Come on. Want to go closer and see if we can spot it?"

Jace grinned. "You're done with my lectures on grass-fed certification…and parenthood?"

"For now. I truly appreciate all that you're teaching me, Jace. I'm learning a lot, being here on your ranch. I guess I'm just a little distracted today."

"Well, it's not like you have much on your mind."

Liam smiled at his sarcasm. "Yeah, just a few things."

They walked quietly toward the edge of the pasture where they'd both seen the bushes move. It was difficult to spot, but the coyote was there. Staring at them from behind bushes the same gray-brown color as its fur.

Golden eyes, big ears and a front paw it was holding up off the ground, just a little.

Liam's chest ached with relief and something else. A deep current of joy and admiration. It had gone to ground, licked its wounds and survived. And now it was back—a wild embodiment of strength and courage. Silently, fiercely demanding that they return the pups.

I didn't realize what you were, when I pulled out the gun, Liam told the animal silently. *I didn't understand.*

They watched it for a few minutes, then Jace put a hand to Liam's arm, indicating they should leave. Liam took one last, long look before they walked back to where they'd left their horses.

"I think that was your coyote," Jace said. "Did you see how it wasn't putting weight on its paw?"

"It sure seems like the same one." Liam's legs felt a little shaky with all the unexpected emotion. "I never thought I'd say this about a coyote, but I'm truly glad to see it."

"Let's see if someone from the wildlife center can come out and take a look. I'd ask Vivian, but she took the kids shopping in town this afternoon. Apparently Amy is desperate for some brand of shoes that all the other girls are wearing."

"Left that job for Vivian, did you?"

Jace grinned. "She offered. But yeah, she has a little more sympathy for that kind of thing than I do."

Liam hoped he could get Trisha to see that he had something to bring to Henry's life. A kid needed a father, just like Jace's kids needed Vivian. Like those pups needed their coyote parent.

Jace pulled his phone out of his pocket. "I think I'll try Emily. It seems like that coyote is doing okay, but I'd like her to get a look at it, if possible."

Liam walked a few paces back toward the coyote while Jace made his call. It was still there, staring at him through the bushes, and it was easy to read accusation into its golden eyes. "I'm sorry," he whispered. "So sorry."

After a few moments, Jace came to join him. "Emily and Trisha are on their way. They were pretty excited. Their last appointment of the day canceled, so it's perfect timing."

"I hope it sticks around."

"Why don't you stay here and wait for them? If it moves, try to see which way it goes. I'll head back and get going on the chores."

"You sure you don't want to stay? I can do the chores."

"I figure you're better off spending any time you can get with Trisha." Jace tipped his head toward the coyote. "She may even like you, after this."

"I can always hope." He wasn't counting on it. But maybe this could make a difference.

Jace swung up on his horse, gave Liam a final wave and trotted back toward the barns. Liam went to comfort Wild Bill, who would rather have gone home with Jace. "You'll get your hay soon enough, W.B.," he told the big bay horse. "Just stick around here and help me redeem myself." He scratched Bill between the ears and in the spot the horse liked best, under his thick black mane. It was nice to be quiet for a few minutes, to just hang out with his borrowed horse and take in the rolling green hills, the dimming blue of the afternoon sky, the whistling of the blackbirds that were ever-present around here. Liam's mind had been racing ever since he left Trisha's on

Sunday. Four days later and this was probably the first time he'd felt calm, accepting even. Maybe the coyote's return was a sign that he and Trisha would figure something out. Somehow.

It didn't seem long before Emily and Trisha came rattling up the lane in Emily's truck. Liam went to open the gate for them and they parked near Wild Bill.

"Is it still here?" Emily practically fell out of the driver's side of the cab in her excitement.

"It's sitting in the bushes over there." Liam pointed. "It hasn't moved."

"It's probably waiting for you to clear out of here so it can catch some dinner in peace." Trisha lugged a big tripod around the side of the truck. "Hello, Liam."

He swallowed hard. She was so pretty, her thick blond hair braided into pigtails for work, a baseball cap on her head. Though, unfortunately, it advertised the San Francisco team. They'd have to talk about that another time. No way could Henry grow up cheering for anything but Texas.

"Liam, will you take this spotting scope?" Emily pulled something that looked like a giant telescope out of a case and handed it to him. "Please don't drop it."

He took the big scope carefully in his arms. "Follow me."

Emily grabbed her medical bag and the three of them walked toward the coyote. "Can you see it?" Liam pointed. "Right there in that brush."

"Oh, how cute," Trisha said softly. "That brush is actually called coyote brush."

"Let's get the tripod set up," Emily said. "I want to see if it's hurt. Jace said it wasn't putting much weight on its paw?"

"One of its front paws," Liam said. "I think it might be my coyote."

"Which means it survived." Trisha was practically beaming. "This is really good news."

"Let's not celebrate until we get a look at it." Emily fastened the scope to the tripod and peered through the narrower end, turning various parts of it until she seemed satisfied. "Okay, I've got it. Do you guys want to take a look?"

Liam motioned for Trisha to go first and she took off her cap and peered through the lens. "Oh wow, it's gorgeous. Look at those golden eyes and how it's peeking through those branches. It has no idea how well we can see it with this scope. Here, Liam, take a look."

Liam stooped down to look through the scope, startled by how close the coyote seemed. He could see its mottled fur, its big ears. "I can't see its leg."

"Let me watch it for a bit." Emily hunkered down to peer through the scope. "I wonder if you all could go downhill from it and make some noise. I don't like having to scare it, but if I can see it move, I can see how bad its leg is."

"We can try." Trisha motioned to Liam. "Come on."

The afternoon was turning into evening and the air was getting chilled. Trisha was still in her scrubs from the vet clinic, and that was it. She wrapped her arms around her front, as if to block the cold.

"Take my jacket." Liam removed the fleece-lined denim. "Please."

"No, I'm fine." She waved him away and then shivered.

"You're freezing. I've got more meat on my bones. Just wear it."

"Okay." She pulled his jacket on and instantly looked more relaxed. She glanced up at him. "Thank you."

He shouldn't feel proud that she was wearing his jacket. This wasn't high school and that wasn't his letterman's. But she'd accepted something from him, let him help her in some way, and it felt good.

"Let's climb through here." Trisha pointed to a section of barbed wire. "Then we'll go just a few yards toward the coyote. If we can move it uphill, Emily can get a good view."

They slipped through the sharp wire and started slowly back up the hill, stomping their feet just enough to get the coyote's attention. From where they were, they could only see its ears, upright and alert, facing them over the tall grass. And then it turned and trotted uphill, and they got a better view.

"Perfect. Can you see its paws? Is it limping?" Trisha jumped up, as if the extra height would help.

"Honestly, no. I can't see much because of the bushes. Let's go back and talk to Emily."

They ran back down the hill and went through the fence again.

"This is kind of fun," Trisha said.

"It is." He couldn't help but hold her gaze just a little longer than necessary. Seeing her smile at him like that, with warmth in her eyes and excitement parting her lips just a little, it was hard to look away.

But she did, jogging lightly uphill to get to Emily. "Is it okay? What did you see?"

Emily didn't look quite as happy as Liam hoped. "You definitely hurt its right front paw, Liam. I can see the wound. But since she was running, I think you just nicked it. And it can't be infected…or at least not too badly."

"She?" Trisha brightened. "Do you think it's their mother?"

"Well, I didn't see anything that made me think it's a male."

"So what do we do?" Liam was glad it was the pups' mama. But he'd hoped for better news about the wound.

"I want you to keep watching for her. As long as she's active and out hunting, then there's a good chance she will make it. There are a ton of small animals she can catch at this time of year. And since it's only early spring, she has a whole summer ahead to heal."

"Do you think we can try to introduce the pups back out here?" Trisha shaded her eyes to better see the coyote on the hill. "She abandoned them. Will she accept them again?"

"I think it's worth a try, but Maya and Vivian will need to make that call. I'm sure they'll want to observe her for themselves."

"Thanks for coming out here this evening," Liam told them. "I made this mess, and this gives me some hope that it can all come right in the end."

"Fingers crossed." The vet trained the scope on the coyote, who'd stopped farther up the hill and was watching them.

"I should probably get going so I can help Jace with the chores." Liam tipped his hat to the women. "Hope to see you soon."

"Can I walk you to your horse?" Trisha fell into step beside him. "I feel awful about the way things went between us at my house on Sunday."

"It was a rough day. For both of us." An understatement. He'd replayed it over and over, wondering if he could have said it all better, in a way that would have reassured her more.

"I talked to my friend Becca. The one I was with in Texas the night we met. She's pretty smart about life, when she isn't talking me into ridiculous stuff like crashing weddings."

"I think Becca was smart that night, too."

He caught a flicker of a smile on Trisha's face, and there was a sweet warmth in her blue eyes. "It's true. She helped get us to where we are now."

Where they were now was complicated, and scary, but would he wish it any other way? Wish there was no Henry? Never.

"Anyway, Becca lived here in Shelter Creek in high school. Her family moved away before our senior year, but she was here when I was in a bad car accident."

He stopped walking and turned to face her. "What happened?"

She looked away for a moment, and when she spoke again her voice was quieter. "My friend Julie and I had been at a concert in Santa Rosa with some older guys I'd met. They'd given us alcohol and then they started getting pretty aggressive, you know? So we ditched them, but then we didn't have a ride home."

Liam pressed his palms into his thighs,

wanting to step back through time and smash his fists into those guys' faces.

"Julie was Caleb's sister. You know Caleb, who's married to Maya? Well, Julie called him and asked if he'd pick us up. Maya and Caleb were dating at the time, and Caleb was busy, so he sent Maya."

Liam hadn't realized that these people he'd gotten to know in the past couple weeks had such a tangled past. "So Maya came and got you?"

Trisha nodded. "Julie was really drunk, and on the road back to Shelter Creek, she took off her seat belt and leaned over into the front seat to change the music. Maya told her to stop, but Julie wouldn't listen. She lost her balance and fell onto Maya, and Maya couldn't see the road, and couldn't steer properly. We went into a tree. Julie was killed."

Liam swallowed the emotion rising from his chest. She'd been through such a tragedy. So had Caleb and Maya. It was amazing they were all still here, making their lives work, despite something that must haunt them every day. "I'm really sorry, Trisha. That must have been terrible."

She'd been staring at the ground as she

spoke. Now she looked up at him and there were tears on her cheeks, sliding down like melted diamonds. He brushed one away with his knuckle, but another took its place.

"I was badly hurt. My leg was broken in a bunch of places, and for a while the doctors weren't sure if I was going to be able to keep it. And I was haunted by guilt. Everyone blamed Maya for the accident, since she was driving, but I knew inside that it was really my fault. If I hadn't wanted to impress those older boys, if I hadn't brought Julie with me, she'd still be alive."

He couldn't believe she'd been holding all of that on her small shoulders all these years. "It sounds like Julie made some choices of her own, too."

"I try to remind myself of that, but I have wished every day since that I hadn't begged her to go with me that night."

No wonder she was so careful with Henry. It must be daunting to care for a tiny helpless baby when you already felt responsible for someone's death. And yet, she'd been brave enough to become a mom all on her own. To raise Henry so well, despite her fears.

The unfamiliar sting of tears had him blinking hard.

"Anyway, last night on the phone, Becca reminded me that throughout my surgeries for my leg, and my healing, I had my parents monitoring every dose of painkiller I took. I didn't have access to my own pills. If I had, things might have been different. I know what it's like to crave oblivion."

Liam could barely trust himself to speak. There was so much he wanted to say, words he wanted to give her, of comfort and praise, but he'd probably say it wrong. "I wish I could take away all that pain you went through. But I'm grateful that you understand a little."

"I think that's why I reacted so harshly. Because I can imagine how you might want to go back to them sometimes."

"I don't. Those pills turned me into a different person. Someone I never want to be again." He squared his shoulders to say the hard part. "But I won't make false promises. They told me in rehab that relapsing is always a possibility for an addict. I'm going to start going to some meetings with Caleb, to try to keep to the right path."

She nodded. "I have to learn to trust that you've got it under control."

"I'd appreciate it if you could." They were both silent for a moment, awkward after such heartfelt confessions. Liam glanced around, realizing how much time had passed. Emily was packing up the scope. The coyote was nowhere to be seen. "I should let you two get going. It's getting late."

She nodded. "I have to pick up Henry from the babysitter." She glanced at him shyly. "Would you like to spend more time with him?"

Liam felt a few pounds lift off his shoulders. "I'd like that a whole lot." *And with you*, he wanted to add. But he bit that part back.

"Saturday, then? Come by in the morning? Around nine?"

He'd get up at dawn if he had to, to get his chores done on time. "I'll be there."

"Maybe we can go for a walk with Henry. Or to the beach, or the park or whatever you'd like. Let's just hang out together, as friends. Maybe that's the best way to figure this whole thing out."

"Sure. Friends." He could do that, though she was more to him. So much more.

Trisha studied him for a long moment, her blue eyes looking into his as if she were trying to find something in them. Maybe she did, because she nodded. "Okay. I'll see you then."

"Looking forward to it."

"Oh. Your jacket." She pulled it off and handed it to him. "I'll be fine now. Thank you."

He pulled it on, aware of her body heat still warming it. Her scent lingered and it smelled like flowers.

Trisha flashed a shy smile and turned back toward Emily. Liam went to Wild Bill with unexpected nerves in his stomach. Saturday. It wasn't a date, though it felt a bit like one. Mainly, it was progress. And they could use some of that.

"Hey, W.B." Liam untied Wild Bill and the horse nuzzled his shoulder, impatient to get back to the barn, to dinner, to free time. Liam tightened the cinch before swinging into the saddle. When he turned the horse to leave, Trisha was watching him. She gave him a wave and he returned the gesture. It was only a wave, but it felt like more. A sign that maybe things were better between them, and might get better still.

CHAPTER TWELVE

"THIS USED TO be part of Jace's ranch." Trisha pulled her car into the parking area for the Long Valley Nature Preserve. There was only one other car here, which surprised her. Usually this trail was more crowded on a Saturday morning.

They got out of the car and Trisha was grateful for the cool morning air on her skin. Her little car felt like close quarters, with Liam sitting beside her. She could still feel the pull when she was near him, the same feeling she'd had when she first met him in Texas. She was trying to ignore it, but it was hard when they were sitting elbow to elbow.

"Is this the area the community bought for the elk? He told me about that." Liam shaded his eyes and looked out over the valley with a low whistle. "I can imagine he wasn't too happy about losing this land."

"It's gorgeous, isn't it?" Trisha studied

Liam as he surveyed the valley. His brown hair fell in tousled waves over his forehead. His denim jacket sat easily on his broad shoulders.

He glanced down at her and she hoped he hadn't noticed her close scrutiny. "I don't know how I'd feel if I bought this valley and was told I couldn't use it."

"Jace wasn't too happy about it at the time. But it's how he met Vivian. She was assigned to survey the wildlife in the valley. When she found an endangered salamander, she didn't think Jace was ever going to speak to her again."

Liam smiled down at her. "Guess they were able to work something out, though."

"Yes, they did."

"So maybe we can, too?"

Trisha flushed under his teasing glance. He had a way of unnerving her with that smile. "Let's not get ahead of ourselves." She walked over to open the rear passenger door. "Ready for your first walk with Henry?"

He grinned. "Ready as I'll ever be."

"I'll get him out of his car seat. Why don't you get the stroller from the back." It was actually nice to have some help. Usually she had to wrestle the big jogging stroller on her own, unless one of her friends was with her.

Liam opened the trunk and pulled out the stroller. “This thing is awesome. It’s like a mountain bike for babies.” He set it down on its front wheel and wrestled to unfold it.

“Hang on, there’s a lever.” Trisha set Henry on her hip and went to help Liam, showing him where to press.

He unfolded it and then pushed down until the latch clicked into place. “Is that it?”

“Looks good.”

Trisha went to put Henry in the stroller, but Liam held out his arms. “Can I carry him for a bit?”

She hesitated, anxiety whispering vague warnings in her ears. “Well, I guess. Just watch your step.”

He shot her an amused look. “I’m fairly good at walking.”

“I know, I’m just—” she sighed, hating to admit it “—overprotective. Everyone teases me about it. Maya, Vivian, all the ladies in my book club.”

She set Henry carefully in Liam’s hands and he nestled Henry on his hip, his arms around him, just like she carried him. At least he'd been watching her. He was trying.

"Does he look comfortable?"

It was sweet that he cared so much. "Yes. He looks happy." And Henry did. Maybe he felt Liam's magnetism, too, because her baby seemed perfectly content, looking around at the trailhead and chewing on his fist.

Still, it was hard to relax, knowing how little experience Liam had with babies. What if he did trip, what if he dropped little Henry into one of the ponds… *Stop.* She was imagining totally implausible catastrophes. She channeled her worry into action, getting the diaper bag and loading it in the stroller and locking the car.

"The trail is this way." She pushed the empty stroller toward the wooden boardwalk, built over the valley so people could enjoy the views without damaging the salamanders' habitat.

"You are stressed right now, aren't you?" Liam was teasing her, but his eyes were kind. "I promise you I will take the best care of our son."

They stared at each other, both of them startled by those two words. *Our son.*

"That's pretty crazy to say out loud, isn't it?" Liam tilted his head for a better look at Henry. "What do you think about that, little guy?"

"Can I hold him?" She was like a kid, not willing to share. Except Henry had always been hers. Still felt like hers. She wasn't ready for team parenting.

Liam handed the baby to her without a word, but Henry had something to say. He fussed and reached back toward Liam.

"It's okay, little one." Trisha bounced him gently, trying to stay cheerful though her petty heart hurt. *For shame.* She should be happy that her baby had already bonded with his daddy.

Henry settled at the bouncing, and Liam took up stroller duty, pushing it along as they walked into the valley. It was pretty adorable, actually. Liam wore a straw cowboy hat and his denim jacket. He looked like he should be on a horse chasing after cattle, not pushing a stroller along a trail.

They went a little farther along before Liam broke the silence. "I didn't mean to upset you back there. I don't know how to handle this. I don't even know if you want me to be around or if you'd rather I had never shown up here."

"Of course I'm happy." But Trisha's words sounded empty, even to her. "I guess it's going to take me a while to relax. Or, who knows… Maybe I never will." She decided to be totally honest, as he had been with her about his addiction.

"It started after the accident. I was paralyzed by anxiety. My mind was full of all these *what-ifs*. What if I was in another accident? What if I talked with someone who blamed me for Julie's death? What if I made another mistake?" She blew out a long breath. Just telling him about this was making her anxious. "I went to therapy, but it didn't help much. Then Maya came back to town and we became friends. And she welcomed me into The Book Biddies book club. Vivian moved here and I became better friends with Emily. Once I had a community of people I cared about, I started to relax a bit. But becoming a mom made the anxiety come back tenfold."

"I wish I'd been there." Liam's glance met hers, then he looked away out over the valley. "I wish I could have shared all that worry you must have had while you were pregnant and when Henry was first born."

Trisha's pride rebelled at the hint of pity. "You didn't miss much. I wasn't one of those cute pregnant ladies who looks like herself but with a basketball under her shirt. I was basically a big lump."

"I bet you were the cutest lump this town has ever seen."

"That Texas charm. Do they teach that in school where you're from?"

He laughed and gently touched Henry's nose when the baby laughed, too. "We've all got to pass an exam in compliments and manners before they let us out of high school."

"I suspected as much." It was a relief to be light. There was so much between them that felt heavy and confusing.

The boardwalk wound through the valley circling between the first two of the spring-fed ponds that made this area such an oasis for wildlife.

"Did you see the coyote this morning?"

Liam shook his head, his mouth quirking to one side. "I went up there and looked around, stayed for as long as I could, but didn't see it."

She wanted to reassure him. "Maybe we'll catch a glimpse of it on Maya's camera feed. It might start using the den, if it needs a place to rest and lie low."

"I hope so. If it really is back, how long before we could try reuniting the pups?"

"Maya thinks we could do it at almost any time, really. But I wonder if we should wait until it's completely healed. If it's in pain, it might be less likely to want to socialize."

Liam laughed softly. "I can understand that. My social skills sure went out the window after I was injured."

Trisha had to smile. "I guess mine did, too."

Liam was quiet, just pushing the stroller and looking around, so Trisha looked around, too. There was a lot to look at. Wildflowers were everywhere, especially the golden California poppies. The sun was out and the sky was a bright, rich blue. The green hills always felt like a miracle this time of year. They wouldn't stay green for long under the scorching summer sun.

"How come there aren't more elk, if this is a preserve?"

Trisha glanced at the small band of tule

elk grazing near the hills on the far side of the valley. "Most of them won't come until the fall. When water gets scarce everywhere else, they'll all show up here."

"I'd love to see it."

He'd be gone in the fall. He'd be gone by summer, really. She had to keep that in mind. He was here playing daddy and then he'd be back on his family's ranch in Texas. She wanted to ask how they'd handle it, living so far apart, but decided against it. It would open up the idea that there was something to discuss, and might imply that he could share custody. That was not happening. Nope. He could fly out from Texas if he wanted to see his son.

"And the salamanders? Are they around?"

"They come out in the rainy season and lay their eggs in the ponds. There could still be some around, but they'll be heading underground soon, if they haven't already."

They were near the first pond. Everything was newly washed, clear and cool, the whole valley rich with spring. Trisha stopped walking to take it all in, and Liam came to stand next to her. He reached for Henry's little hand

and Trisha watched her son's tiny fingers curl around his daddy's.

"What do you think, buddy? See any small crawling critters out there? Don't underestimate them—they cheated Jace out of some pretty fine real estate."

Trisha laughed, surprised by his humor, so Henry laughed, too. It felt good to stand there, the three of them, connected just a little, finding something funny together. But when she glanced up at Liam, he was watching her with a serious expression.

"It's good to see you smile."

She didn't answer, just looked out over the pond wondering how to go forward with him. They had a world of issues to figure out, and her smile wasn't one of them.

She looked down at Henry. His head was nestled on her chest. "He's getting really sleepy." She knelt and carefully set him in the stroller, fastening the straps and tucking a blanket around him.

Liam came around the front of the stroller to see. "He's cuter than anything I've ever seen."

Trisha smiled. "I'll have to agree with you there."

"Can I push him? You can just walk and not be responsible for much of anything for a little while. Bet that doesn't happen for you too often."

He was right. She had a lot of help, of course, from her friends and The Book Biddies and Patty, the babysitter. But she'd never felt right asking for help just so she could stroll along like this, listening to the blackbirds and the wind in the rushes that grew near the pond, taking in all the beauty in Long Valley. "That's really thoughtful. Thank you."

They walked the boardwalk in companionable silence. It was almost like they were just two regular parents, out for a walk with their child.

After a while, Liam spoke. "So has Henry said 'Mama' yet?"

"I think he might have said it the other night. But I wasn't sure. I tried to get him to say it again, but he just did some funny little babbling noises." She looked at Liam in surprise. "Hang on. How do you know he's supposed to be saying Mama right about now?"

"I've been reading those books you gave me. I also know that he can probably feed himself some finger foods, that his hand-eye coordination is improving rapidly and he'll probably be walking soon."

She eyed him, reluctant to admit she was impressed. "You're taking this seriously?"

"Of course I am. I have a kid. I need to study up."

It wasn't what she'd expected, even though he'd asked for the books. His easygoing manners were deceptive. She kept assuming he'd take this lightly. Or not follow through.

Her phone buzzed in her pocket. Pulling it out, she saw the text from Maya. "Oh no."

"What's going on?"

"Someone brought some bobcat kittens into the wildlife center. This time of year, everyone is bringing babies in. Mostly babies who would be fine if left alone. They're not abandoned—their parents are just out hunting."

"Do you need to go?"

She sighed. "Yes. Maya just got a call about a possible mountain lion attack at a ranch about an hour south of here. She needs to drive over and check it out. Vivian is at Amy's dance recital today, and Emily's doing vaccinations out at Creek Canyon Ranch."

"Sounds like we'd better get going. This stroller jogs, right?"

"It's all terrain."

"Race you." He started running, and she realized then that he wasn't wearing his usual cowboy boots under his jeans. He wore trail running shoes.

She jogged after him, pushing herself to catch up. "You run?"

He glanced at her with a teasing grin. "I don't go fast enough to call it running. With a leg like mine, all pieced together, I've got to be careful."

She nodded. "You know what's weird? My leg feels better when I jog than it does when I walk. My doctor said it's something to do with the way the tendons healed."

"I noticed your limp."

She looked up at him, ready to take offence, but the warmth in his eyes was affectionate, not cruel. "I don't notice yours at all. Is it your left leg?"

"Yup."

"My right one is the bad one." It was good right now, though, settling into the rhythm of their jog.

"Well, what do you know? Between us we have one good set of legs."

"You're ridiculous." But Trisha was smiling. It was true, actually.

He grinned down at her. "Maybe. But now, more than ever, I have to keep running. I've got to be careful not to get a dad bod, right?"

Trisha let out a sharp laugh at the idea. He was lean and strong, and he knew it. She glanced down to make sure she hadn't woken Henry. He was still sound asleep, the fancy stroller The Book Biddies had bought for them making his speedy ride over the boardwalk smooth.

"Maybe this could be one of our things," Liam said after a moment.

"What do you mean, *our thing*?" And why wasn't he even out of breath? Trisha tried to get out running with Henry a few times a week, but she was still huffing and puffing.

"You know, a thing we do together, with Henry. Aren't families supposed to have that?"

Whoa. *Family?* She decided to ignore that reference. "We can go running again sometime, for sure." Thankfully, the boardwalk's half-mile loop through the valley was coming to an end, and Trisha could see her car. She wasn't ready to think of Liam as family, or to even let her mind get too far ahead of where they were now. She was still just trying not to panic about him being in Henry's life at all.

"Can I load Henry in the car? I could use a car seat tutorial."

All this enthusiasm was charming, but it also put her on edge. Every little step Liam took into parenthood was a step into their lives. And what would happen when he went back to Texas? "He's sleeping. Maybe I should do it."

"Please?"

She relented. "Okay." She opened the door to the back seat and watched as he unfastened the stroller buckles and gently lifted Henry up to his chest. The sight of such a big, tough-looking man cradling her baby caused her heart to do an odd squishy flop in her chest. Then she remembered the first few times she'd tried to load a sleeping Henry in the car. "Hang on. I'll go around the other side and help."

Trisha climbed into the back seat and slid over so she was next to the car seat. She held the straps apart as Liam gently lowered sleepy Henry into the seat, one big calloused hand supporting his head as he set him down.

She put the strap closest to her over Henry's little shoulder and Liam did the same on the other side. She showed him how to pull the lower strap up between the baby's legs and hook the shoulder straps into the buckle. Then she slid the fuzzy strap covers up, so the baby could rest his head against them as he slept.

Liam put his palm up and they shared a silent high five.

Trisha slid out of the back seat and closed the door with a thick feeling in her throat. Liam was trying so hard, but what did it mean? Was he trying this new dad role out? Or was he thinking of the long-term? It was hard to say, and she was grateful, suddenly, that Henry was so young. If Liam decided not to stick around, Henry would never remember this.

They got into the car and Trisha headed for her house, where Liam had left his truck. She'd drop him off and then take Henry to the wildlife shelter with her, to meet Maya and take over care of the bobcat kittens.

They were quiet on the drive so Henry could sleep. But at the house, Liam turned to her before getting out of the car. "Want me to take Henry inside? I can take care of him while you're at the center."

"No thanks." Her response was automatic. "He comes to the wildlife center all the time. If he wakes up or gets restless, I can have a friend come help out."

"Or you can put him to sleep in his own bed and let his father take care of him."

Trisha stared at him in shock. "I barely know you. I'm not leaving my baby with you. Plus, you don't know how to take care of Henry."

"Won't he be sleeping?"

"Maybe. But what about if he wakes up? Do you know how to change a diaper?"

"It can't be that hard. Plus, isn't it in one of your books?"

"It's not hard, but it's not simple either. Even if I was comfortable leaving Henry with you, I'd want to show you how I do everything first. There's feeding him, what he drinks, what clothes he wears, safety issues..."

She felt guilty. Like she should be accommodating his need to jump into parenting. But why was she guilty? She hadn't done anything wrong. "Look, I know you had your reasons for walking out on me that night. But you made a choice then, and you can't just waltz back in and act as if you have the right to care for Henry. I'm not putting my baby at risk just to gratify some whim you have to suddenly step up and play daddy."

His mouth pressed into a flat line for a moment, as if he were holding back words he wanted to say. When he spoke, his voice was low and calm, but she heard the edge of anger there. "I get that maybe I don't know enough about babies, and about Henry in particular, to care for him today. But this isn't a whim and I'm not playing daddy. I take this responsibility seriously."

Something in her heart twisted, and it hurt. "That's just the thing. Henry isn't just a responsibility for me. He's a person I love with my whole heart, who I carried in my own body, who I'd do anything for." She tapped her fingers on the steering wheel, trying to think clearly, trying not to just kick him out of her car, but right now, his kindness and his good intentions felt like threats.

"I think if you start feeling the same way about Henry, I'll be more comfortable with you taking care of him."

"Then let me spend more time with him. Time with both of you."

It was only fair. She couldn't refuse Liam's help with Henry because he had no experience, then deny him the chance to gain that experience. "Okay. What about tomorrow? It's Easter and they always have a big celebration in the square downtown. Henry's a little young, but they have the Easter Bunny there, and some other fun stuff. I thought I might get some cute photos of his first Easter."

"I'd like that. What time should we meet?"

"Meet me here at nine? We can walk to the square."

"I'll see you then." Liam turned in his seat and blew a kiss to Henry. Then he got out of the car and blew her a quick kiss, too. He quietly shut the door behind him, so as not to wake the sleeping baby.

Trisha watched him walk to his truck, her hand on her cheek as if she could feel where his kiss landed. As if she could hold it there for a while. The realization washed over her slowly, in a chill wave of clarity. She wasn't just lashing out at Liam to protect Henry. She was trying to protect her own heart, too.

CHAPTER THIRTEEN

THE SHELTER CREEK Easter Celebration was in full swing. Kids were running around clutching empty baskets for the upcoming egg hunt, vendors were selling food and drinks. People had brought picnics and set up blankets and chairs around the edge of the grassy town square. There was a long line at the gazebo, where people were waiting to get their photo with the Easter Bunny.

Trisha, always organized, had gotten them there early, so they hadn't had to wait for Henry's Easter photo. Then they'd had one taken with the three of them together. Their very first family photo. Liam figured both he and Trisha looked pretty awkward in it, but maybe that was okay. At least it was honest.

Now he was standing with Trisha and all her friends, watching Jace's younger kids participate in the egg-rolling event. Carly, their older sister, had wandered off a while ago, disappearing into one of those clumps of teenage girls who seemed to function as one big blob, moving around the town square together in a conglomeration of color and motion and high-pitched giggles.

Trisha was leaning on the handlebar of Henry's jogging stroller. "Jace is taking this egg roll really seriously," Liam whispered to her. He was rewarded with a smile as she looked at Jace to see what Liam meant.

Jace was on the sidelines coaching Alex in the best way to push his egg forward with the long-handled wooden spoon.

"He might even be turning into a helicopter parent," Trisha whispered back, only half joking. "I think he's trying to give those kids everything they never had before they came to live with him. He goes all out for every holiday."

"That's cool. I want to be like that. Super dad." Liam knelt down next to Henry, who had a front row view of the egg roll from his stroller. "What do you think, buddy? Me and you, winning this egg roll in about three years?"

His son looked at him with huge blue eyes.

"Gah ma," he said, which Liam decided to take as meaning "I'm in."

Trisha was watching him with a look he couldn't decipher. It was strange being in such an intimate situation, learning to parent with someone you barely knew. But Liam was determined to relish these first days with his son.

It was all still sinking in. He'd wake up every morning in his little cabin on Jace's ranch, sleepy and stretching, and then it would hit him. He was a dad. But without any immediate daddy duties and responsibilities, the thought seemed almost abstract. He was a dad, but nothing had really changed in his life except the baby books he'd been studying like Scripture.

He hoped he'd find a way to get Trisha to trust him, but right now she was still reluctant to let him take on any real responsibility. Even here, at the Shelter Creek Easter Celebration, surrounded by her friends, who all considered Henry family, she hovered like a moth, fluttering around Henry every moment, and especially any moments where Liam tried to pay attention to the little guy.

A cheer rose from the crowd and Liam refocused on the egg roll. An older kid had come in first place, but Amy was right on his heels with a lucky shot across the finish line. Alex was still pretty far back, but he was laughing at something Jace said, so that was good.

Vivian left her spot next to Trisha and ran to help collect the kids. A pang of envy ambushed Liam. He wanted that with Trisha and Henry. That ease. That solid knowledge that they were a family, and they had each other's backs.

But how could he have that? He owed it to his family to return to Texas and help transform the way they ran the ranch. His brothers and father had given him a new chance at life, paid for rehab, forgiven his stealing, his lying, his betrayals. He could probably move to California eventually, but not now. Not until he'd done his part in Texas.

He glanced at Trisha, wondering if she'd be willing to come to Texas. If he could just make her see that they were a family, that she and Henry were better off with him in their lives, she might do it. Trouble was, she saw him as a kid, not ready for responsibility. He wasn't even sure she really liked him at all, though their walk yesterday had seemed to ease things a bit.

The weather today had started out cool, but now, getting close to eleven, things were warming up a bit. Liam removed his jacket, surprised when Trisha took it from him. "You can put this in the stroller. That's one great thing about having a baby." She folded it neatly and placed it in the bottom compartment.

"I'm assuming that's not the only great thing," he teased.

He loved her self-conscious smile. It was that sweetness he'd fallen for that first night, like she had all these amazing ideas inside of her that she'd share if you just paved the way for her a little. "There are a lot of great things. Right now it's all the firsts. The first time he laughed, rolled over, sat up, crawled, made a sound that might be a word…and his personality, starting to shine through. He's funny. He tries to make people laugh. Now I'm realizing that might be something he inherited from you."

"He got your pretty eyes, though."

She flushed. "No compliments, please."

"Why not?"

She shrugged. "I'm not sure if they're real. It could just be you, doing that cowboy charm thing again. Or it could just be because I ended up having your baby."

He glanced at her, startled that she'd even think that. "You don't think I'd find your eyes pretty if we just met?"

"Maybe, but how can I know that now?"

That was one more layer of complication he hadn't thought of. He'd be drawn to her no matter what, just like he was the night they first met, but how could he convince her of that?

Maya approached, a welcome interruption. "Are you two going to take Henry to find some Easter eggs? I think they're starting the hunt over at the park soon. Let's all walk over there."

"That would be fun." Trisha glanced Liam's way. "Sound good?"

"Of course."

They were a big group, walking together to the egg hunt, which looked to be at the same park with the redwood trees where Trisha had told him about Henry not too long ago. All of the women Liam had seen the night of the Spring Art Fair were there, the ones Trisha called The Book Biddies. They seemed to function as a team of surrogate grandparents and aunties for the kids.

Monique, who'd given Liam the pep talk outside Trisha's house that first day, was sipping a lemonade and chatting with Jace and Caleb. Flanked by the two handsome cowboys, Monique seemed to be in her element.

A woman named Priscilla, who he gathered from Trisha was a retired teacher, was holding hands with Alex and Amy and listening to them recount their egg-rolling adventures. Trisha had pulled ahead of Liam. She was pushing Henry while talking with Eva, who owned an art gallery. According to Trisha, she'd also founded the Shelter Creek Wildlife Center.

Maya was in animated conversation with Annie Brooks, the rancher who'd come by Jace's place to get her hoof trimmer a week or two ago. An older guy held hands with Annie. He'd introduced himself to Liam earlier today as Juan Alvaro and said he'd been ranching in Shelter Creek practically his whole life.

Maya's grandmother Lillian, and her friend Kathy, appeared on either side of Liam, a little breathless, as if they'd rushed to catch up with him. "Liam, how are you holding up?" Lillian asked, not standing on ceremony. "I know this must be quite a time for you."

"Something like that." He was inarticulate inside and out when it came to his current situation. He'd called Wyatt last night, intending to tell him, but his feelings seemed to run too deep to surface. He'd ended up gabbing about Jace, and his ranch, and the difference between getting state versus national organic certification, and left it at that. It was almost like Trisha and Henry were too precious to share. Too important to expose them to the way they might be seen by his family—as one more poor choice he'd made while under the influence.

"We have an idea." Kathy glanced his way with a kind smile. "To help you find your feet."

"Lessons," Lillian continued, as if the two were used to finishing each other's sentences. "Baby lessons."

"Diapering. Feeding. Holding. Playing. Laundry. The works," Kathy explained.

"We'll have to use a doll, since we don't have a baby at our disposal," Lillian said.

"And anyway, we suspect Trisha wouldn't appreciate us borrowing Henry for this little project, since she's rather protective of him."

"But this way, when she does give you a chance, you'll amaze her with your baby knowledge." Kathy's smile was full of pride and Liam suspected she'd hatched this plan.

Liam tried to imagine himself with a baby doll. The image was about as dignified as a pig in a dress. "I don't know… I mean, I do appreciate it and all, but you know I'll just look a fool."

"Oh, and you think a woman doesn't feel foolish every time she heads into the hospital for a prenatal exam?" Lillian inflated with indignation. "Or when she's giving birth and there are a bunch of strangers in the room looking at her girl parts? If you're man enough to get someone pregnant, seems like you should be man enough to do what it takes to be a good daddy."

There was no answer to that except "Yes, ma'am." She was absolutely right. He had to do what needed to be done, just like Trisha had. "Tell me where and when. I'll be there."

"Well, we're hopeful that you'll be busy with Henry and Trisha for the rest of today.

So how about tomorrow evening after work. My house at seven?"

"That would be fine."

"Give me your phone. I'll enter my address and phone number in your contacts."

Man, these ladies took their meddling seriously. Liam tapped in the security code and handed Lillian his phone. "Why are you all doing this for me?"

"Because you look a little pathetic?" Lillian's grin softened her sharp words.

"Lillian, be nice," Kathy admonished. "The truth is, Liam, we love Trisha very much. She hasn't had the easiest time of it, what with her accident and her parents leaving and all. We want her to be happy. We want her and Henry to have the best life possible. And since you're now in their lives, we want things to go well."

"You all are mighty kind. First the cookies, and now this."

"So we'll see you tomorrow night, then?" Kathy patted his arm. "I bet we can turn you into daddy material in just a few hours."

"That's all it takes, huh?"

"If you pay attention." Lillian handed him

his phone. "There will be pizza. See you at seven."

The two veered off to look at a display of hand-painted Easter eggs, leaving Liam to walk on his own for a few moments, letting the group get ahead of him. Lillian and Kathy's tough love reminded him a little of Wyatt, and how he'd always pushed Liam to be a little more, to try a little harder. It had been Wyatt who'd encouraged him to pursue his love of bull riding, saying that if Liam had the talent, he shouldn't waste it. Though now, Liam suspected that Wyatt felt somewhat guilty about encouraging something that had led to Liam's injury and addiction.

But sometimes a little encouragement, or a solid shove forward, was just what Liam needed. And he'd received that, courtesy of those two cookie-wielding Book Biddies today.

CHAPTER FOURTEEN

"He's really sweet, Trish." Maya had fallen into step beside Trisha as they crossed the road to the park.

"Maya!" Trisha glanced behind her to see if Liam was anywhere near, but he was walking at the back of their group, chatting with Lillian and Kathy.

"I'm just saying that if you had to have Henry's daddy show up unexpectedly, at least he's handsome, kind and funny."

Trisha drummed her fingertips on the padded handle of Henry's stroller. "He is, right? But it's so complicated, you know? I don't feel like there's any room for my personal feelings, when it really needs to be about him building a relationship with Henry. And what if he decides he doesn't want to be involved after all? He might just lose interest." Glancing around again, she moved closer to Maya.

"He's only twenty-six. That's practically a baby in guy years."

Maya let out a snort of laughter. "He's only two years younger than you!"

"But come on. You and I got old fast, after what we went through."

"Well, still. That should just show you that one person's twenty-six is different than another's. He seems like a responsible guy."

"He's a guy who lives in Texas. He has to go back there, you know. He's supposed to use all the stuff he learns at Jace's ranch to improve his family's business."

"Think about it this way. A couple weeks ago you thought you'd never see him again. Now he's here and trying to be involved. A lot can change in a short time. Try to relax and have some faith. You could even try flirting with him a little. I mean, you were attracted to him at one point, right?"

"Clearly." Trisha pointed down to Henry in the stroller. "Do you think I'm awful for the way this happened? For crashing a wedding and meeting a guy and getting pregnant like that?"

Maya shot her a wry smile. "I figured it

must be something like that. Henry didn't just appear out of nowhere."

Now that she'd asked, Trisha needed to know the entire answer. "Do you think less of me?"

"No! I'm not judging you, Trish. We handled the car accident and Julie's death in ways that seem different at first glance, but the truth is, we both hid. I hid out in the wilderness, doing science, and you hid out here in Shelter Creek, living a very quiet, simple life. It makes sense that eventually you'd need to break out of your shell. But how could you do it here in Shelter Creek, where everyone knows your past? Where you felt like they might be watching and judging? Being in our situation makes us feel guilty for having fun, because Julie won't ever do those fun things."

"It's such a relief to know that you understand."

Maya smiled gently. "I live with the guilt, too, remember? It makes sense to me that when you finally left town, you cut loose. It was your chance at a little freedom."

Trisha looked at her friend with wonderment. "Our lives are tangled together, aren't they? There aren't many people who've been through something like what we've experienced."

"I understand how hard it is, Trish. And I know we both get busy, and maybe me being your boss now makes it a little weird, but I am always here for you whenever you want to talk, or just hang out or anything."

"Thanks, friend." Trisha stopped the stroller and reached for Maya, giving her a quick hug. "I don't know what I'd do without you."

"You'd probably have a much more peaceful life. I wouldn't be calling you in the middle of your weekend to go deal with bobcat kittens. How are they doing, by the way?"

"They're so cute. I'm having a hard time not cuddling them after I feed them."

"Is the formula working?"

"Two are thriving." Trisha's heart ached when she thought of the smallest baby. "One seems a little listless. Emily said she'd come look at it later today."

Maya sighed. "I wish we could afford a full-time vet at the center. Emily already runs a busy practice. I feel guilty that she has to give up part of her Easter Sunday. It's probably her one day off this week."

"Yeah, but she loves it. She comes to the wildlife center on days when I'm already there, just to hang out. She's fascinated by those coyote pups. And if we're not careful, she'll end up taking Peanut the rabbit home with her."

Maya laughed. "She can't have him! Peanut is going to be our wildlife education bunny, right?"

"That's the plan. Vivian has started spending time with him. She'd like to bring him out to the schools with her."

Liam caught up to them. "Maya, have you seen the coyote on your cameras?"

Maya put a hand on his shoulder and looked right at him. "Hi, Liam, how are you enjoying the Easter celebration?"

He grinned. "Sorry. That was abrupt. And yes, maybe I'm a little coyote obsessed. The celebration is really nice, thank you. How are you today?"

"I'm fine. And I caught sight of the coyote last night, but not near the den. She showed up on that other camera we set up, closer to where she was shot. She was moving pretty well, so fingers crossed that she'll make a full recovery. Vivian and I are thinking that if she stays around the area for another week or so, we can try releasing the pups and see if she'll bond with them again."

"Why not now?"

"An animal's behavior is unpredictable when they're in pain. The last thing we want is for her to turn on the cubs, to attack them or scatter them. It's best to wait."

Liam nodded. They'd reached the park and he looked at Trisha, his eyes warm with enthusiasm. "Can we take Henry out of the stroller? If we park it here, we can walk him around and see if he can point out the eggs. I read that babies his age are gaining more object permanence, so they can find things that are hidden much better."

"I think that's more like if you take his toy and hide it under a blanket," Trisha corrected, then noticed Maya's chastising look. Her friend was right—she had to go easier on Liam. "But yes, let's definitely get Henry involved." She moved the stroller to a picnic table at the edge of the park and lifted the baby out. Henry seemed relieved to be free of the stroller. When she held him against her chest, he grabbed a fistful of her hair and looked around eagerly.

"Ouch." Trish tried to dislodge her hair from her baby's grasping fingers.

"I've got it." Liam picked up Henry's squeaky giraffe from the stroller. He carefully untangled the strands from Henry's hand and replaced the hair with the giraffe. "Here you go, big guy."

Henry gripped the giraffe and it squeaked. He laughed in delight and squeaked it again, waving the giraffe in the air.

"Thank you." Trisha smiled at Liam. "The hazards of wearing my hair down."

"It looks nice, though."

His compliments threatened to seep into her heart. It didn't feel safe, but it did feel good.

"I'm going to go find Caleb." Maya winked at Trisha. "Have fun. That's an order."

"Yes, boss."

Maya waved and wandered off in search of her husband.

A horn sounded. The mayor had one of those funny long plastic ones. She blew it two more times.

Kids started running everywhere. The Shelter Creek Business Association had hidden plastic eggs all over the park, each filled with a sweet, or a toy, or even a gift certificate for one of the shops downtown. When she was about ten years old, Trisha had found one with a gift certificate to the ice-cream store. She'd taken Julie and Becca for ice-cream sundaes the following weekend and they'd felt so grown-up, sitting at the table in the ice-cream shop all by themselves.

It was a bittersweet memory now. Just like Maya had said, every moment of happiness was tinged with guilt and sadness, because Julie would never have any more moments like that.

"You ready?" Liam pointed to a spot by the creek, close to where they'd sat when they talked last week. "I think I see an egg."

"Would you like to carry Henry?"

There was relief in Liam's smile. Like he'd thought she'd never offer him even this. "I'd really like that." He took Henry and settled him carefully on his hip so the baby could easily look around. "Do you see any eggs, Henry?"

"Gah." The baby looked up at Liam and smiled, far more interested in the big tall cowboy than in anything going on around them.

Trisha retrieved an egg hidden under a picnic table. “This is an egg, Henry.” She showed the baby the purple plastic egg. Henry took it in his free hand and shook it. It made a gratifying rattle, so he shook it again.

“I wonder what’s in there.” Liam eyed the egg. “It sure is noisy.”

“It could be jelly beans,” Trisha guessed.

“We’ll have to be careful.” Liam frowned. “It could be a choking hazard. I know babies Henry’s age like to stick things in their mouth.”

Trisha looked at him in amazement. “You’ve been reading again.”

His gaze met hers and held for a moment. “I’m behind, so I’ve been cramming.”

It was so hard to look away, when every instinct was ordering her forward, wanting to be closer to him. That chemistry that had initially brought them together was still there and getting stronger with every smile he gave her, every moment of sweetness they shared. But this wasn’t the right time for chemistry. Their situation was too complicated for that. Trisha swallowed hard and made herself take a step back instead. “I’m glad you’re taking your studies seriously. Come on. Let's see what else we can find."

They wandered around the park, watching kids hunting eggs, listening to the happy shouts and laughter. Henry seemed to adore watching the big kids, pointing to them and even offering them a chance to squeak his giraffe when they got close.

After a while he seemed to tire of the excitement and reached his arms out to Trisha. "Mama."

Trisha brought her hands to her mouth to try to contain her astonishment. She looked at Liam. "Did you hear that?"

His smile was so wide it carved a dimple in his cheek. "Did I ever. Henry, is that your mama?"

Henry reached out his arms even farther. "Mama."

His first word. Tears rose in Trisha's eyes and she took Henry from Liam and held him close. "Oh, you sweetie." She kissed the soft curls at the top of his head. "Here's Mama." He laid his cheek on her shoulder and gave a sleepy sigh.

"So he really does know the word," she

said to Liam. "I thought I was just imagining it."

"Guess you weren't." Liam pulled out his phone and took a photo of her and Henry. "There. Now you have it documented. The first moment he called you Mama."

Something welled warm and new inside her. She'd never had this. Someone who'd think about taking photos and making memories together. "Thank you," she told him softly. "That's really thoughtful."

Liam was 100 percent proud daddy. "Can you believe it? He's eleven months old." A stricken look took the joy out of his expression. "I don't even know the day he was born."

"April 30." Trisha kissed Henry's curls again, swaying slowly back and forth to relax him further.

"I wonder what I was doing that day. Probably just fixing a fence or moving some cattle or something. It's so strange to think that I was just going about my business the day our son was born."

"You didn't know," Trisha said. "You couldn't have known." She put a hand on Liam's arm. "Let's just try to enjoy this time, and not worry about what you missed. Not right now."

All this time she'd been so worried about herself and Henry. In a way, she'd figured that whatever Liam had missed out on was his own fault. He could have left his name and number that night. In her fear and resentment, she hadn't thought much about what it was like for him, knowing he'd missed out on so much. Knowing he'd have missed out on everything, if he hadn't come to work with Jace in Shelter Creek.

When she thought about it, the enormity of what he might have missed was staggering.

Henry was floppy on her shoulder, losing interest in the crowds and bustle. "I think he's pretty sleepy."

"Should I walk you guys home? He might sleep better in his own bed."

Liam was too sweet. Too thoughtful. He was going to make her want to be with him, and she didn't want that. Not when he wasn't going to stay in Shelter Creek. But he was right. It was time to walk Henry home.

"Want me to load him in the stroller? You can go say goodbye to your friends?"

Trisha hesitated just a moment, then nodded. "That would be nice." She passed Henry over to Liam and stood watching while he carried the drowsy baby over to the stroller. He buckled his son in, and tucked the blanket around him. He actually looked like he knew what he was doing.

She went to say goodbye to Vivian, Maya and the rest of the group.

"Tell Liam we'll see him tomorrow," Lillian said, giving Trisha a kiss on the cheek. "And if you need any Henry care this week, I'm your gal."

"Or me," said Priscilla, squeezing her hand.

"Or me." Kathy gave Trisha a hug. "Just call us the Henry Fan Club."

"Thank you so much. You all are so good to us."

"And now you have someone else who wants to be good to you." Monique tipped her head in Liam's direction. "You should let him."

"It's a lot to get used to," Trisha said.

Monique's slow smile contained reams of mischief. "Honey, I could definitely get used to a handsome cowboy looking at me the way that boy looks at you."

"He isn't looking at me as anything more than the mother of his kid." Trisha glanced toward where Liam was waiting. He smiled and tipped the brim of his hat in her direction.

"That little hat tip..." Eva sighed. "I could get used to that. Maybe he has an uncle who likes older artsy women."

"Or an older brother," Monique added.

"Monique!" Eva looked shocked.

"Some men like older women," Monique countered, totally unabashed.

"Cougar," Eva said, and she and Monique burst out laughing.

"Okay, you two cougars, knock it off." Lillian put a hand on Trisha's arm. "This young lady and her young cowboy have to get their baby down for a nap."

Shaking her head, Trisha made her way back to Liam.

"What is going on over there?"

She glanced back to see Monique and Eva still laughing, leaning on each other for support.

"They're just The Book Biddies. They've always got something to say about everything. They were checking you out and then calling each other cougar. Which makes them laugh because when Maya first returned to live in Shelter Creek, she was here studying mountain lions. Some of the locals weren't supportive of her work, so The Biddies decided to become her support group. They named themselves Cougars for Cougars and went around passing out flyers about how to coexist with lions."

Liam shook his head. "I don't think I'm following."

"Don't even try. Just accept that The Biddies are always up to something. Speaking of which..." Trisha eyed Liam suspiciously. "Lillian said to tell you she'd see you tomorrow."

"Oh, that." Liam's shrug was a little too casual. "She just offered to feed me some pizza. How could I say no?"

"Smart boy. It's best to not even try to refuse when The Biddies get an idea in their head."

They started across the busy square toward the side street that led to Trisha's cottage.

"I had a lot of fun," Liam told her as they approached her house.

"Me, too." Trisha realized she was telling the truth. She'd been nervous about today, being out with Liam and all of her friends, but it had felt pretty natural, almost as if he fit right in.

Liam stopped in front of her gate. “Let me carry the stroller up the stairs?”

She could use the help. Half the time she just left it in her garden, so she didn’t have to haul it up the steep porch steps. “Thank you.” Trisha lifted sleeping Henry out and watched Liam pick up the heavy jogging stroller like it was nothing. He carried it up the steps and put it down on the porch, carefully setting the brake so it wouldn’t roll away.

She held Henry against her chest, climbing the steps slowly and carefully so as not to wake him up.

“Keys?” He kept his voice to a whisper and she answered the same way.

“The outside pocket of the diaper bag.”

The bag was in the bottom of the stroller and he pulled it out along with his jacket. “Almost forgot this.” He fished the keys out and opened her front door for her, setting the bag down in the hall.

“Thank you,” she whispered.

He came back out on the porch. “Do you need any more help? Want me to come in?”

"I've got it from here."

He looked like he wanted to say more, but he caught his lower lip instead, as if to stop himself. "I'll see you soon, then."

"When?" She hadn't meant to ask it. Didn't want to care when she saw him again. But suddenly, she did.

His eyes sparked with interest. "How about Tuesday evening? Any chance one of those Book Biddies can watch Henry long enough for us to get some dinner?"

"Us?" He'd taken her by surprise.

"Yeah, us." His gaze riveted to hers, intense in its purpose. "Because this isn't just about Henry, though he matters most. It's also about you and me. I want to take you out. On a date."

Her heart just about stopped. A date. Normally she'd say no. In fact, *No* was right there on the tip of her tongue, but then she heard Maya's words from earlier today. *Try to relax and have some faith.* Why not try to get to know him? Why not see what there was between them? Maybe they were just co-parents. Maybe not even that. But maybe there was something more, and maybe she was ready to try to reach for it.

"Tuesday night would be fine. I'd like that."

"Okay, then." Liam reached out and brushed his fingers lightly over Henry's curls. Then he brought his hand up to touch Trisha's wavy locks. "I think he may have gotten those curls from my mother. She had thick curly hair."

"No one on my side has curls. And you have a little curl in your hair, too."

"It's nice knowing there's something that was handed down from my mom."

"You must miss her." Trisha tried to imagine the woman who'd held Liam close, just like she was holding Henry now.

"I do. I wish you could have met her. I wish she could have met Henry." They both stood quietly, looking at the baby cuddled on Trisha's chest. Then Liam swallowed hard and took a step back. "I'll see you Tuesday, Trisha. And Happy Easter."

"Happy Easter, Liam." She watched him as he jogged lightly down the steps and headed for his truck. Easter. A holiday of renewal. Of revitalization. Maybe she was just being silly, but it seemed like something in her was rekindling, and coming alive. Trisha took a deep breath, acknowledging the excitement flickering inside her. Yup, it was true. Things were changing. She felt hopeful and awake, and she just might have a little crush on Henry's daddy.

CHAPTER FIFTEEN

"OH NO, POOR BABY." Trisha put her hand to Henry's forehead for what must have been the tenth time in five minutes. "You've got a fever, for sure." She walked slowly around her living room, bouncing her sick baby gently, trying to get his crying to stop.

Glancing down at her carefully curated outfit, she sighed. The dark jeans, the heels, the pretty red sweater—they'd all have to go back in the closet for another time. Henry gave a little cough that just about cracked Trisha's heart in two. It must have hurt because he screwed up his mouth and wailed.

"It's okay, Henry, love." She took another lap around the living room, watching him carefully, trying to figure out if bouncing made him feel better or worse. He cried louder and she stopped the bouncing. Maybe the poor guy had a headache.

Trisha moved Henry onto her hip and

held him with one arm while she wrestled the phone from her purse with the other. She called Kathy, who'd been planning to come over and babysit so Trisha and Liam could go to dinner. When Kathy answered, Trisha told her what was wrong.

"Oh, the poor baby. Do you want me to come over there and help?"

"We're okay right now. And I don't want you to catch it."

"Do you have some of that infant pain reliever?"

"I do." Trisha swayed gently back and forth with Henry. The motion seemed to soothe him a little and he quieted. "I'll give him some if he doesn't settle down soon. Thank you for offering to babysit tonight. I really appreciate it. May I take a rain check?"

"Of course. And don't hesitate to call if you need some backup."

"Thank you, Kathy. Will do." Trisha set her phone down and chewed on her lower lip. She'd never thought to get Liam's phone number, and now she had no way to call and tell him that their date was off. She tried Vivian's phone number, thinking that she'd know how to reach Liam, but it went straight to voice mail. Vivian had probably set her phone aside to spend time with the kids and Jace.

Henry started crying again—she shifted him higher up in her arms so he could look out over her shoulder, which he usually liked. Instead he put his head down and clung to her. Trisha pulled up his favorite playlist of kid songs on her phone and stuck it in the dock. The happy beats of "Baby Beluga" filled the room and she danced slowly, hoping his favorite song would bring him some comfort.

It seemed to work, so she put the song on repeat and she and Henry danced to it a few more times. When she shut the music off, intending to try putting him in his crib, he started crying again.

"All right, one more time." She started up the song again but it was interrupted by a soft knock on the door. She danced over to answer, and there was Liam, standing on her porch, looking amazing in dark jeans, a black T-shirt and a leather jacket. A wave of disappointment washed over her. She'd been looking forward to seeing him tonight—she hadn't realized how much until it wasn't actually going to happen.

She was about to tell him that their date was canceled, but he raised the bag he was carrying. "Takeout from the barbecue place. We can eat here."

"How did you know I couldn't go out?"

"Kathy called Lillian, and Lillian called me." He grinned. "I am dialed into the local gossip network."

"I didn't have your phone number or I would have called. I tried Vivian."

"She and Jace and the kids are having a movie night. I bet she has her phone off. I'm glad you didn't reach her. This way I can still see you."

"But Henry is sick."

"And I'm here to help." His smile was a little shy. "Isn't that what fathers do?"

"I don't know." She thought of her own dad, so formal and brisk. He'd left most of the nurturing to her mom, who hadn't been much better at it. She'd seemed to find most aspects of childcare an annoying burden, especially when her almost-grown daughter had become so needy after the accident. "You don't have to stay. Henry and I will be fine. We've been through this before."

"Of course you have," he said reasonably. "But now you have me."

"You don't need to take the trouble..."

"It's not trouble. Where else would I want to be right now except here with the two of you, trying to help?"

She couldn't argue with that, and she didn't want to because the truth was, she wanted to see him. "Come in."

He kicked off his boots and set them inside the door, which she appreciated. She liked to keep the floor as clean as possible for Henry to crawl around on. Not that poor little Henry would be up for much crawling tonight.

Liam set the bag down on the dining room table. "Nice music. How is the little guy?"

"He cries every time I shut this song off. He's got a low fever, a hundred and one."

"That's low?" He looked at her with concern furrowing his brow. "That seems like a lot."

"It's not great, but it's not terrible for a baby."

He whistled low. "Man, babies are tough."

"So are their parents. I'm not sure how much more 'Baby Beluga' I can take."

He laughed quietly and pulled off his

jacket, setting it on one of the dining room chairs. "Want me to take him? I can dance, if you want to change into something more comfortable."

Gratefully, she handed him the baby. She wasn't used to wearing high heels and tight jeans.

He got Henry settled on his shoulder and then caught sight of her outfit. "You look amazing. Can we try this date another time?"

Trisha felt her face heat. It had been so long since she'd seen open admiration on a man's face. "Sure. That would be great." She fled to her bedroom and changed into comfortable yoga pants and her favorite pink sweatshirt. She chose some pink fuzzy socks and pulled her hair back in a ponytail, to keep it out of Henry's way. She glanced in the mirror a little ruefully. So much for trying to look like someone who was more than just Henry's mom.

She stopped in the kitchen for plates and silverware, just in case they got a chance to eat. The barbecue smelled delicious. In the dining room, she stopped and stared.

Liam was in the living room, swaying to yet another round of "Baby Beluga." He held Henry close to his shoulder and his head was bent over the baby's, like he was singing along quietly. He was completely immersed in his son, dancing in the dim golden lamplight, his big frame and long legs making Henry seem even tinier in his arms.

It was beautiful and perfect, and father and son looked just right moving around her living room. Tears burned behind Trisha's eyes. This was what she'd almost missed out on. What Liam had almost missed out on. And more importantly, what Henry had almost missed out on—having a daddy to love him like this.

"Baby Beluga" wound down for the umpteenth time and Liam reached for the volume. "I think he's sleeping," he whispered.

Trisha motioned for him to follow and led him back to the bedroom. He went to lay Henry down in his crib and Trisha almost intervened to tell him how to do it, except he handled the baby like a pro, supporting his back and neck with his hands and forearms.

"You're a natural," she breathed.

He winked and said nothing. Just took the baby blanket she offered and put it over Henry's legs. Then he removed the toys that had ended up in the crib earlier today, when Trisha had set Henry down for a few minutes.

"You really have been reading the baby books," she told him as they made their way back down the hall to the dining room.

"Something like that." He opened the bag of food, allowing heavenly smells to escape. "Are you ready to eat? It might be a long night."

Their first meal together. She was nervous as she opened the containers of meat, while he dished potato salad and coleslaw onto the two plates.

"Barbecue tofu?" She stared at the skewers in disbelief. "How did you know?"

"I asked Lillian what you'd like. She said you're not a big fan of meat. Which makes sense, I guess, since you're such a big fan of animals."

He opened a second container. "I got chicken. I hope that doesn't upset you."

"No. Not at all."

"Tell me why you like animals so much."

"They're cute." It was her standard answer and he saw right through it.

"And…?"

She studied him, deciding what she wanted

to reveal. "After that car accident, I didn't want to be around people much. It was so awkward. I worried nonstop that they blamed me, or felt sorry for me, and I guess I blamed myself so much, too. And I missed Julie a lot. She'd been my best friend forever."

"Did you have pets already?"

"No, my parents didn't like pets. They said they made the house dirty. But I was so lonely after the accident and I begged and begged. Eventually they let me adopt a poodle from the animal shelter, because poodles don't shed. Frenchie was about nine years old when I got her. She lived to be sixteen and she was such a good buddy. She's the reason I decided that I wanted to work with animals." Trisha took a bite of her barbecue. "Oh my gosh, that's so good."

A thin cry came from the bedroom. Trisha stood up. "I guess he's really not feeling well, if he can't sleep."

Liam rose, too. "You eat a few more bites. I'll go get him."

Doubt warred with hunger. "Are you sure? Just pick him up and try dancing with him again. Call me if he's wet."

"No problem." Liam disappeared into the

bedroom and Trisha indulged in a few more delicious mouthfuls of food. She heard Henry cry a little harder as Liam picked him up, and then the cries quieted.

It felt absolutely decadent to just sit and eat while someone else saw to Henry's needs. If she set aside her worries, and her need to be in control of every little thing when it came to Henry, she might actually get used to this.

LIAM GAVE HENRY the little bear he found near the changing table and removed the baby's soggy diaper. He tossed it into the diaper pail, then reached for the wipes just like Lillian had shown him with the doll last night. One hand on the baby's belly at all times, one hand setting the clean diaper over the baby in case he had an accident on the table. He found the wipes, cleaned Henry up and wrestled the fresh diaper on. It was definitely harder on a real baby than a doll, but in the end, it didn't look too bad.

"Okay, let's get you in some dry pajama bottoms." Liam scooped Henry up and went to the dresser, opening drawers until he found them.

"What are you doing?" Trisha came

through the doorway, looking shocked that her baby was only half dressed. "Does he need changing?"

"I just changed him." Liam motioned to the dresser with his free hand. "Can you point me toward clean pajamas?"

She looked completely mystified but she rummaged in a drawer, then handed him some soft cotton pajama pants with dogs on them.

He took Henry back to the changing table and laid him down again. "I wasn't sure what to do with his wet pants," he said conversationally. "Should I rinse them in the hall bathroom?"

"Um…sure, that would be great." She was watching him slide Henry's clean pants on with the funniest expression on her face. Part disbelief, part protective mama bear. "How do you know how to do all this stuff?"

"Oh, I guess I'm not completely inept, that's all." It was way more fun to pretend like he was a natural baby whisperer than to reveal the baby lessons he'd had last night.

Once Henry's pants were on, Liam picked him up and handed him off to Trisha. The baby coughed a couple times and Trisha felt his forehead. “His fever doesn’t seem worse. Maybe this is a cold.”

“Do you have a humidifier? That might help with his stuffy nose and cough.”

“You know about those, too?” Trisha shook her head like she couldn’t believe it. “There’s one in the closet right there. Be sure to—”

“Add salt. Yeah, no problem. Is there some in your kitchen?”

“In the cupboard to the right of the stove. But how did you know about that?”

“I’ve learned some things.” The truth was, when Lillian had called to let him know that Henry was sick, he’d asked her questions about what he could do to help the baby feel better. She’d told him about the humidifier. And the salt.

He got the humidifier, went to the kitchen to add water and salt, and brought it back into the bedroom. “Where should I plug it in?”

Trisha indicated the table near the crib. “That will be fine.” She was swaying back and forth with Henry, as if there was music on. Their son was snuggled against her chest and when she bent to kiss his head Liam’s heart went all soft and he had to hold himself back from going over there and wrapping his arms around both of them. They were becoming a part of him so fast, it was scary.

"I'll just wait out in the living room," he told her and hurried out of the bedroom, down the hall and straight out the front door. The night air smelled like wet leaves and earth and he breathed it in, trying to catch his mind up with the feelings growing inside. It was a lot to fathom, how much he was starting to care.

When he stepped back into the house, Trisha was leaving Henry's room. She tiptoed toward him down the hall. "He's sleeping for now." She went into the living room and flopped down on the couch. "Thank goodness."

He went to sit next to her. "You're a good mom."

"Thanks. I appreciate all of your help."

"It's what I'm here for." They sat in silence for a moment and he thought about saying what was in his heart. Maybe it would scare her off, but maybe it would make her see that he really was here for her, in more ways than just as Henry's daddy.

"There's one thing I left out, when I told you about my past."

She looked at him with wide, worried eyes. “Uh-oh.”

He smiled at the dread in her tone. “It’s nothing that bad, I promise. It’s just that I didn’t tell you the whole truth, when I told you why I left you that night in San Antonio. It wasn’t just that I was taking drugs and was unreliable. That night was a catalyst for me. It made me want to get help.”

“It did? How?”

“It’s hard to explain. You were so pretty and sweet, even when you’d had way too much champagne.”

She pressed her palms to her cheeks. “I still can’t believe how I behaved.”

“Is it terrible to say that I’m glad you did? It got us Henry, and I think it might have saved my life. I realized that night that I wanted to be the kind of guy someone like you would love. I could suddenly see a future that I wanted so badly. A future where I was clean and sober and in love with a woman as classy and smart and beautiful as you. I wanted it to *be* you, but I knew I had a long journey ahead of me if I was going to get clean. We’d just met. I couldn’t ask you to stick around for that.”

She glanced at him with compassionate eyes and he held out a hand. After a moment's hesitation, she put her hand in his and he held on, savoring the connection.

"I left the hotel that night and drove back to the ranch. I got there just as my father and brothers were starting the day. I told them the truth about my addiction and begged them to get me some help."

"I had no idea." She turned her body to face him, as if she wanted to study his face for the meaning in all this.

"Ever since that night, I've thought of you as my angel. As the person who made me realize how much I wanted to change, and how sweet life could be if I did."

Trisha put her free hand on top of their clasped ones. "I'm so glad you got the help you needed."

He looked down into her blue eyes, feeling like he could live or die by what was reflected there. He feared her pity, wanted her admiration. He was relieved to see a flicker of the latter.

"It makes me happy to think that I might have made a difference for you."

"You did. And you do now."

He shouldn't. There were a thousand reasons why he shouldn't. They were just figuring out the situation with Henry. They didn't need to make things any more complicated. But he gave in to the pull, leaned down and pressed his lips to hers, relishing the softness of her mouth and the way she kissed him back.

Pulse speeding, he ran his fingers into her hair and kissed her again and again, not wanting to stop. But he had to. The voice of reason was unwelcome, but it was right. Having Henry meant they had to take things slow. *He* had to go slow, build trust between them and help her see all the reasons they should be together as a family.

He kissed her one last time, softly, and pulled away, studying the dazed look in her eyes, hoping it was a sign that she'd liked their kisses as much as he had.

Her slow, satisfied smile was his sheer relief.

"I'd like to date you," he said. "Really date you. Take you places, spend time with you, get to know you. Can we do that?"

Her *yes* was spoken on a shaky breath, but he heard it loud and clear.

"And I'd like to help with Henry, however I can. I want to learn to be his daddy. Can I do that, too?"

Her smile faded a little. "Yes. But I think Henry is already pretty crazy about you. Please don't break his little heart." She didn't say it, but he heard it loud and clear. *Or mine.*

"I won't. I know we can figure out any obstacle in our way." He'd show her that they belonged together. Even if it meant they'd live in Texas for a while. He kissed her one more time, on the forehead. "But for now, let's take it easy."

"You mean no more kissing?" The glance she shot him was a combination of shy and flirty that could annihilate the best intentions of any man. But he wasn't just any man. He was Henry's daddy and he was going to get this right. "How about we finish our food, and then watch a movie? It's not the most exciting first date, but it's something."

She smiled and pushed herself off the couch. "It sounds like a nice way to spend an evening when we're home with a sick baby."

He followed her to the dining room. "I'll take that as a yes."

She turned to face him and put her hands

to his chest to stop him. Going up on tiptoe, she kissed him lightly on the cheek. "*That's* a yes."

She went into the kitchen to reheat their food. Liam put a hand to his cheek and felt her kiss still lingering. A blessing from an angel, his angel, saving his life back then in San Antonio, and rebuilding it tonight, here in Shelter Creek.

CHAPTER SIXTEEN

THE FOG WAS thick this morning and gave the still-dark hills a mysterious aura. The sound of the horses' hoofbeats, Vivian's and Carly's voices, and the early-morning birdsong were all muffled by the blowing clouds. Through the mist, Liam spotted the gate to the pasture.

"Let's leave the horses back here," he said to Vivian and Carly. He dismounted and led Wild Bill over to the fence. "We don't want to disturb the coyote, assuming it's around today.

"I hope it is," Vivian said. "It will be a bummer if Maya, Trisha and Emily bring the pups up here for nothing." She slid off her horse and tied it near Wild Bill, then turned to Carly. "Are you good?"

"I'm great!" The teenager slid easily off her horse. "Life always seems a lot more interesting before dawn, doesn't it?"

"That's because you're young," Vivian said with a yawn.

But Liam knew what Carly meant. It was one of the things he loved about ranching. *The early pearly light*, his mama had called it. The way the colors hadn't seeped into the landscape yet, and the Texas heat hadn't either. It was like being in an old photograph.

He missed Texas suddenly, with a sharp feeling that went beyond the dusty hills and enormous sky. He missed his mom. Maybe realizing he was a parent brought the emotional things to the surface. He sure wished she'd lived to meet her grandson. Cancer stole so much. Not just someone's life but all the good they might have done, all the connections they would have made.

The sound of a truck coming up the dirt track pulled him back to the present.

"There they are." Vivian waved to the approaching pickup. Carly ran to open the gate, and Maya pulled the truck into the pasture. Trisha and Emily were crammed into the cab next to her. There were five crates in the back, a coyote pup in each.

"Good morning," Maya said through her open widow. "Any sign of the adult yet?"

"We just got here," Vivian answered. "We haven't gone close to look, in case we scared her off."

Yips and yowls rose from the back of the truck.

"They sure are chatty," Carly said.

"That's a good thing," Maya said. "If the adult coyote hears them, she'll be intrigued. She'll most likely stick around to see what's going on. I'm going to drive right on over to where we've seen her."

"We'll walk over and meet you," Liam said. He caught Trisha's eye through the window and tipped his hat to her. "Nice to see you."

She blew him a kiss and waved as Maya drove on across the pasture.

"Aw, aren't you two so sweet." Vivian took him by the arm as they walked along the track, following the truck. "It's good to see you so happy."

Carly had gone back to close the gate. Now she jogged up to walk alongside them. "Are we talking about how cute Liam and Trisha are?" She pressed her hands to her chest. "It's so romantic."

Liam was pretty sure just about everything was romantic to Carly. She was going on seventeen, pretty as a picture and, according to Jace, had her first boyfriend. The kid was the star of the high school rodeo team, something Jace was none too sure about.

"How about you not talk about our cuteness and spare your old friend Liam some embarrassment."

"Oh, come on, you know you're a total romantic." Vivian nudged Liam with her elbow. "I heard how you took Trisha and Henry on a tailgate picnic to the beach on Saturday. Trisha said you thought of everything. Champagne, blankets in case the fog came in, sand toys for Henry… Maybe you can give Jace a few lessons in romance." She smiled fondly just mentioning her husband's name. "Well… no, he does okay, actually."

"Ugh! Please don't mention Uncle Jace in the same sentence as the word *romance*," Carly protested. But she was smiling at Vivian. The two of them had a tight bond.

"Sorry. I'll spare you the details."

They'd reached the truck. Trisha and Emily had the tailgate down and were inspecting the pups to make sure they'd fared okay in their carriers.

"They've gotten big." Liam hadn't seen

them, except on the video feed, since the day they'd caught them. In just a few weeks, they'd tripled in size. "They look like smaller versions of adult coyotes now. They're not fuzzy little pups anymore."

"They're so cool looking," Carly said. "I love their ears."

Maya had walked over to the pasture fence with her binoculars. She turned and headed back to them. "I see her," she said. "She's up pretty high on that cliff, watching us." She pointed. "See that small scrub oak growing about halfway up? Look to the left."

They all squinted through the dim light, and then Liam saw her, sitting perfectly camouflaged in the dirt like one of those optical illusion puzzles that looked like one thing, but when you stared at it, was really something else. The coyote was watching the truck intently, her ears perked way forward. Surely she could hear the pups.

Trisha came over to Liam's side and put her arms around him. "It's good to see you," she said quietly.

Liam returned the embrace and kissed her hair, inhaling the scent of her shampoo. After three weeks, it still felt like a dream to him, that he could do this. Hug her. Kiss her. Spend time with her and Henry. They were growing into a family, and he and Trisha were growing into so much more. It wasn't just Henry that connected them. It was something deep down, as if his heart and mind and muscle and bone, his very cells, knew her. Like they'd been waiting for her to show up in his life, so all his pieces could fall into place, just right.

"Here's what I want to do." Maya started toward the back of the truck. "I want to release the biggest pup first. The gray one with the big attitude."

"Boss Hogg?" Trisha said. "Good idea."

"That's what you call him?" Liam looked down at her in surprise. "I thought you weren't going to name any more animals. You got so attached to those bunnies, you almost had a nervous breakdown when we set them free."

"I wasn't, but old habits die hard. And Boss Hogg was so piggy, trying to get all the food, I couldn't resist."

"Wasn't Boss Hogg a character on some old TV show?" Emily slipped on thick leather gloves and reached for the pup's crate.

"Can we focus, people?" Maya put a hand to her forehead in mock distress. "I swear, sometimes you all forget that we're supposed to be scientific around here."

"We haven't had enough coffee to focus," Vivian said. But she pulled on her gloves and reached for the other side of the crate to help Emily.

"Are you doing okay?" Liam brought his mouth close to Trisha's ear and kept his voice low. "I know you get all emotional about coyotes."

Trisha jabbed him in the ribs with her elbow. "Only when dumb ranchers shoot them."

"This dumb rancher is a lot smarter now." He kissed her hair one more time, then let her go. "We'd better get to work or Maya will get even more riled up."

"I heard that," Maya said, flashing him a dry smile. "Here, big guy. You can unload the second-in-command." She pointed to a crate holding a pup that had a lot more brown in its fur than the first one.

Liam pulled his gloves out of his back pocket and headed for the truck, then glanced back at Trisha. "You have a name for this one, too?"

She sighed and came toward him, yanking on her gloves. "Lieutenant."

"Busted. And the other three?"

They each took one side of the crate and lifted it down to the ground. "The small gray girl is Minnie Mouse. The larger girl is Tulip, because she walks on her tiptoes. The blue-eyed boy is Wolf."

"You've gotten attached." He couldn't help but tease her. "Will there be tears tonight?"

"No." She caught his look of disbelief and caved. "Okay, maybe a few. But I'm okay letting them go. We did this thing right, I think. Look at Wolf snarling at us. They're not used to humans and can't wait to get away from us. That's a good outcome. Plus, hopefully they'll have their mama welcoming them home."

"I'm so glad she's stopped limping." Liam glanced at the coyote up on the hill. "I feel like a weight has been lifted from my conscience."

"I'll feel better if she moves toward us." Maya was looking through her binoculars again. "I was hoping she'd show a little more curiosity about the pups."

"We could move the pups' crates to the other side of the fence," Liam suggested. "So it's clear to her that they're in her territory."

Maya lowered her binoculars and regarded him with surprise. "Look at you. From coyote hunter to coyote behaviorist."

"I've done a lot of reading since some folks I know told me I couldn't shoot them anymore. I figure if I have to live with them, I'd better understand them."

"You need to meet my friend Aidan Bell, up north of here," Maya said. "He's been pioneering wildlife-management practices on his ranch for a while now. He taught Caleb a lot. He's kind of a wildlife whisperer."

"Sounds like an interesting guy. I'd like to meet him." Liam went to stand beside Emily. "Want me to help move Boss Hogg over the fence?"

Emily looked at Maya. "What do you think?"

"I think it's a good idea. Let's put all the crates over there."

Liam climbed through the barbed wire and helped Emily lift Boss Hogg over. He walked the crate close to the base of the hill, since they were going to release him first. Then he went back and helped Trisha lift Lieutenant, and Vivian and Emily lift Wolf. Finally, Maya and Carly passed him Minnie Mouse's and Tulip's crates. He set those down farthest away from the mama coyote and climbed back through the fence.

"What do we do now?" he asked Maya.

"We sit and wait." She sat down in the grass and gestured for them all to do the same. "Welcome to the world of wildlife biology. Hard ground, cold air and no breakfast."

Emily sat down next to Maya and pulled a small pair of binoculars out of her pocket. Vivian went to the truck and came back with a big black duffel bag. She opened it and pulled out a tripod and video camera. "For the website," Vivian explained. "And to educate our donors and visitors about what we do."

Carly retrieved a digital camera from the bag and Vivian helped her focus. "Try to get some action shots," Vivian advised. "Those will look amazing on the blog."

Liam sat in the grass and Trisha sat next to him. He put an arm around her and she leaned in close. "How's our boy this morning?"

"He was sleeping when I left. It was so nice of Monique to come watch him. She says she always gets up early to do yoga anyway. When I left, she was rolling out her mat in the living room."

"You've got some amazing friends here."

"*We've* got amazing friends. They all really like you, Liam."

That was the problem. He liked them, too. And he adored this woman beside him and their baby boy. But he owed it to his family to go home, at least for a while. Whenever he mentioned Texas, Trisha changed the subject. It was like this big gap between them. They talked about pretty much everything else. But not that.

"She's moving," Carly whispered, snapping a couple photos. "She's coming down the hill."

"Thank goodness." Maya breathed a sigh of relief and handed her binoculars off to Liam. "I think it's time to let Boss Hogg out of the crate. I hate to use him as a guinea pig, but if mama doesn't recognize him and gets territorial, he's got the best chance of holding his own."

Trisha buried her face in her hands. "I don't think I can look. What if this goes badly?"

Liam pulled her closer into him. "Have faith," he whispered in her ear. "We've come this far. This can work." He wasn't quite sure, when he finished talking, if he was thinking about the coyotes or their own situation. Mama coyote was standing still as a statue, watching Maya's every move. Its wounded paw was up, and Liam could see dark fur where the wound had been.

Maya moved slowly and calmly toward the fence, slipped through and stood by Boss Hogg's crate. From here it looked as if she was saying a quick prayer, and maybe she was. Maya understood predators better than pretty much anyone on the planet, according to Trisha. So she probably knew how easily things could go wrong out in the wild. Maya knelt and opened the crate, then climbed back through the fence and returned to where they were all sitting in the grass.

Liam realized he was holding his breath. This was his personal moment of reckoning. He'd set these events in motion with one impulsive shot, and now, with the help of everyone here, he had a chance at redemption. So far, luck had been on his side. The adult coyote's wound had healed up. She was partway down the hill now, staring at the pup, who hadn't seemed to notice his mama yet. Instead, Hogg had run to Lieutenant's crate and was nosing at it, yipping for his brother to come out and play. Lieutenant let out a low, frustrated yowl.

From the hillside, mama coyote howled back. She started on a low note and ended in a series of sharp yips.

Boss Hogg froze. Lieutenant went silent. One pup, maybe it was Minnie Mouse, let out a startled bark, then was silent, too.

Hogg's tail lowered between his legs. His ears went down and back. He slunk forward a few steps and waited.

"Perfect submissive posture," Vivian breathed. "Good boy."

The adult came down the hill quickly now. She circled the pup, sniffed it, then backed away.

Liam glanced at Maya, looking for clues as to how this was going. She was looking through her binoculars, chewing on her lower lip.

Trisha reached for his hand and squeezed it tight.

The pup crouched low and whined. It must have been the right move because the adult returned, sniffed it again, then nuzzled it. When it turned to walk back up the hill, Boss Hogg followed.

"Oh fantastic," Maya breathed, lowering her binoculars and glancing at Vivian. The two biologists exchanged relieved smiles, and Liam realized that he wasn't the only one completely invested in this reunion. Maya and Vivian must have had many discussions, plotting how to make this work.

"Let's wait a few minutes before we release another one," Vivian said quietly. "Let's make sure this is really okay."

Liam watched the adult and pup circle each other. It seemed like there was a lot of sniffing and yipping, a noisy dance of recognition. Maya must have understood the steps because she said, "Okay, let's send Minnie Mouse in."

"Wait, she's the weakest," Vivian said. "Are you sure?"

"Yes. We don't want her going in last because they might be more likely to reject her." Maya rose, squeezed between the barbed wire strands and let little Minnie out of her crate. Liam glanced down at Trisha and caught her wiping a tear from under her eye. "Hey," he whispered, and she looked up at him. "They're a family. Reuniting. That's a good thing, right?"

"Happy tears," she whispered.

Surprisingly Minnie, who Trisha had described as cautious, went bounding up the hill toward her brother and mother with no reservations. She was accepted easily, without going through the crouching and submissive behavior that Boss Hogg had displayed.

"Is that because she's a girl?" Carly asked Vivian.

"I think so." Vivian was filming the reunion, peering into the camera lens intently. "I hope the others go just as well."

Maya let Tulip, the other female, go. Then the blue-eyed male.

"Goodbye, Tulip. Goodbye, Wolf," Trisha breathed as the two coyotes went up the hill to join the growing pack. Wolf and Tulip both imitated their big brother's behavior, crouching low, tail and ears down, waiting for their mama to come to them. A few sniffs, a conversation of yips, and they were happily bothering their brother and sister as if nothing new was happening in their lives. Maya released Lieutenant last. He went slowly toward the pack and was accepted almost immediately.

They all watched for several minutes. Liam couldn't take his eyes away. The mother coyote still limped a tiny bit, but she seemed happy and relaxed as her pups played around her. Her serenity was his redemption. He'd look at coyotes, and other wildlife, very differently from now on.

Maya picked up Lieutenant's crate and climbed back through the fence.

"Let's give her a hand." Liam got up and pulled Trisha to her feet. Emily joined them, and they carried the crates back to the truck.

Vivian was still filming the reunion.

"It seems like it's going well, right, Maya?" Carly snapped a photo of the milling pack as she asked her question.

"I think it is. Anyway, it's out of our hands now. The hope is that they'll stick together and the pups will be able to copy their mother's hunting behavior."

"Should we keep the cameras up by the den?" Vivian looked at Maya.

"Let's leave them for at least a week. Hopefully we can get some footage of them."

"I guess that's it, then." Vivian shut off her camera and pulled it off the tripod.

"Let me help you with that." Liam folded the tripod and put it back in the duffel. He held it open so Vivian could put the video camera away, too.

"Thanks, everyone." Maya put the last of the crates back in the truck. "Mission accomplished."

"I appreciate everything you all did, to try to fix this situation." Liam looked around at the strong women surrounding him. "I've learned a lot from you."

"You can take it back to Texas with you," Vivian said. "Maybe your ranch can become an example to others, of how to manage wildlife humanely." Then she seemed to realize what she'd said. Her cheeks flushed. "I mean, if you go back to Texas. Which I hope you won't."

Liam glanced at Trisha, but she was suddenly busy with the zipper on her jacket. "That's a good idea." He changed the subject.

"I'd better get on with the chores. Jace and I have a long list of things to get through today. Vivian, Carly, are you ready to ride back?"

"Sure." Vivian sounded relieved. "Maya and Trisha, I'll see you at the wildlife center in a couple hours."

"See you then." Maya started for the truck.

Carly put the camera into the duffel and loaded it in the back. "I'll get the gate."

Vivian smiled at her adopted niece. "Thanks, Carly."

Liam turned to Trisha. "Give our boy a big hug from me. Can I see you guys for dinner tonight? I'll cook, if you want."

Trisha smiled, but he could see the worry in her eyes. Vivian's comment about Texas had gotten to her, too. But all she said was, "I'd love that. But I'll cook."

He grinned. "Aw, come on, I'm not that bad at it."

"Your attempt at vegetarian cooking was interesting, to say the least. And very much appreciated. But let me take care of dinner tonight."

He kissed her, as thrilled as ever when she kissed him back. "I'll see you then."

"See you." She gave a little wave and

climbed in the truck with Maya and Emily. Liam watched as they drove off.

Before he left, he turned to watch the coyotes one more time. The pups were wrestling, falling down the hill and climbing back up to wrestle some more. The mother was sitting up, watching them, and Liam could swear there was a slightly bemused expression in her eyes.

"I'm sorry I hurt you," Liam said quietly. "I'm glad you've got your family back." For a heart-thudding instant, the coyote looked straight at him.

"Good luck out there." Liam turned away to go get Wild Bill and head back to the ranch with Carly and Vivian. As he walked, the sun finally made it through the fog, turning the mist golden, promising a bright day ahead.

CHAPTER SEVENTEEN

TRISHA LOOKED AROUND at the friends assembled in her backyard. Even Becca had flown home from Texas for Henry's first birthday. She was deep in conversation with Maya and Emily, while she cuddled Henry on her lap.

Jace was sitting on Trisha's outdoor sofa with Amy and Alex, reading a story. Carly and Vivian were inside, putting icing on the cake they'd insisted on making for Henry's special day.

All The Book Biddies were there. Annie and Juan were in charge of the barbecue, though Liam couldn't seem to stay away. He and Juan were debating the merits of smoking meat versus regular old grilling. Eva and Monique had taken over the bar and were making potent margaritas. Trisha had taken a sip or two of hers and immediately switched to water.

Lillian, Priscilla and Kathy kept clearing

plates and doing dishes, and Trisha kept going back in the kitchen to kick them out and tell them to just relax. Ranger was sleeping in the sun just a few feet away. She'd started thinking of him as her dog, he and Liam spent so much time at her house. The shepherd had quickly made himself at home and was great about tolerating Henry's clumsy affection.

Trisha picked up a spoon and clinked it against her water glass to get everyone's attention. Conversations faltered, slowed and stopped, and Liam made his way over to her side.

"I just want to thank you so much for being here today," Trisha said. "And for all that you've done to get me through Henry's first year. From holding my hand in the hospital—Becca, Vivian and Maya—to keeping me employed—Emily and Eva—to endless amounts of babysitting, hand-holding and advice—" she raised her glass to all The Biddies "—I could never have made it through this year without you all."

She turned to Liam, suddenly aware of how this might feel to him. A list of all the things he'd missed out on.

But he just put an arm around her, kissed

the top of her head and raised his glass of water to the group. "Thank you for everything you've done for Trisha and Henry. And for me. You all could have run me out of town when you found out who I was, but instead you've made me feel like a part of your lives. I'm grateful to know you all."

Tears stung in Trisha's eyes, but she had one more thing to say. "And now, here's to our son, Henry. Happy first birthday, baby boy. We're so glad you're here."

"To Henry," said Liam.

"To Henry," everyone responded.

Henry lifted his arms toward Trisha. "Mama," he said. Trisha went over to Becca and scooped up her baby. "Here's Mama," she said, and brought him back to Liam. "And here's Dada."

"Dada." Henry raised his arms to Liam.

Liam glanced at Trisha, a wide grin starting across his face.

"I think he wants his daddy." Trisha felt like her whole heart was in her smile.

Liam reached for Henry and held him up in the air for a moment, making Henry squeal with laughter. "I guess that's me," he said. "I'm Dada."

Trisha heard the buzzing from Liam's pocket. "Your phone."

Liam handed Henry back, and Trisha kissed his curly head, wanting to cuddle, but he was wiggly after the excitement of his daddy. So she lifted him up and blew on his tummy, making him laugh again.

She glanced over to see if they'd made Liam smile, but he was gone, disappearing through the side gate toward the front yard, as if he needed privacy.

Vivian came over. "Let me see this little one-year-old."

"Can you believe it's been a year since he was born?"

Vivian tickled Henry's tummy, eliciting delighted giggles. "In some ways no, it's gone so fast. But in other ways it's hard to imagine life without Henry. I feel like he's a part of all of us, you know? By the way, Jace thinks you should get him a pony as soon as he's old enough. You can keep it up on the ranch. We'll take care of it for you."

Trisha gaped at her friend. "That is the sweetest offer. So generous. But Henry won't be ready for a pony for a while."

"Liam told Jace he was riding by the time he was three."

"Well, I'm going to have a little talk with Liam about that." Trisha looked around, but there was still no sign of him.

"The truth is, I think Jace just wants this baby around as much as possible. He didn't really know our kids when they were young. He and his sister weren't exactly close. I think he's hoping to get his baby fix with Henry."

"You two aren't trying for a little one?"

Vivian shrugged. "We're talking about it. But it's a little tricky with my health issues. And we do already have our hands pretty full with the three we've got."

"It's a big decision." Trisha bounced Henry up and down a couple of times, trying to get him to settle down. "You seem so healthy, sometimes I forget about your lupus."

"It's nice to forget about it sometimes, trust me." Vivian sighed. "Speaking of young ones, I don't know how much more good behavior Alex and Amy have left in them. Maybe Carly and I could bring out the cake now?"

"That would be amazing. Let me go track down Liam first."

"Can I keep Henry here with me?" Vivian reached for the baby. “I don’t think he’s had enough Auntie Viv and Uncle Jace time today.”

Trisha laughed and passed Henry over. “Of course. Please take him. He’s such a wiggle worm.”

“You must know it’s your special day,” Vivian told Henry, settling him on her hip. “You must know that it’s your birthday and you’re one year old and everything is about you today.”

Her singsong voice and the little dance she was doing with Henry had Trisha laughing. “Babies must think the world is full of cute voices and being bopped around in grown-ups’ arms. It must be a rude awakening when they get older and adults start using a normal voice with them.”

“Maybe so.” Vivian bounced Henry along with her words. “Maybe that’s true, right, Henry? Let’s go ask Uncle Jace.” She waltzed him off across the patio.

They were all so silly when it came to the baby, herself and Liam included. Liam had started making up little country songs about Henry’s day, which he sang to him whenever he helped put Henry to bed.

Ranger brushed against her legs. Maybe he was worried about his master, too. The dog and Trisha went through the gate and around the side of the house. Liam was there, sitting on the front porch steps. The phone was at his side and he had his hat in his hands. He was turning it around and around, staring down at the brim.

"Liam? Are you okay? It's time for cake." Trisha climbed the stairs, sat down beside him and put an arm around his shoulders. Ranger lay down on the path below the steps.

Liam leaned into her a moment, as if absorbing her warmth and energy. Then he kissed the top of her head. "Thanks. Let's go eat some cake."

"Did you get bad news?"

He nodded. "My dad's sick. He should be okay eventually, but he's not okay right now." He stood up and offered her his hand. "Can we talk about it later? I don't want to mess up Henry's party. It's a first for all of us."

Trisha studied him, trying to read the feelings he was hiding. But if he wanted them hid, that was his right. "Okay." She took his hand and followed him back to the party. "I'm here for you, though. Whatever you need."

Liam stopped before the gate and put his hands to her shoulders. He kissed her suddenly, fiercely. "I need you," he said when he pulled away. "You and Henry." He looked down at Ranger. "And you, too, squishy buddy. Of course I need you, too."

Trisha laughed and bent down to cuddle Ranger's silky ears. "You're a good boy, Ranger. And not *too* squishy. Don't listen to that mean old cowboy."

Laughing, she led the way back in to the party, but she noticed Liam wasn't even smiling as he followed her back to their friends.

LIAM FINISHED WIPING out the serving bowls and set the dish towel down with a relieved sigh. The last of the guests had gone and the patio was clean. Ranger was sacked out in front of Trisha's fireplace and Henry was in bed, tuckered out from all the partying.

His son's first birthday. Little by little the surreal feeling was wearing off. And in its place was a love for Henry that grew with every minute Liam spent with him. In the past few weeks he'd grown from incompetent, brand-new dad to somewhat-bumbling father, and he figured that wasn't too shabby.

He was a long way from getting it all right, but at least he wasn't getting it all wrong.

Trisha came into the kitchen after checking on Henry and turned on the burner beneath the kettle. "I need a cup of tea and a chance to just sit down for a moment. How about you?"

"I'll skip the tea, thanks, but let me make you some. You put on an awesome party today. Go put your feet up."

Her smile was full of gratitude and she came over to kiss his cheek. "Thanks."

She went into the living room and Liam heard her land hard on the couch and let out a sigh of relief. He smiled. She was usually so composed and ladylike, it was cute when she wasn't.

He boiled the water and made her favorite mint tea. Stepping into the bathroom, he washed his face in cold water and ran fingers through his hair. He looked tired, but hey, it had been a long day. All he could do now was be honest about how he felt. "You got this," he muttered to his reflection in the mirror. He hoped that was actually true. Heading back into the kitchen, he grabbed Trisha's tea and went to find her in the living room. "Here you go." He set the tea down on a coaster on the coffee table.

"Thank you." She patted the couch next to her. "Come sit down and tell me how you're doing."

Liam took a deep breath and knelt on the floor in front of her. He was a little shaky but he was determined to say what was in his heart. "Trisha, you must know how I feel about you and Henry. I love you two. You have my heart and I am here for you 100 percent."

She sat up straight, looking a little worried. "You have our hearts, too."

Liam pulled in a little more oxygen. "I think we should get married. I want us to be a family. Officially."

"What?" She put her hands to her face, over her mouth, like she'd just won some big prize. Except her eyes didn't look that happy. "Liam, are you sure?"

"I've told you how I feel. I've held you in my heart ever since that night in Texas. You were my angel. You inspired me to get better. And getting to know you this past month has shown me that my instinct was right that night. You are so special to me, Trisha. You grew me up. You changed me so much, for the better. You are the person I want to spend the rest of my life with."

There were tears welling in her eyes and he sure hoped they were happy ones. But he had a sinking feeling he was getting this all wrong.

"I love you, Liam. I'm sure I do. But we don't know each other that well. We're still trying to find our way, with Henry and with each other. We've only been on a few dates..."

"But they were great dates, weren't they? We laughed—we loved being together." He studied her pretty blue eyes, looking for clues. "I didn't imagine all that, right?"

She reached out and ran her fingers over the stubble of his beard. "No, you didn't imagine it. They were great dates."

"And we've had weeks now to figure out how to care for our baby together. You've even survived my bad cooking once or twice. We're a couple. A happy couple."

A weak smile softened her serious expression and gave him the hope he needed. "We are. We really are. A happy family, even."

"Look." He took her hands in his. "I've

got to go back to Texas. My brothers need my help, now that my dad is sick. So let's get married. Let me take you home to my family, as my wife."

Her lips parted as if she meant to speak, but for a moment, no sound came out. Then she said, "Please don't ask me to do that."

He'd been afraid of hearing it and he had his reasons ready. "We belong together. The three of us. And I have to go back to Texas. At least for a while."

"I understand. Your family needs you. Go to Texas, then come back here to us."

"It's not that simple. My dad's having heart surgery, so I have to be home for that. But there's also this commitment that I made—to learn from Jace, and to come home and help them transition the ranch to organic." He tried to explain what he owed. "My family dropped everything to help me when I needed it. Now they need my support."

Tears were spilling down her cheeks. "I understand, but I don't know what to do. I can't move to Texas. I have two jobs that I care about here. My friends are like my family. Henry and I have our whole lives here."

He was losing his grip on the situation. He

grasped harder. “You can have a life in Texas for a while. Then maybe we can come back. And we can always visit.”

“No.” She stood and took a few steps away from him, wrapping her arms across her chest like she was cold. “I love you, Liam. I do. But I belong here in Shelter Creek.”

“How do you know that when you’ve never lived anywhere else?” He stood, too. “We can be a family, Trish. Why can’t you just trust what we have together? Why are you always so cautious?”

Her eyes widened and her hands went to her hips. “You have to ask that? Let me tell you about the two times in my life I wasn’t cautious. The first time my best friend was killed. The second time, I got pregnant with Henry.”

“But you don’t regret Henry, do you?”

“I could never. But I had to build a life for us, all by myself. And I built that life here. I had no family, but my friends became my family. I’m not going to throw that all away, just because you happened to wander into my life again.”

“You don’t think me wandering in means something? That maybe we were meant to be?" He was getting desperate. He wanted them all to be together. Though it was becoming clear to him that he'd been naive. That he'd been walking around Shelter Creek feeling like somehow, magically, love would conquer all.

"I think we got really lucky." Her hands went to fists at her thighs. He'd never seen her angry before. She was pale and furious. "You know what would have meant something? It would have meant something if, after rehab, you came looking for me. You knew my first name. You knew I was from California. You knew I'd stayed at the hotel, and when. If you'd *tried* to find me, *that* would have meant something. Because then I'd know that you'd actually *chosen* me."

Her words cut deep because there was truth there. He'd been so weak back then. A coward hiding behind his guilt and self-blame, afraid to go after what he'd truly wanted. "I wish I'd looked for you. I missed so much of your life and of Henry's. But I didn't feel like I was worthy of you. You were this unattainable goddess in my mind."

"But now you have me and you're choosing Texas instead." She sat back down on the couch like all the fight had gone out of her and used her sleeve to swipe at the tears on her cheeks. When she spoke, her voice was hollow. "I love you, Liam. I want to be with you. I want all of us to be together. But I can't leave here. This is my home. My life."

He'd been so sure they were going to be okay, but that illusion was crumbling around his feet. His heart might be crumbling, too. "Then we're stuck. You're basically telling me that the only way I can be with you is if I abandon my family and my obligations to them, and fit myself completely into your world. I can't do that right now. I have to go back to Texas."

"But can't you go and then come back here? To us?"

"I don't know how long I'll be in Texas. It could be a year, or even more, before I've helped transition the ranch to organic. I've got to be there for my brothers and my father." He didn't want to go. If he walked out the door without her, this thing they'd built, their connection, their tentative family, could be shattered. He couldn't face that. "There has to be a way to figure this out."

"I can't think of a way right now." She buried her face in her hands for a moment. When she looked up she was composed, but there were tears in her eyes. "Go back to Texas. Do what you need to do. We can figure something out. I'll wait for you. You can come visit us."

It was something at least. "A long-distance relationship? It's not enough."

"It has to be." She seemed so tired. There were shadows below her eyes, and a dullness within that he'd never seen before. Like her spirit was crushed.

"I'm so sorry, Trisha. The last thing I want to do is hurt you."

She went to the door and opened it for him. "Have a safe trip home. Keep me posted on how it's going. We'll miss you."

"I'll miss you, too." Liam grabbed his hat and his boots and stumbled out onto the porch, gripped by that same surreal feeling he'd had when he first found out about Henry. Except then he'd been gaining something unexpected, and now he was in danger of losing what he loved the most.

CHAPTER EIGHTEEN

TRISHA PUT TOGETHER a dish of raw meat for the bobcat kittens. They were getting bigger and eating so much. Now that they were more grown-up, they were using the same shelter the coyote pups had been in. The one Liam had worked so hard on. The bobcats hadn't been thrilled with the scent of coyote all around, so she'd carpeted the floor with thick wood shavings, which seemed to help.

Trisha went into the shed and slid the tray through the slot in the wall. She shook it so the meat fell into the trough below. Back outside, she glanced up and saw the clouds getting thicker. It was supposed to rain tonight, and usually she'd be glad. Rain in drought-ridden California was always something to be thankful for. But right now, the gray clouds just added to the sense of depression she'd felt for over a week now. Ever since Liam got on a plane for Texas.

She yanked open the door and went back into the clinic. If she hurried, she could get cleaned up and be on time to pick up Henry from Patty's. Though the prospect of another night at home alone didn't sound great either. She used to think of her life as cozy and quiet. But that was before she knew what it was like to cook dinner with Liam. To have him help with the bedtime routine and sing Henry silly songs. To curl up on the couch and watch a movie after Henry was asleep, or play Scrabble, or just talk and laugh.

Maybe she'd been content with her simple life because it was all she knew. But now she knew different.

She was wiping off the counters and putting things away when Vivian walked in.

"Do you need any extra help here?"

Trisha shook her head. "No thanks. I'm fine. Just getting ready to head home."

"Would you and Henry like to come up to the ranch and have dinner with us?"

It was tempting to have some company. But it was the ranch. Where Liam had lived until so recently. "Maybe another time? I think we'll just have a quiet night in."

"This weekend?" Vivian picked up a

sponge and began scrubbing the front of the cooler.

"Sure, that might be nice."

"Trish, help me out. I'm trying to find a way to cheer you up."

Trisha leaned on the counter. "I don't know what to do. I guess I just need to get used to missing him."

"Liam might come back, you know. He left to help his dad and show his brothers how to get the ranch on the right track. Once he finishes that, he'll feel more free to be with you and Henry."

"I hope so." Trisha studied the pattern in the linoleum. "I'm sure I must seem like the biggest baby to you. Moping around, when Liam left for a good reason. I think it's just that I finally risked my heart, you know? I never really have before. I told him I loved him, I jumped into a relationship with him with everything I had, and it felt like we were becoming this sweet family. And then he left."

Vivian gave up her pretense of cleaning and set her rag down. "Like your parents left. I see the connection now."

"I don't want to be someone who is so easy

to leave." Trisha blinked back tears. "But when I say that out loud, I sound like I'm having a pity party."

"No, you're scared. You've lived a pretty quiet life, maybe to protect yourself from the losses you've experienced. You're not used to taking risks with your heart."

"You're right. I keep thinking that it's not worth it. That it's better to stay here, where I feel safe. Except being safe doesn't feel very good if I don't have Liam. But he left me, so why should I go chasing after him?" She buried her face in her hands. "Viv, this is all so confusing."

"I'm sure it wasn't easy for Liam to go," Vivian reassured her. "The way he looks at you? He adores you. He asked you to marry him. I'm pretty sure that's a sign that he's crazy about you."

"You're right. My anxiety is taking over. I'm not used to wanting someone like this. I used to be happy, just being on my own."

"No one ever said that love was a comfortable emotion," Vivian said. "Have you heard from him?"

Trisha shuddered at the memory. "One very awkward conversation. And after just a few minutes, he said he had to go. It sounded like someone was coming and he couldn't wait to get off the phone."

"Weird." Vivian studied her quizzically. "Maybe he had something cooking in the oven and it was ready."

"Or maybe he has a wife back home in Texas and she was coming to find him."

"Trisha!" Vivian looked genuinely shocked. "Of course he doesn't have a wife."

Trisha knew she was being silly, but her mind couldn't seem to settle. "That's the thing, though. I don't know him *that* well. Maybe he does."

"Okay, that's it," Vivian said. "I am calling an emergency Book Biddies meeting. You are making yourself so anxious, and it's too much for me to handle on my own."

"Fine. As long as there are cocktails."

"You barely ever drink."

"Maybe I'll turn over a new leaf."

Vivian rolled her eyes. "Yeah, right. Saturday night, okay? I'm not sure whose house yet, but I'll send an email around. And you have to be there. No more hiding at home, feeling sorry for yourself." Vivian held out her arms. "Now, give me a hug, you brokenhearted bozo. And try to have faith that everything will be okay."

Trisha went to her friend and gave her a big hug. "Thank you for trying to cheer me up. I'm sorry I am such a mess."

"You fell in love and then you got hurt. You have a right to be a mess." Vivian hurried for the door. "Call me if you start imagining more upsetting things. And trust me, the guy doesn't have a secret wife."

"Good to know," Trisha muttered. She made the rounds of the building, locking doors, shutting off computers, turning out lights. She was often the last person out of here because she had to feed the animals their dinner.

Vivian was right—she had to get ahold of herself. Her fears were taking over. But she missed Liam so much, her bones ached with it. She wanted him with her. She wanted his kisses, the way he held her, his silly jokes and his way of smiling that came straight from his eyes.

And then there was the fact that without him here, it felt like a piece was missing. Not just from her and Henry's lives, but from her heart.

"LIAM, SEE IF you can get that heifer in the chute. She's the last one that needs vaccinating, and no one can get her to do anything."

Liam turned his horse, King, toward the heifer. Her brown ears were up and she was darting around the pen as if avoiding her shots was some kind of a game. But King was a champion and turned on his hindquarters faster than any horse Liam had ever had. When the heifer veered right, King anticipated it and cut her off. When she tried to get around him, the big quarter horse danced back and turned right to stop her again. After a few minutes of this, the gal gave up and went into the chute where the vet was waiting.

"It's good to have you home." Boone grinned at him from the fence. "We need someone else besides me who's a decent rider."

"I heard that." Tommy glared at Boone from where he was closing the gate behind the heifer. "And I'll remind you about who around here takes first place in steer wrestling at the rodeo every summer."

"Wrestling ain't riding. It's just hanging on to the back of a horse until you're ready to throw yourself off it."

Liam shook his head at their endless banter. "I don't think I ever realized how noisy you two are. Do you ever stop giving each other a hard time?"

Tommy looked at Boone. Boone looked at Tommy. "Nope," they both said at the same time and burst out laughing.

"I don't even know what to say." Liam guided King out of the corral. "You two are a couple of characters."

"I know what you can say." Tommy walked over to the fence and climbed up to sit next to Boone. "You can tell us what her name is."

Liam looked at his brother with as much innocence as he could muster. "I don't know what you're talking about."

"Oh, come on. You've been moping around here ever since you got back two weeks ago. And there's the way you're always looking down at your phone as if you're hoping for a message. Who is she, Liam? Some pretty California girl?"

"Yeah, whatever. I'm taking King back to the barn. We're done here for the day and I still have to meet with Wyatt."

Liam let King walk to the barn on a loose rein. He pulled off his hat and used a bandanna to wipe the sweat and grit off his face. It was only mid-May, but the temperature was creeping up into the eighties and the air was dry.

An image of waking up in Shelter Creek flashed in his mind. Early morning and the air all misty from the coastal fog that crept over the hills at night and left everything damp and rich. Liam had known he'd miss Trisha and Henry, but he hadn't thought he'd miss Shelter Creek as much as he did.

He thought about it a lot. The picturesque town with its lively square. The way the whole community turned out for the art fair and the Easter celebration. Jace had told Liam that in the summertime, the Shelter Creek Rodeo was a big event. He'd love to show that to little Henry, with Trisha by his side.

But Trisha didn't seem to want to be by his side. She hadn't called, though she'd texted him a few photos of Henry. She hadn't emailed either. And when he'd phoned her, their conversation was stilted. All the remnants of their last bitter conversation had settled like ash, covering all that was good between them.

He unsaddled King, rubbed him down and

put him in his stall with a flake of alfalfa. Tommy was feeding tonight, but King deserved an extra snack for his hard work today. Then Liam went to meet Wyatt, to go over the steps they'd take to install a manure digester.

Wyatt was reading a web page when Liam got to the office. "We need to dig a big holding pond. And then we'll need a separator for that," he said by way of greeting.

"Hello to you, too," Liam quipped. "And as for the digester, Jace was only just getting started on it, so I don't have much personal experience. I just know what he explained to me. And that it's expensive to set up."

"But if we can get it set up, we can power our own ranch. With manure." Wyatt's inner geek was showing. "That's so cool."

Liam grinned. "It's rare you show so much enthusiasm about something out on the ranch. Maybe you can be in charge of this process. Ranch and Manure Manager. I can see it written across a business card."

Wyatt laughed. "I think I'll leave that particular title off my card, if that's all right with you. But it's good to see you smile. You've been pretty serious since you got home."

"Well, it's felt pretty serious, with Dad having bypass surgery and all."

"He's out of the woods now, though. I bet he'll be up and about and bossing us around any day."

"Good to know." Liam slumped back in his chair. "Maybe he'll want to supervise the manure digester."

"I sense a lack of enthusiasm. I thought your time in California would get you all revved up about this stuff."

"It did. I'm sold. Glad we're going organic and grass-fed." Liam thought about what he'd gleaned in California. "Have you ever thought about how we manage predators out here?"

"Not really. If we see them, we shoot them. Why?"

"They do it differently out in California. Jace's ranch, and the ranches around them, are trying to coexist with their coyotes and mountain lions, rather than shooting them on sight."

"They've got a lot of rules out in California that we don't have. Mountain lions and coyotes aren't classified as game animals here.

Which means we don't need permits or anything to shoot."

"But what if we didn't shoot? What if we just scared them off?" He explained to Wyatt what he'd learned. "If you kill one coyote, other packs move into the territory. Then they have more young because they've got this new food supply."

Wyatt shrugged. "You'll have to talk to Dad about it. I don't see him changing his ways about predators too quickly, though." Wyatt looked at Liam with mild curiosity. "Did you like it out there in California?"

It was the perfect opening. A chance to tell his brother about Trisha and Henry. But Liam held back, just like he had ever since he'd come home. He'd told himself it was because they were all worried about their dad, and dealing with the hospital and the surgery and the aftermath. But now that Dad's health crisis was under control, Liam had to admit that wasn't the only reason.

If he told his family about Trisha and Henry, they'd see it differently than him. They'd see it as one more mistake he'd made when he was addicted to the pills. And he knew he wouldn't be able to keep his cool if they started making jokes and comments. Or if they saw the people Liam loved the most as consequences he had to live with.

Yet he'd made Trisha feel that exact way. He hadn't meant to. He'd tried to speak from his heart that night, but either it had come out all wrong or she just couldn't hear him. Maybe she didn't want to hear him. She was so self-protective—maybe she was incapable of feeling deeply for someone.

Except she clearly adored Henry. And she said she loved Liam, too. But she didn't trust him. Not enough to truly commit to him. Maybe she still saw him as the young guy who didn't know himself well. Who went along with whatever impulse grabbed him next. Who didn't have the guts to go after what he wanted.

He stood up suddenly, disturbed to the core. He *was* that guy. Sitting here in his brother's office, when what he really wanted was to be in California.

"You okay, Liam?"

Liam winced at the worry on his brother's face. Wyatt, too, saw him as incompetent. As needing constant worry and watching so he didn't go off the rails again. He needed to get out of here. To think about who he was, and what he needed to do, and how he was going to do it. "I think I'll go for a ride," he told Wyatt. "I've got to clear my head."

"All right. Suit yourself. See you in a while."

"See you." Liam jogged to the barn with a sense of urgency he hadn't felt in a while. Not since he'd left Shelter Creek and Trisha and Henry and everything that really mattered to him. At the barn he threw a saddle on Delta, a big black quarter horse that he'd ridden for years. He slipped the bridle on and mounted, taking the trail out to the bluff overlooking the ranch. It had been his mom's favorite spot and it was where Liam came whenever he wanted to feel close to her. Her spirit was here, at least for him. He'd come here after rehab, to apologize for his weakness. For his lack of care for the body she'd grown and nurtured so carefully with square meals and love.

He stopped at the edge of the bluff, where it was all view and sky and air. He closed his eyes, remembering his mother's voice, her laugh, her smile. "I've got a son, Ma. I've got a baby boy. His name is Henry, and he's got your curls and his mother's big blue eyes. He's the cutest little guy."

He waited. For what, he wasn't sure. Maybe her voice, wrapped up in the whisper of wind that rustled the grass out here.

"I want to be a good dad," he confessed to the empty space. "I want to take care of both of them, but I'm twenty-six years old and all I know is this ranch and the rodeo and I don't think I can do either of those anymore." He was breathing more heavily now, fighting back tears he didn't even know he had in him, it had been so long since he'd cried.

"And, Ma, I keep asking myself, how can I be a good dad? Less than two years ago I was strung out on drugs, living from pill to pill. I stole, Ma. You know that. I told you out here, after rehab. But it haunts me, you know? I'm someone who is capable of committing a crime, and now I'm supposed to be an example to a kid?"

Tears ran down his face and he let them come. Just sat on Delta's back and looked at the view and cried, the dry wind wicking at his damp skin, hissing gently through the grass, as soothing as his mom's hand on his back. He could almost hear her telling him it would be okay.

The first stars were glimmering when Liam turned Delta back toward the ranch. Despite the dark, the sure-footed gelding knew the way, so Liam gave him a loose rein and let him find the path. By the time they reached the barn, Liam felt more clearheaded than he could remember being in his entire life. He hadn't just come back to Texas to fulfill his past obligations—he'd been scared about his new ones. Returning home wasn't just about loyalty to his family—it was about his fears about starting a new one. Fear that he couldn't be a good father or a good husband. Fear that he didn't have as good a handle on his addiction as he thought. Fear of striking out on his own, on a new ranch in a new place.

The wind, his mom's hand, whatever it was that he'd felt this evening, had assured him that he could do this. He could create the life of his dreams, if he only mustered the courage to start.

Liam led Delta into his stall and slipped the bridle off him. The big horse immediately went to his manger to start in on the hay waiting there. As Liam pulled off the saddle, he knew it was time to move on from his life here in Texas. He could see his future so clearly, in Shelter Creek, with Trisha. He could even see the path he'd need to take to get himself there.

CHAPTER NINETEEN

TRISHA LOOKED AROUND at The Book Biddies, gathered in Lillian's living room for the emergency meeting Vivian had called. Trisha was sitting on the couch, with Vivian on one side of her and Lillian on the other. Annie was cuddling Henry in the armchair by the fireplace. Everyone was drinking the margaritas Lillian and Emily had concocted. They were looking at Trisha expectantly and she was trying to think of what to say.

"I love Liam," she blurted out.

"Well, of course you do," Lillian said mildly.

"He wants me to live in Texas," Trisha told them. Just saying the words twisted her stomach in knots. "And I don't want to leave Shelter Creek." She looked at Emily and Maya, who were sitting across the room. "I love working for you two."

"We love having you." Maya's smile was kind.

"But I'm considering moving to Texas anyway." There. It was out. And from the stunned looks on everyone's faces, it wasn't what they'd been expecting. "I want to visit and see what it's like."

"Good for you." Monique raised her glass. "It's a great idea. You two are meant to be together. Anyone can see it."

"You certainly deserve a vacation," Kathy said. "How long has it been since you took time off work?"

"Maternity leave," Trisha said. "And before that was the trip to San Antonio. Where I met Liam. And got Henry."

"How romantic," Kathy said. "Flying across the country in pursuit of love."

"But if I go, what about my jobs? Emily, Maya, who will assist you?"

"We'll find someone to substitute while you're gone," Emily said. "I have a roster of substitute assistants for my clinic. Maybe one of those people can cover for you at my practice *and* at the wildlife center."

"And Carly loves to help with the animals,"

Vivian added. "I can give her some part-time work caring for wildlife, if we need extra help."

Trisha felt as if they'd removed weights from her ankles, and now she could suddenly fly free. It was frightening, but she was so tired of letting her fear keep her tethered.

"Okay, then." Trisha squared her shoulders. "I'm going to go to Texas to show Liam that I love him. It's not a solution, but it's a start."

"And then come back here as soon as possible." Lillian put her arm around Trisha. "Because we will miss you, very much."

"But what if I hate it there?" Trisha looked around at her friends. "I don't think I can stay unless it's a nice place."

"Don't borrow trouble." Monique's voice was firm. "Cross that bridge when you come to it." She burst out laughing and looked at the margarita in her hand. "This magic elixir is making me speak in clichés."

It eased the tension in the room perfectly. Everyone laughed and Emily raised her glass. "To Trisha. Being strong."

Trisha took a deep breath and looked at Henry, who was bouncing on Annie's knee. "Henry, I think we're heading to Texas."

"Let's look at plane tickets," Vivian said. "Lillian, can we borrow your computer?"

"I'll help you pack," Eva offered. "I've got the capsule wardrobe down pat."

"We'll drive you to the airport," Priscilla said. "Me, Lillian and Kathy, since we're retired. Do you want to leave tomorrow?"

Trisha looked around the room in astonishment. "Why are you all so excited to get rid of me?"

Vivian put an arm around her and squeezed. "Because you're in love with Henry's daddy. And we want you to be happy. Even if you have to go to Texas to do it."

"I'VE GOT SOMETHING to tell you all." Liam looked around the old pine table in the main house dining room. They still gathered there for Sunday night supper, even though Liam, Boone and Tommy shared a bunkhouse now, and Wyatt had an apartment over the garage.

Dad leaned back in his chair, looking so much thinner and older than he had before. "This doesn't sound like good news."

"Depends on how you look at it, I guess." But his father's words caused Liam some unease. Maybe it was wrong to spring this on

Dad suddenly. What if it caused another problem with his heart?

But how did you ease into telling someone that you had a kid? He'd just have to do his best.

"Almost two years ago now, I went to my friend Clint's wedding in San Antonio. I met a woman there and we hit it off pretty well. But then I left and we didn't stay in touch."

Liam realized he was sugarcoating things to make himself look better, one of the things he'd learned not to do, back in rehab. "Well, the truth is, I spent the night with her, then walked out without leaving a note or anything."

"You dog," Boone said.

"It's not an excuse, but I was using at the time. I wasn't on my best behavior anywhere I went."

"I remember this," Wyatt said. "This was the night before we took you to rehab. You were going on and on about this woman."

"That's right." Boone ran a hand through his hair. "We all thought you'd had a hallucination or something."

"Nope. She was real." He took a breath and went for it. "Turns out she's from the same town as Jace. Shelter Creek, California. And she had a baby. A son named Henry. He's my kid."

Liam watched his dad carefully, looking for signs of cardiac arrest. But his father just looked shocked. Then, unexpectedly, he smiled. "A son? You have a son?"

His brothers seemed stunned into silence, something Liam could not remember happening in their entire family history. He addressed his father. "You have a grandson. His name is Henry and he just turned a year old. He's cute as a button. And he's got Mom's curly hair."

His father stared at him with an interest Liam was not used to seeing there. "Well, I'll be. Why are you here, and not there?"

"You had a heart problem, Dad. Remember?"

"I'm fine now. Is she coming out here? Are you moving there? You'll take responsibility for this, Liam."

Liam put his hands out to try to stop his father's impending lecture. "I asked her to marry me. She hasn't said yes yet. I'm hoping I can convince her, though."

That woke his brothers out of their trance.

"You mean you two have a kid together and she *still* doesn't want to marry you?" Tommy grinned. "That must sting a little."

"Ouch," Boone echoed.

Wyatt was looking misty-eyed. "That's amazing. Congratulations, little brother."

"Thanks, Wyatt." Liam turned to his father. "I want to sell my share of this ranch. I want to start my own operation, out in Shelter Creek. It's where Trisha wants to raise Henry. And I respect her enough to go along with that."

A silence settled on the table. "If that's what you want, Liam, we'll work something out," his father said. "But we'll be sorry to see you go."

"I don't love the idea of living so far away from you all," Liam told him. "I never thought I'd live anywhere but Texas. But my home is where they are. I've realized that now." He glanced over at his brothers and grinned. "And the weather sure is a lot nicer out in California. I'll be thinking of you all while I'm riding through that cool summer coastal fog, and you're out here sweating in 105 degrees."

"Okay, now I pretty much hate you," Tommy said, and Boone busted out laughing.

They talked a little more, asking questions about Henry, and what Shelter Creek was like. Liam tried to explain it all, and showed them photos, too. But it was hard to paint the whole picture—the pretty houses, the nicely maintained streets, the redwoods, the hills. And how he felt about Trisha and Henry. There were no adequate words for that.

Mostly what he felt was his mother's spirit, that sense of having her blessing, which he'd carried with him since his ride the other day. He was stepping up, taking control of his life, and she was proud of him, wherever she was.

His phone buzzed and he pulled it out of his pocket. It was a text from Lillian, back in Shelter Creek. He looked up at his family, stunned. "Trisha and Henry are on their way here from California. They're supposed to land in San Antonio in two hours."

"You'd better get to the airport, then." His father stood, more energized than Liam had seen him since the surgery, and started barking orders like a drill sergeant. "Boone, you can work on cleaning up the kitchen. Tommy, run upstairs and put fresh sheets on the guest bed. Wyatt, you make sure the bathroom up there is clean as can be."

He paused, realized his sons were all staring at him in shock and raised his voice even more. "What are you all gaping at? We've got to get to work. We've got a baby coming to stay."

THEY'D MADE IT. Trisha carried Henry down the airplane aisle, trying not to bump into anyone with her baby, his diaper bag or her purse. Thank goodness Henry had only cried during takeoff and landing, so overall, flying hadn't turned out to be as difficult as Trisha had feared. Mostly Henry had slept, after he'd spent some time flirting with the woman seated next to them. He must have inherited his daddy's cowboy charm.

Henry's stroller was waiting for them when they got off the plane. Trisha set him in and gave him his blanket and squeaky giraffe. It was ten at night, Texas time, eight o'clock California time, past Henry's bedtime no matter where they were. But with his airplane nap, the little guy was in pretty good spirits. Trisha leaned over the stroller and blew him a kiss, making him smile. She set the diaper bag in the bottom compartment, settled her purse over her shoulder and started up the gate to the terminal.

She'd get their baggage and then check into a hotel near the airport. Tomorrow she'd call Liam and tell him they were here to see him. Hopefully he'd think it was good news.

This was so unlike her. She'd got caught up in The Book Biddies' excitement and enthusiasm, and before she knew it, she was on a plane to Texas. She wanted to believe that this was the right thing to do, but spontaneous events outside her comfort zone had never ended as planned.

She followed the signs to the baggage terminal, wondering if it would be smarter just to turn right around and fly back to California. What if Liam wasn't happy to see them? Or what if he thought that her being here meant she'd caved, and was willing to give up her entire life for him?

She stopped to read the message board that listed her baggage carousel, then followed the signs to the baggage area. And there he was. Liam. Standing there waiting, with his hat in his hand. Trisha's heart sped up in her chest. He was as handsome as ever, but more than that, he was hers. She was sure of it now. Sure of them. Maybe because she'd been brave enough to fly across the country in pursuit of love.

"What are you doing here?" She pushed Henry toward him. "How did you know we were coming?"

"Lillian texted."

"Of course she did. My friends love to stir the pot." But she wanted to hug her friend because this felt so much better than arriving on her own and heading to a sterile hotel room.

Liam smiled that slow wide smile she'd come to love. "I appreciate the stirring, personally. I'm glad I could be here to pick you up."

"I was going to get a hotel. I didn't mean to cause you any trouble."

Liam knelt down to get a good look at Henry and his whole expression beamed with fatherly pride. "This isn't trouble. This is great." Henry tossed his giraffe in excitement and Liam handed it back to him. "Hello, son, it's good to see you." Then he stood and surprised Trisha with a kiss on the cheek. "It's amazing to see you."

She flushed, surprised at her own shyness.

She was supposed to be brave. But that kiss, the love in his eyes… It was hard to find the right words. "I thought about calling you first but I was worried you were really mad at me. That you'd tell me not to come."

"I wasn't mad. Disappointed. Sad. But not angry. I know you have your reasons to want to stay in Shelter Creek. I don't blame you. I like it there, too."

She wanted to run into his arms. To hold on so tight, he'd never get away again. But that wouldn't solve their problems. He had to choose her. He had to want to be with her. She had to decide if Texas was right for her.

"How's your father doing?"

"Right now he's barking orders at my brothers, who are getting the house all cleaned up for your arrival. He can't wait to meet you and his first grandson. Honestly, I think it's the best thing that could have happened. He was feeling a little listless, post-surgery."

"So you finally told them about me. Were they shocked?"

"Of course. But, Trish, I didn't just tell them about you. I told them I'm moving to California to be with you. I love you. I'd want to spend my life with you, even if I just met you tonight and we didn't have amazing Henry here. I promise you that. And I'll try to show you that, every day."

Trisha put her hands to her ears, as if she could capture his words and study them. It was hard to take it all in. "You want to move to Shelter Creek? Are you sure?"

"I've never been more sure. I really thought about it and it became so clear. I was afraid, deep down, that I wouldn't be a good enough father to Henry. Or strong enough to make my own life, away from here. But I know now that I can."

His words were her dreams come true. Still, she had to let him know that she was willing to make changes as well. "I came here to tell you that I'm considering moving to Texas. Now you've taken all the wind out of my big declaration."

Liam took her hands in his and pulled her close. "I know what your home means to you. How hard you've worked to build your community of friends. How much you love your work. I'm honored, beyond words, that you considered leaving all that behind for me."

"I guess I love you." Trisha wrapped her arms around him and held on tight. "A whole lot."

"And I love you. You're it for me, Trisha. You and Henry are my life, from now on."

If Trisha hadn't been hanging on to him for dear life she'd have tipped over, she was so dizzy from relief. "If you're sure..."

"Trust me. I'm sure. I've thought it through and it's what I want more than anything. I choose you, Trisha. Over everything else."

She was going to cry. Just lose it right here in the middle of the baggage area. "I..." She went on tiptoe and kissed him. Some feelings she didn't have words for.

"Dada."

They released each other and knelt down to see what Henry needed.

"Here's your dada," Trisha said, catching her son's little hands in her own. "Do you want to cuddle with him?"

"Dada."

Trisha looked at Liam. The lines of his face were soft with love as he gazed at his son. "I think somebody has missed his daddy."

Liam unbuckled the straps, lifted Henry out and settled him in the crook of one arm. Henry whacked him on the nose with the rubber giraffe. "I missed you, too, son." Liam put his free arm on the handlebar of the stroller and smiled down at Trisha. "Let's go get your bags. I want to take my family home."

CHAPTER TWENTY

LIAM TUGGED AT the unfamiliar suit jacket. “I can’t believe some guys wear these things every day.”

“Hold still.” Wyatt was trying to pin the rose that Trisha had picked out onto Liam’s lapel. “Ouch. Got my finger.”

“Some best man you turned out to be.”

“A best man who flew all the way out from Texas to get stuck with a flower pin.”

Liam glanced over at the guests making their way into the barn for the wedding ceremony. He spotted Monique picking her way carefully in very high heels. He waved frantically, and fortunately she spotted him and teetered over.

“Do you gentleman need some help?”

“Trisha wants me to wear this flower. How do you pin this thing?”

Wyatt looked up from where he was trying

to jab the pin back through the tape-wrapped flower stem. "Oh, hello, ma'am."

"That accent." Monique fanned herself with the tiny handbag she carried. "Just keep talking to me and I'll help you with anything you want."

Wyatt looked a little taken aback, and Liam laughed. "Monique, go easy on my big brother Wyatt. He doesn't get off the ranch much."

"Okay, fine. Always glad to assist the handsome groom on his wedding day." Monique took the flower from Wyatt and attached it in one quick motion to Liam's lapel. She patted his chest. "All set."

"You made that look pretty easy." Wyatt stared at her, astonished.

"And I did it in heels, too." Monique flashed him a sultry smile and teetered off.

"Who *was* that?"

"Monique. She's part of that book group I told you about. And she's much too old for you."

"I'm not sure she is." Wyatt stared for a moment longer, then seemed to remember his best man duties. "So, is everything else ready?" He patted the pocket of his suit jacket. "I've got the ring."

"Good to know. Where are Boone and Tommy?"

"Inside already. They want to know why Trisha's bridesmaids are all married."

"Those are Trisha's friends. And Emily's not married. But she's so smart, she'd run circles around guys like Boone or Tommy."

Wyatt looked mystified. "This town has a lot of smart people. It takes a little getting used to."

"That it does." Liam glanced around the property. His property. The idea also took some getting used to. He'd bought the beautifully maintained ranch from Juan Alvaro just a couple months ago. Juan and Annie Brooks had finally stopped pretending they weren't an item and eloped to Vegas. Now they lived together on Annie's property.

Trisha had wanted to have their wedding right here in their own barn, to celebrate the future unfolding before them. The Book Biddies had decorated the place so it looked like one of those photos in a wedding magazine, all golden lights and flower garlands.

"You ready to go inside and get hitched?" Wyatt pulled his phone out of his pocket and glanced at the time. “I think Trisha will be arriving any minute.”

It was hard to believe this day had finally come. About a year after Trisha showed up in Texas to tell him she was willing to move there, they were finally making it all official. Getting married, on their own land, in the town they loved—Shelter Creek, California. “I’ve been ready a long time. Let’s do this.”

Wyatt led the way into the barn and Liam took his place next to his brothers, by the makeshift altar. Ranger lay near Boone, a flower garland draped around his neck. A harpist started playing the wedding march and the guests grew quiet.

Henry came in first, with Liam’s father behind him, helping to guide his beloved grandson in his flower boy duties. Two-year-old Henry took his petal-throwing seriously, chucking the petals high in the air so they fell like confetti. Liam couldn’t contain his grin. “That’s my boy,” he whispered to Wyatt.

When Henry reached the front of the room, he set down his basket and dashed for his daddy’s arms. Liam scooped him up, much to the audience’s delight, and kissed him on the cheek.

Liam's dad collected the tiny basket of rose petals and went to sit down in the front row.

Next came the older generation of Book Biddies. Dressed in beautiful mother-of-the-bride dresses, they came down the aisle two by two, first Monique and Eva, then Priscilla and Annie, then Lillian and Kathy. They all waved at Henry as they took their seats in the front row.

Maya, Emily and Vivian walked the aisle wearing matching silver dresses. They looked radiant, smiling at Liam and waving to Henry as they came to stand in the front, opposite Liam and his brothers.

And then there was Trisha, walking down the aisle with her mother and father on either side of her. They'd come back to Shelter Creek for the wedding, and even if Liam thought they were a little odd, he knew that their presence here today was important to Trisha.

She was beyond beautiful. She'd chosen pale pink for her dress, a color she'd called dusty rose. Whatever it was, it suited her. She looked like an exotic flower, moving gracefully down the aisle. His angel. So sweet and loving, he could only stare and marvel at his luck.

"Mama," Henry called, and folks in the audience laughed. Liam set him down and he ran to his mother on his stubby little legs.

Handing her bouquet to her mother, Trisha scooped her baby up and carried him the rest of the way down the aisle. The two of them were the embodiment of Liam's whole heart.

"Let's get married this way. With Henry right here with us." Trisha's wide smile warmed Liam like the California sun.

"I'll marry you any way you want." Liam glanced at the minister. "Is that okay with you?"

"Absolutely."

The ceremony began, and Liam tried to listen to the traditional words, tried to take in the guests and the decorations, and the importance of this special day. But all he could focus on was Trisha, with their baby in her arms, promising to spend forever loving him.

Way back when, in Texas, a short straw had sent him to California. It had seemed like bad luck at the time, but now Liam knew that he was the luckiest man on earth. He intended to remember that, every day of his life.

* * * * *

Get 4 FREE REWARDS!

We'll send you 2 FREE Books
plus 2 FREE Mystery Gifts.

Love Inspired books feature uplifting stories where faith helps guide you through life's challenges and discover the promise of a new beginning.

YES! Please send me 2 FREE Love Inspired Romance novels and my 2 FREE mystery gifts (gifts are worth about $10 retail). After receiving them, if I don't wish to receive any more books, I can return the shipping statement marked "cancel." If I don't cancel, I will receive 6 brand-new novels every month and be billed just $5.24 each for the regular-print edition or $5.99 each for the larger-print edition in the U.S., or $5.74 each for the regular-print edition or $6.24 each for the larger-print edition in Canada. That's a savings of at least 13% off the cover price. It's quite a bargain! Shipping and handling is just 50¢ per book in the U.S. and $1.25 per book in Canada.* I understand that accepting the 2 free books and gifts places me under no obligation to buy anything. I can always return a shipment and cancel at any time. The free books and gifts are mine to keep no matter what I decide.

Choose one: ☐ **Love Inspired Romance Regular-Print** (105/305 IDN GNWC) ☐ **Love Inspired Romance Larger-Print** (122/322 IDN GNWC)

Name (please print)

Address Apt. #

City State/Province Zip/Postal Code

Mail to the **Reader Service:**
IN U.S.A.: P.O. Box 1341, Buffalo, NY 14240-8531
IN CANADA: P.O. Box 603, Fort Erie, Ontario L2A 5X3

Want to try 2 free books from another series? Call 1-800-873-8635 or visit www.ReaderService.com.

*Terms and prices subject to change without notice. Prices do not include sales taxes, which will be charged (if applicable) based on your state or country of residence. Canadian residents will be charged applicable taxes. Offer not valid in Quebec. This offer is limited to one order per household. Books received may not be as shown. Not valid for current subscribers to Love Inspired Romance books. All orders subject to approval. Credit or debit balances in a customer's account(s) may be offset by any other outstanding balance owed by or to the customer. Please allow 4 to 6 weeks for delivery. Offer available while quantities last.

Your Privacy—The Reader Service is committed to protecting your privacy. Our Privacy Policy is available online at www.ReaderService.com or upon request from the Reader Service. We make a portion of our mailing list available to reputable third parties that offer products we believe may interest you. If you prefer that we not exchange your name with third parties, or if you wish to clarify or modify your communication preferences, please visit us at www.ReaderService.com/consumerschoice or write to us at Reader Service Preference Service, P.O. Box 9062, Buffalo, NY 14240-9062. Include your complete name and address.

LI20R